Dear Reader,

Joy Revolution's growing library of love stories gets its
first sci-fi addition with Jill Tew's *The Dividing Sky*, and we
couldn't be more excited that it's finally in your hands. We
were immediately intrigued by Jill's intricately detailed twin
worlds: the dark dystopia of the Metro Boston of the future,
where wealth and poverty sit farther apart than ever, and the
bright, wooded Outerlands, ruled by chaos but also graced
with hope.

The whole story is wrapped up in an unlikely romance
between a renegade memory dealer and a green, earnest cop,
keeping the story rooted in swoony emotion while managing
to drop truths about where our society is and where it could
be headed. It's an absolutely thrilling combo that equals pure
reading pleasure. Sci-fi writers of color don't get seen enough,
so it's an honor to collaborate with and publish someone
as talented as Jill. She and her wonderfully poignant novel
both embody our mission of presenting irresistible stories
featuring characters of color exploring the full breadth of
their humanity.

Happy reading!

Nicola & David Yoon
Founders, Joy Revolution

RANDOM HOUSE CHILDREN'S BOOKS

TITLE:	The Dividing Sky
AUTHOR:	Jill Tew
IMPRINT:	Joy Revolution
PUBLICATION DATE:	October 8, 2024
ISBN:	978-0-593-71035-7
TENTATIVE PRICE:	$19.99 US / $26.99 CAN
GLB ISBN:	978-0-593-71036-4
GLB TENTATIVE PRICE:	$22.99 US / $30.99 CAN
AUDIO ISBN (download):	978-0-593-94365-6
EBOOK ISBN:	978-0-593-71037-1
PAGES:	352
TRIM SIZE:	5-1/2" x 8-1/4"
AGES:	12 and up

THE
DIVIDING
SKY

JILL TEW

joy revolution

GetUnderlined.com

Educators and librarians, for a variety of teaching tools, visit us at
RHTeachersLibrarians.com

Library of Congress Cataloging-in-Publication Data is available upon request.
ISBN 978-0-593-71035-7 (hardcover) — ISBN 978-0-593-71036-4 (lib. bdg.) —
ISBN 978-0-593-71037-1 (ebook)

The text of this book is set in 11-point Charter ITC.
Interior design by Debbie Glasserman

Printed in the United States of America
10 9 8 7 6 5 4 3 2 1
First Edition

FOR MY FAMILY, MY STARLIGHT

MAP TO COME

Creating a World of Value

Job Title: EMOTIONAL PROXY ("EmoProxy")

Long-standing LifeCorp VP of Supply Chain Operations Arthur Preston seeks experienced EmoProxy on a part-time, fee-for-service basis. Ideal candidate is highly motivated and excited to provide a wide variety of emotional memories ("Scraps") for Mr. Preston. This will further enable him to support LifeCorp's mission of sustaining the Metro through the production of affordable, high-quality goods and services.

Due to the personal nature of this support role, applicants should expect to match client's schedule. Client has singular tastes, and this role is best suited to a proactive self-starter.

Compensation
- Up to 250 credits per emotional memory ("Scrap"), at client's discretion
- Generous productivity score bonuses available in exchange for satisfactory performance

Responsibilities
- Meet with client to gather requirements for Scraps
- Discover and record media and/or life experiences and ensuing emotions as requested
- Maintain EmoProxy neurochip according to LifeCorp guidelines and regulations
- Travel to client's home on demand at employee's expense
- Collaborate with other in-home staff to ensure Scraps are aligned with current client needs

Minimum Requirements
- Five years' experience
- Must be able to provide all documentation of EmoProxy chip installation and any subsequent enhancements upon request

Team (Additional Household Staff)
- 2 RelaProxies (Sophie and Marco), who manage Mr. and Mrs. Preston's personal relationships, respectively
- Freelance SprinterProxies for delivery of household goods as needed
- RepairProxies as stipulated in estate's maintenance schedule
- Various domestic droids

Disclaimer
Applicant accepts that commuting time, expenses, and hazards are applicant's sole responsibility and that neither LifeCorp nor Mr. Preston is liable for any injuries or damages sustained in pursuit of emotional memories ("Scraps").

We are an equal opportunity employer.

LIV

THIS HAD BETTER BE WORTH IT.

With a grunt, I help Celeste push a piece of warped sheet metal aside to reveal a rusted drone. It's almost half her height.

"No way is that going to hold my weight," I say, rubbing my arms. The sun's not up yet. Wind whips across the sky-scraper's cluttered rooftop.

"I know it doesn't seem like much," she says, chewing the inside of her cheek. "But the specs are good. These drones used to carry nets full of fish, and those are heavy! You'll be fine, Liv. I'm pretty sure, anyway." She mumbles to herself as she does some math on her fingers. My nerves flicker. Celeste's inventions can border on genius—for anyone, let alone a nine-year-old—but this wouldn't be the first time her enthusiasm outpaced her calculations.

I eye the flaking LifeCorp logo on the drone's hull. "Surer than the compost incident?"

Her face twists in disgust at the memory before she switches topics. "Check out this harness! Kez helped me make it from old fishing nets." She slips one strap over my shoulder.

"He did? Doesn't really sound like his—ugh!"

The stench of fish guts overpowers me. I hold on to a tiny sliver of hope that the scent won't set into the fabric of my EmoProxy uniform: a thin amber jumpsuit with a wide hood and long sleeves that end in fingerless gloves. I sniff the front of the jumpsuit, right above the stenciled LifeCorp logo, and grimace. Celeste's flying machine better work, or my client Mr. Preston won't pay, and I'll end up smelling like a cannery droid for nothing.

Celeste takes a step back from her handiwork and nods, satisfied. She's wearing a jumpsuit like mine—except hers is dark gray—under a worn fuchsia puffy jacket two sizes too small. She reaches into the jacket's pocket and pulls out something that looks like two cans of jellied VitaBar soldered together.

"And here's the remote," she says proudly. I bite my tongue as I eye the crude contraption, but sure enough, when she switches it on, the drone comes to life, humming against my back.

"Can I *please* ride along? I'm small; you won't even notice!" She peers up at me with round dark brown eyes, the wind gently blowing the tops of her Afro puffs.

I shake my head firmly. "No way. For one, Thea would kill me. Two, this isn't a joyride, it's my *job*. Mr. Preston says he wants his Scraps 'pure.' I can't have you wriggling and screeching when I'm trying to channel my emotions. And thirdly, after Thea kills me, she'll have a droid replica made, Liv two point oh, so she can kill me all over again."

Celeste pouts. I do feel the teeniest bit of guilt; she did all this for me. If this works and Mr. Preston likes the Scrap, I'll get her something nice with my earnings. After LifeCorp takes its requisite cut, of course—forty percent off the top.

In the meantime, the least I can do is give her a good show.

"Fire it up, Celeste!"

She beams as she mashes the remote's buttons, and I'm airborne. One foot, then three, then five, hovering above the western tower's rooftop junk pile. Celeste squeals with delight, her jacket a bright spot surrounded by the dingy gray remains of decades' worth of furniture, clothing, and other forgotten LifeCorp purchases. At fifteen feet above the roof, I'm as ready as I'll ever be.

I shake out my hands and lift my wrist screen to my mouth. "Nero, begin Scrap," I tell the screen's AI software. The device chirps a confirmation that my EmoProxy neurochip is now making a Scrap: a recording of everything I see, smell, taste, touch, hear, and feel, and all the emotions that go along with those sensations.

I push past the fish smell and center myself on the thrill of weightlessness, the excitement of flight. The wind whooshes in my ears as Celeste zips me from one edge of the Fenway Towers to the other, and I marvel at the labyrinth of winding walkways and bridges that connects the cluster of buildings. A self-made community, built by the Lowers—the people who carry the Metro on their backs but enjoy almost none of its progress. *My* people. My home.

In the distance, the sun begins to rise over the Bay, transforming the glittering black water into a fiery orange. The whole of Sector Ten is ablaze. My neighborhood glows as molten gold spills onto the harbor, making the LifeCorp oil rigs off the coast look like gilded monuments. Celeste spins me south. From here, I can see all the way downtown. Sunlight bounces off Boston's chrome skyscrapers. The Citadel—home to LifeCorp's police force, the Forcemen–towers over the rest. I have to shield my eyes from the glare, but even I can't deny the beauty of the polished high-rises that house some of the Metro's most wealthy—the Uppers. An ache blooms in my chest. Someday we'll be there, or in a lavish apartment in New York, Philadelphia, or any of the Metro's other four boroughs, once cities in their own right. I've got six thousand credits saved up for proof of income already. Only nine thousand to go.

"Let's have some fun, Liv!" Celeste shouts. Before I can respond, I'm hurtling out over the Perimeter, the wide pedestrian avenue that encircles the Towers. The empty road hugs the wall that LifeCorp built around the Towers to contain our sprawl, forcing us to grow in on ourselves—tighter, closer—instead of outward. Celeste whoops as she enters some elaborate combination on the remote, and I do a full flip in the air. We both yelp with glee. My heart hammers against my chest as she flips me over and over. I can hardly breathe, I'm laughing so hard. Mr. Preston's going to *love* this. I can already picture his face as he experiences my exhilaration, feels his stomach do somersaults as if he himself were soaring over the Towers. Beats being stuck at a computer sixteen hours a day, that's for damn sure.

Over my shoulder, the drone's exhaust sputters.

"Uh, Celeste . . . ?"

I dip precipitously to the right. Below me, Celeste's eyes become saucers.

"Do something!" I shout.

"I'm trying!" She fumbles frantically with the remote, but it's not responding anymore. The Towers blur as I tumble toward what I *think* is the Perimeter. My eyes sting so much from the speeding air I can barely open them. I can't find the breath to scream as the ground lurches closer. I'm only eighteen. My life can't end like this. Can it?

Honestly, what a stupid fritzing way to die.

I'm not sure if Celeste figures something out, or maybe it's dumb luck, but the right-hand stabilizer suddenly fires just enough for me to reorient myself. I'm still falling, but now I can see my surroundings. Story after story of the Towers whizzes by, each fire-escape platform another number in the countdown to oblivion.

Or maybe a lifeline.

I unclip one strap of the harness, against every survival instinct. Clutching the drone with one arm, I sling the loose strap and pray to whoever's listening that its clip will catch onto something.

It works.

With a *thunk,* the clip hooks around a railing, jerking me upward, before it slips loose again. My dismount onto the landing below is not gentle, and a protruding rusty bar rips a wide gash in the sleeve of my uniform. But it's better than splattering onto the sidewalk.

Dozens of feet above, Celeste peers over a roof ledge at

me, panting with relief. I wave to show her I'm alright, then bring my wrist to my mouth.

"Nero, end Scrap."

Reality sets in. I almost died just now. . . .

If that doesn't sell, I don't know *what* will.

■ ■ ■

THE CLOTHING STALL IN THE TOWERS IS OUT OF EMOPROXY UNIFORMS, SO I have to settle for a plain gray Lower jumpsuit to replace the amber EmoProxy one I tore on my fall. It might have been faster to patch the hole, but making modifications of any kind to LifeCorp uniforms is strictly prohibited. Even an alteration that small would defeat the purpose of a uniform, I guess.

Now I'm half an hour behind schedule for my appointment with Mr. Preston, but even that can't stop me from humming with excitement. The wonder of taking flight, the death-defying plummet—there's no way my Scrap's not exactly what Preston's into. Last time we met, he told me he wanted something "pure." I can't think of anything purer than abject terror. Around me, Lowers of all kinds head to their first shift, wearing gray jumpsuits like the one I've got on. Most are on their way to LifeCorp's warehouses and factories, to create and package everything from toothbrushes to televisions—the goods that keep the entire Metro going. Among the sea of gray are a few pops of color: other Proxies like me, members of the lower class who have been mechanically modified to make the Uppers' lives more convenient so they can squeeze every last drop of productivity from their workday. Each Proxy wears a colored jumpsuit based on their specialty. Unless, of course, you rip a giant hole in one trying to impress a client.

My wrist screen buzzes. Kez's smartass grin appears on the screen before I accept the call. He's handsome, I suppose, but I've spent way too much time with him over the past ten years to ever see him as anything but an older brother.

"Hey," he yawns as he zips up his reflector-silver Sprinter-Proxy jumpsuit. "Did you take my last VitaBar?"

I freeze mid-chew. ". . . mo." Crumbs fly from my mouth.

"Come on, Liv! My shift starts in twenty. Now I'm gonna be hungry all day. I bet you've got more stashed around here somewhere. Somewhere private . . ." He scans the small apartment we share with Celeste, eyes settling on my corner of the single room.

"David Marquez, so help me, if you go anywhere *near* my library—"

"Relax!" He laughs. "I know better than to touch your precious books. Damn, busting out my government name and everything . . ."

"If you're really out of VitaBars, I'm sure one of your little girlfriends will spot you." I smile and take another exaggerated bite of the chicken-flavored kelp. "Mmm, tasty."

Kez responds with a taunting sneer. "Cute. We heard about your little stunt this morning, by the way. You should've seen Thea. I had no idea she knew so many curse words."

Whoops. "Damn, those CareProxy instincts are strong. She needs to find a new client, and a new gaggle of Upper kids to watch so she can stop mothering *me.*"

We laugh. In the crowd, another CareProxy—judging from his navy blue jumpsuit and kind, tired face—scowls at me.

I shrink. "I mean, uh—CareProxies are a vital part of our society." Which is true. I would love to have been raised by someone like Thea, instead of LifeCorp's Employee Care team, who took custody once my parents' work leave ran out at the six-month mark. After that trial period, parents decide if they can balance the two—work and childcare. Like most, mine apparently weren't up to the job.

"Glad you're okay," Kez says from the screen.

"Me too. And I'm sorry about your VitaBar." I frown. "But it wasn't your last. When I took it, there was still one left."

Confusion contorts the golden skin of his face, blossoming into frustration. "Celeste!" he shouts over his shoulder. The call ends.

Thirty minutes later I'm on the T's Green Line as the train glides toward the wealthy Sector One, commonly known as the Estates. After I left the Towers, most of the other Lowers trickled off, either going on the Red Line train to the canneries or to the factories via a fleet of LifeCorp shuttles. While other Lowers work double-shifts for LifeCorp, Proxies scatter throughout the Metro to run someone else's errands, stand in for someone else's appointments, or enjoy someone else's tee time.

I grab a window seat on the right side of the car so I can take a Scrap of the glimmering Boston skyline as we pass downtown. Decades ago, the subway lines of the T switched to elevated tracks, after sea levels rose too high to maintain the underground lines.

"Nero, end Scrap," I say.

The skyline is a view Mr. Preston has probably seen thousands of times. But other clients of mine—clients I prefer to keep off the official record—aren't so privileged and might appreciate the scene. Sometimes I feel strange calling these memories Scraps—"for the scrapbook of your life," the old LifeCorp benefit ads used to say—when the simplest image can hold so much meaning.

We pull into the Estates station. "Have your wrist screens ready," the Forceman at the checkpoint grumbles to the handful of non-droid passengers. The lanes at the checkpoint are color coded for each type of Proxy entering the Estates:

Lane 1 in the SprinterProxies' reflector-silver.

Lane 2 in the oil-slick black of the RepairProxies.

Pale pink *Lane 3* for the RelaProxies. A couple of them canoodle as they wait in line, clearly on a date for their respective clients.

Lane 4 is marked by the CareProxies' soothing deep blue.

And an amber-colored *Lane 5,* for the EmoProxies like me. My lane's the only empty one. EmoProxies are fairly rare, a perk reserved only for LifeCorp's most senior executives.

Proxies are the only Lowers permitted in the luxurious Estates—one of the perks tied to our higher productivity scores, along with better pay. The benefits aren't too bad, if you can get over these corporate thugs—the Forcemen—checking your status at every turn.

"Hood down," the Forceman commands as I reach the front of my line. I do as he says, lowering the hood of my jumpsuit and letting my thick black curls fully expand. The guard's eyes narrow as my ID pops up on his holographic display. His gaze darts from my face to the hovering image as he makes sure I check out: Liv Newman, eighteen, five foot five, brown-black eyes, deep brown skin. He pauses when he gets to my hair, and the part of me that everyone's curious about, whether they have the gears to ask or not.

I quirk an eyebrow. "Yes, Officer?"

He clears his throat gruffly. "You're out of uniform. That'll be a penalty of two hundred credits."

"It's not my fault; I was on a job for a client—"

Before I can finish explaining, he swipes the display, and my wrist screen confirms the fine's been paid. *Make that nine thousand two hundred credits to go until we can afford a home outside the Towers.*

"Never seen a Feele—er, an EmoProxy—in person before. How do you sleep with that thing?" He nods to my chip.

If only I had a credit for every time someone asked me this question. For a second, I regret not following Thea's advice to wear a twist-out whenever I go through the checkpoints, but that would be an invitation for Forcemen to put their fingers in my hair under the guise of a security screening. No thanks.

Everyone in the Metro's got some sort of chip, but most are embedded under the skin. Mine's a larger unit, a silver disc about an inch and a half in diameter that protrudes from the skin at the base of my skull. Three silver wires connect it to an additional sensor over my left temporal lobe, on the bone behind my ear. It's an upgraded model, designed to enhance my emotional responses, then capture and transmit those larger data packets. Feelings are more complicated than facts. *Same way you sleep with that LifeCorp leash around your neck* would be my preferred response to the Forceman. But I don't like to keep clients waiting.

"You get used to it." I pull my hood up, tight, and move along.

The Preston estate is massive—eight townhouses face one another in two neat rows, the wall around them creating a courtyard in the center. In school, they taught us that before LifeCorp formed the Metro by merging every major city from Atlanta up to Boston, multiple families used to live in each of these buildings, in condos barely bigger than the one-room apartment I share with Kez and Celeste. But that hardly seems like enough space for the Uppers, knowing how they like to live: an in-home movie theater, multiple kitchens, a guest home for entertaining—not that anyone ever comes to visit.

"You're late," Sophie, Mr. Preston's RelaProxy, taunts in a singsong voice as I sprint over the square's moss-resistant artificial cobblestones. Her pale pink jumpsuit brings out the natural blush on her light brown cheeks. I assume she's on her way to Mrs. Preston's house across the courtyard, for a date with Mrs. Preston's RelaProxy, Marco. RelaProxies stand in for their clients when it comes to maintaining their personal relationships—everything from cuddles to coffee chats. So Sophie meets up with Mr. Preston's friends and family—or rather, with *their* Proxies—and transfers her experience to Preston when she's done. In some ways, it's a lot like what I do, transferring emotional memories for pay. But the Prestons have such a busy social calendar, I doubt Sophie has any of her own personal relationships to maintain.

"Still got thirty seconds," I pant. "Catch you after!"

"Good luck!" she says. RelaProxies are trained in advanced interpersonal dynamics, and their brains are modified to maximize their empathy response. Who knows if Sophie would actually care if I'm late without her mods, but I'll take all the support I can get. I sprint past her and into the house, up the grand staircase to Preston's office.

"There you are," he says from his desk in the corner. His light brown skin is tinged with blue from the computer holoscreen's glow. The dark hollows under his eyes aren't hidden at all by the patchy concealer he's applied, which typically matches his skin tone perfectly but today seems too yellow. His hair, as always, is meticulously combed into shiny gray waves.

"Sorry, I'm late—" I begin, but he shushes me with a hand. He sets a small contraption on top of his desk. It almost looks like a pair of droid hands, except the endoskeleton's exposed; only the ten finger pads have texture. He activates the device, and it begins moving across the keyscreen, typing words, causing spreadsheets to open and close.

"Can't let my score drop. I'm on a tight deadline for this deliverable," he says. I nod, hoping he won't go into more detail about his workload. Mr. Preston tried to explain exactly what he does for LifeCorp once—logistics optimization something-or-other . . . I don't remember—but my eyes glazed over and I started thinking about how many credits I could get for pawning one of his paperweights.

I sit and wait on the pale mauve couch opposite his armchair. Everything in Mr. Preston's office has the suggestion of color—the faint lilac walls, the ivory of his shirt and pants—without coming too close to the real thing. Mr. Preston looks away from his screen and rubs his hands together, dark eyes shining bright. "Okay. What do you have for me?"

My nerves swarm like a cloud of nanobots. When I first started working for Mr. Preston three months ago, he had one request: books. Not the leadership drivel or pop psychology crap that clients have asked me to read in the past. *Real books*—classics like Brontë and Jemisin. Stuff I never even would've heard of, if my crew leader Silas hadn't smuggled me copies over the years. I could hardly believe my luck. But then, suddenly, Mr. Preston's taste changed. Instead of books, he wanted experiences. The pure stuff of life, he said. So I began with the usual fare: the latest explosion-riddled action movies, trending articles with lofty new philosophies. Things he'd be able to brag to his friends about. But he refused to pay for any of it. Proxies aren't technically bound to clients; I would've dropped him after the first week for an easier, lower fare, if it hadn't meant my productivity score taking a hit for turning down a job. Besides, even with LifeCorp's 40 percent cut, a single sale from him would set my crew up for weeks. All I have to do is crack this latest assignment. But if he doesn't like the Scraps I've brought, he won't pay today either. And if he doesn't pay—

From the corner of the room, an air regulator chimes and puffs a pleasing scent into the air—lavender, maybe? I feel calmer, even though I know it's not the TranquiliMist's floral aroma, but the scentless negative ions underneath that relax me.

Mr. Preston frowns. "You're nervous?" he asks, even though he knows the answer. The regulator is on sensor mode, triggered by the pheromones our bodies release. In this case, *my* body. The perfume in the air is all the confirmation he needs to know that I am, in fact, stressed.

"Just . . . eager to see what you think."

The corners of his mouth lift in a tired smile. "Let's begin, then." He drags his finger across his temple in a slow semicircle, then taps twice. Words appear before me.

ARTHUR PRESTON WOULD LIKE TO PAIR. ACCEPT?

Two taps of my temple, and we're synced.

I pull up the Scrap of the drone flight, knowing he sees the same thing. At first, he's confused by the angle, but I stay quiet and let the Scrap do the talking. The whoosh of the wind as I hover over the Towers. The sensation of floating above the horizon, racing toward the clouds. I wait. When the sun rises and Preston's breath hitches, I know it's hit him. The rush. The thrill. The feeling is his as much as it's mine now. And it's some of my best work.

As the Scrap shifts from wonder to danger, he grips the arms of his chair, panic etching his face. I relive every emotion through his eyes; every bolt of terror reverberates in me as he experiences it for the first time. Finally, the Scrap ends, and he opens his eyes.

"How was it?"

"That was lovely." He removes his glasses and cleans them on his shirt. "You love your home—the Towers—very much." It takes every ounce of restraint to control my face. A veritable blockbuster action sequence, and *that's* what he got from the Scrap? A trickle of affection as I glanced at the Towers for less than a minute, before plummeting to my death?

Preston notices my face fall. "You're upset?"

I sigh. "I'm sorry, sir. I'm trying, really."

"I think that might be the problem," he says, leaning forward. "Will you do me a favor next time? Keep it simple. Hmm?" A sympathetic pat of my hands punctuates his words.

Only one problem: I can't afford to wait for "next time." I want a better life for our whole crew—Celeste, Kez, Thea, even Silas if he'll leave—now. I love the Towers deeply, but I know there's more to life than its messiness and stench and struggle. There must be. Maybe that's why I do something so ridiculous next.

"Wait," I say as he lifts his hand to unpair. "I've got one more you might like." I pull up the new Scrap, the one of the regular ol' Boston skyline. I'd meant it for . . . less sophisticated clientele. But it's worth a shot.

The Scrap's not even fifteen seconds long, but by the end, Preston's in tears. I'd be lying if I said I understood why.

"Excellent. This . . . *this* is what I want."

I eye the regulator to make sure it's not pumping out goofy gas. "It is?"

He nods. "Simplicity. A memory without all the . . . artifice. How does five hundred sound?"

"Five . . . hundred credits? For one Scrap?" It's double his maximum rate, more than I usually make in three months, even after LifeCorp's cut. My heart pounds. Mr. Preston stares at me, waiting.

I clear my throat. "Five hundred sounds fair."

"Wonderful." Casually, he transfers the credits as I try not to float up to the ceiling.

The regulator chimes and sends out a plume of ions so strong, the citrusy smell of glee is almost palpable.

Is Preston "eccentric" enough for you now, Kez?

I think of all the things this money can do for us: for Celeste, a jacket that actually fits; for Kez, some cream for that road rash he swears will heal on its own. And half will be left over for my Liv and Crew Get the Hell Out of Here fund. Nine thousand and fifty credits to go now.

Mr. Preston checks the time. "I haven't taken my Mean break for the day yet. Care for a buzz?"

I pause. "With me?"

"Why not? We've got plenty to spare."

This is what Kez means when he says Preston's "a little off," I guess. Mean is a productivity drug, a stimulant that makes life shine brighter. Uppers and Lowers don't take it together. Ever. As far as I can tell, LifeCorp wants us to believe that Uppers don't take Mean at all. That the lives they've carved out for themselves in the Estates—lives full of meetings and promotions and someone else's thoughts in their heads all day—are enough to sustain them. But I'm not stupid. Anyone who's felt the rush of Mean for themselves could never turn it down.

Mr. Preston waits patiently for my answer. I could refuse, but I can tell he's already noticed the way my grip's tightened on the chair, the shallowness of my breathing. My body betraying etiquette, betraying me.

I nod.

He leads me into a small den next to his office. The sunken floor forms a square pit, filled with large plush cushions, all various hues of pale teal. As soon as we're seated, a small bot rolls in, a tray on its square back. The injectable triangular vials on the tray are still cold, which means Preston must have a stash somewhere in the house. I can already hear Silas's voice in my head, planning a raid he swears will change our futures. But I ignore it as Mr. Preston hands me my dose. I won't tell Silas. Let the Prestons have their stash. Not everything plentiful needs to be plundered.

I tug the patch on the upper arm of my uniform to open it, exposing my bare shoulder. The vial of crystal-clear liquid hisses softly as I click the injector into my soft flesh. It's a sound I've grown to associate with euphoria, the intoxicating buoyancy of this chemical that governs my life. Seconds later, I feel thrilled, hopeful, ecstatic. About everything. About nothing in particular. It's a good hit. Not the watered-down stuff you get in the Towers.

Mr. Preston exhales and lowers his own injector, grinning a hair too wide to be natural. "That's better, isn't it?"

"Definitely not worse." I lean against the cushions and let my eyes drift to the coffered ceiling. Things are working out. Things *will* work out.

We both let the Mean lead our thoughts for a few minutes.

I plan out my Scraps for my off-the-books client this afternoon, bolstered by the fuzzy, assured feeling the drug provides. Mr. Preston absentmindedly taps his fingernail against the glass vial in his hand. He's contemplating something, but he won't say what. At last, he speaks.

"I have an offer for you. A new assignment."

I snap back to attention, the need for more credits stirring within. He continues. "There is something I've been meaning to go see at least once more before . . ." He frowns at his wrinkled hands. "Well, I suppose discretion is foolish at this point. Liv, I got some bad news from Employee Care today. I'm very, very sick. LifeCorp insists I'm fit enough to work, but I'm under no illusions that the next chapter of my life will be a long one. You'd think LifeCorp would grant an old man a little time off. Time I've *earned* . . ."

Careful, I lean toward him. "Sir?"

He's a million miles away.

"'. . . and not, when I came to die, discover that I had not lived.'" He shakes his head slightly and comes back to the room. "You can return tomorrow with more of what you brought today, and I'll pay what's fair. But if you're interested . . . here are some coordinates." He swipes his wrist and a map floats in front of me, in my augmented vision. I furrow my brow, working hard to make sense of the image. There are no markers I recognize, no street names. There are barely any streets at all.

"I don't understand. Where is this?" I look past the augment, at his face.

"My old lake house. I used to spend every summer there, before the Merger. Out in Sunapee." He says the last part like it's supposed to mean something, but it's a word I've never heard before.

I frown. "Is that a southern borough?" I've always wanted to see DC.

He wavers for a moment. "No. It's . . . north."

"North?" I almost laugh. "There's nothing north of— Wait." I do my best to blink away the Mean's rosy fog as the information begins to weave together. I zoom out on the map. *Sunapee*—the word even sounds strange in my mind—is a tiny lake town an hour or two's drive north of the Metro's northern boundary, which is an hour or two north of where anyone I know has ever been. Beyond LifeCorp's jurisdiction, beyond the "protection" of the Forcemen.

Going there would be a death sentence.

"No one leaves the Metro and lives to tell about it," I say.

He grimaces. "That's not *entirely* true—"

"So the stories of feral raiders in the Outerlands are what? Fairy tales?" I've heard about the people who resisted Life-Corp's rule since I was a kid—how they rejected Metro citizenship after the Merger. Turned droids that ventured into their wild woods into mutilated bits of scrap metal with obscenities painted on the side for good measure, and did worse to any human foolish enough to try the same.

"No. No, the stories are real. But they aren't . . ." There's a flash of sadness in his eyes that makes my heart lurch. I make a mental note to review the sensation later, to see if it has any value as a Scrap. What's the going rate for sympathy these days?

I stand to leave. "I'm sorry, sir. I'm not—"

"I'll pay you one hundred thousand credits."

Those words, in that order, make no sense. So I walk on.

"Liv. Stop." He's still seated on the cushions. "Listen to what I'm saying. One hundred *thousand* credits could change your life."

It takes my brain a second to catch up, and even then, I know I'm not fully grasping what his offer could mean. Used properly, a hundred thousand credits is enough to hang up being an EmoProxy forever, not to mention move into a nicer place. I wouldn't qualify as an Upper, but I could leave Boston and settle in a quieter town in the Metro. I picture myself running a cozy little antique bookshop with one of those adorable cat-bots snoozing in a bay window.

"That's a lot of cred. To see what?" I ask.

"The stars."

Risk my life for more credits than I've ever even thought about, to look at the stars? *Could he be any stranger?* "The . . . Okay. And what would you like me to feel when I see the stars?"

He shrugs, a twinkle in his eye. "Just . . . be open. To the awe of it all." *Apparently, he can be.*

A part of me says I should refuse this suicide mission. But if I make it back, I'll have a chance at something much, much more than survival. I could have a *life.*

"I can't leave—"

His shoulders sag. "Of course. I under—"

"—today," I finish. "I have another client this afternoon. Would tomorrow work?"

Mr. Preston's eyes light up, from somewhere deeper than the Mean can reach. "Tomorrow's perfectly fine."

ADRIAN

"YOU DON'T HAVE TO DO THIS," I SAY TO MY PARTNER, NAS, STRAINING AS I push the weights off my chest. He watches me struggle without so much as a glimmer of concern.

"Nonsense, rookie. What kind of partner would I be if—"

"No, I mean literally. It just occurred to me that you don't have to do this." By some miracle, I manage to rack the bar. Nas pulls me up to sit. His synthetic skin is rubbery against my hand. "What do you do with all the time you don't spend staying in shape?"

He shrugs. "Drills, mostly."

"Drills? That's it?"

"What's wrong with that? Should I spend it growing little green friends like you?" Nas shoots a pointed glance at the towers of hydroponic herbs and vegetables that adorn the corners of this room, the second bedroom of my apartment, which I had converted into a home gym. "So inefficient. I don't get why you don't just eat VitaBars like everyone else, instead of blowing your credits on . . . *plants.*" His lip curls at the last word.

"Last I checked, VitaBars are made from kelp, which is *also* a plant. And the lab-made flavors don't taste the same. So, like . . . what *kinds* of drills are you doing? Like endurance runs, or . . ."

"Rule number one of working with a droid, rookie: don't try to compete, unless you like to lose." He smirks as he tosses me a towel, and I note the slight gap between his front two teeth. It's a nice touch by the engineers—a gap here, a freckle there. The slight imperfections in every droid's design that make it even easier to forget they're not human.

"I'm not trying to compete." Even as I say it, I'm watching us in the gym's mirrored wall, comparing our reflections. Nas is a tank personified with golden brown skin and broad shoulders under his uniform that would make you shocked at how fast he is. I'm darker and slender—though I've come a long way from the scrawny kid I was on my first day at the Academy. Young Adrian would have lost his mind if he'd known he'd be working with a droid someday.

Droids aren't all they're cracked up to be, kid. Just smarter, stronger pains in the a—

"Earth to rookie." Nas whistles as he waves a hand in front of my face.

I roll my eyes. "We started on the Force at the same time, genius. If I'm a rookie, what does that make you?"

"Hmm, I dunno. On time for roll call, maybe?" He's out the door before I check the time on my wrist screen. I've got eight minutes to shower, change into my uniform, and get to the Citadel's briefing room.

Fritz me.

■ ■ ■

".. . TO REMIND YOU THAT DETAINMENTS IN THE ESTATES SHOULD BE LIMITED to thirty minutes or less, in order to avoid productivity loss . . ." Inspector Redding's voice drones from the podium. I wait for him to scroll through his notes before slinking in along the back wall.

"*Psst.* Rookie!" Nas whispers, patting the empty seat beside him.

I scoot in and join the sea of diverse faces, each wearing the same white-and-gray Forceman uniform that I am. Everyone in the Metro, from Uppers all the way down, is multiracial in some way. In the Force's Academy, we learned that that wasn't always true, that people used to distinguish themselves from one another using their ethnic backgrounds, religions, and more. Sounds complicated, if you ask me. Nowadays, there are only two differences that matter: what you do for LifeCorp and how productive you are at doing it.

"'Scuse me," I say as I shuffle down the row, toward Nas. A couple of officers glare at me as I pass them, the same way they did when we were kids. As soon as I sit, the girl beside me whispers out of the corner of her mouth. "Not sure how they do it in the *Outerlands,* but in the Metro things start on time," she hisses. *Make that three differences that matter.* Can't believe it's not even 0900, and we're already playing the "blame every mistake Adrian makes on the fact that he's from the Outerlands" game. Like it's my fault I was dumped on the Metro's doorstep by my so-called family—raiders from the Outerlands—as a toddler.

I brush off the insult, like I always do. On my right, Nas rolls his eyes. "Humans. So tribal. Just ignore her, man." As Redding keeps speaking, Nas adds another bullet point to his immaculately organized notes, which he takes for no other reason than to piss me off. No, seriously, he actually told me that once.

"Moving on," Inspector Redding says. "As you know, the borough of Boston is consistently ranked one of the safest and most productive in the Metro—" He pauses to allow a couple of whoops and "hell yeahs" from the crowd. "However, we've begun an investigation into a troubling new development."

He swipes his hand in the air, and the slide projected behind him changes to a side-by-side comparison of two brain scans. On the left, two kidney bean shapes glow yellow and green in the middle of the brain's bright purple hue. On the right, the entire periphery of the brain is aflame—fiery oranges and reds surround the center.

"Who can tell me the difference between these two images?" Redding asks. A junior officer—human, judging by the absence of a data core at the base of her neck—raises her hand.

"The one on the left depicts normal neural activity. The one on the right . . . some sort of disease?"

The inspector nods, satisfied. "As far as we're concerned, yes. Factories in Sector Ten have been dealing with some behavioral challenges over the past month. Declining output, workers disobeying supervisors. Some have even insulted LifeCorp directly—"

Outraged cries fill the room, my own among them. LifeCorp

is singlehandedly responsible for the prosperity everyone in the Metro enjoys today. That goes double for the Lowers. Eighty years ago, the government got into a bind: too much debt, not enough credits to pay it off, unless they wanted a riot on their hands. And it almost came to that, from what I've been told—total societal collapse, like over in Europe. Thankfully, LifeCorp stepped in and offered the US government a deal: redistrict the biggest cities into privatized territories, and they'd take care of the infrastructure, food production, health care—the works. By 2284, their market cap rivaled the fourth-largest GDP in the world, so the choice was obvious. The only catch, if you can even call it that, is that everyone in the Metro is technically a LifeCorp employee, which sounds worse than it is. I'd rather wear LifeCorp's logo over my heart as a Forceman than eat tree bark for dinner as a raider.

Inspector Redding waits calmly for us to settle, but the smirk on his face says that he agrees with our disgust. These workers should be thanking the company for the literal shirts on their backs, not spitting in their supervisors' faces.

He continues. "Brain scans of three different culprits all resembled the image on the right to varying degrees."

"Hang on," an officer behind me says. "Only three? There are thousands of workers in Sector Ten. Who cares about three cases?"

"This type of infliction can spread quickly," Redding explains. "Three could easily turn into three hundred. We're talking about a huge potential threat to LifeCorp, which means it's a threat to the natural order of things. As dangerous as any raider, but within our own walls."

I inhale sharply at his choice of words. Everyone in the room knows how I ended up here. Every day I have to work a little bit harder than the rest of them so they don't question my commitment to LifeCorp. The ironic thing is, I'm more loyal to our employer than any of them could ever be. Without LifeCorp's generosity, I'd be dead.

I ignore my peers' sidelong glances as I raise my hand. "But, sir, what exactly is causing the change in these workers?"

"Analytics believes it's a drug, similar to Mean but clearly meant to disrupt instead of motivate. For now, we're calling it Orange Haze. Getting to the bottom of it—who's manufacturing it, how they're moving it right under our noses—is our new top priority."

The inspector swipes to the next slide, showing a virtual map of the northern half of the Metro. The borough of Boston sits near the top of a gray shaded area that stretches all the way down south to Atlanta. To the west of the Metro's thick black boundary, symbols of trees and wheat represent the droid-operated lumber forests and sorghum fields occupying most of the country. Redding zooms in again on Boston. The borough's thirteen sectors surround our wealthiest sector, the Estates, in concentric circles. Officer names appear beside each sector—our beats for the week. "Chang and Darrow, you're here, undercover in the canneries. Ask around, see if you can find out who's dealing. Costello and Okeke, the riverfront ports. Popov and Simpson, the VitaBar factory on Dudley Street . . ." I rub my clammy hands on my pants as Redding continues down the list. Since I graduated six months ago, Nas and I have mostly been on grunt work—retrieving errant drones from the docks, directing shuttle traffic out of the warehouse lots—when we're not sitting behind a desk waiting for something to happen. This feels like the start of something. A chance for me to prove that I can be useful in the field and defend the company that literally saved my life. Nas glares at me as my knee bounces, his own body perfectly still.

". . . Rao and Davani, Fenway Towers, with me."

There's a beat of silence as everyone processes Redding's final order, then a flurry of whispers descends. Humans and droids sneak looks at me and Nas, but I'm too busy trying to stop the room from blurring to notice.

Nas's hand shoots up. "Sir, the Towers? With all due respect, we don't—"

"We don't patrol there, I know. We do now. Company orders: no stone unturned."

"We'll be walking targets!" Nas continues, artificial veins pulsing on his shaved head. He's out of his motherboard, shouting at a commanding officer like this, and I'm nervous for him. That is, until I remember the ace he's got in his pocket. Redding can't bench him; he'd effectively be junking a million-dollar investment.

"It's not up for discussion, Davani."

Nas isn't happy, but he shuts up after that. Unlike him, I don't have the luxury of telling off our boss and not getting fired, so I keep my protests to myself. *The Towers are a rat's nest, and Lowers don't play fair. The reason we don't patrol there is because they don't believe in law or order. Even if we're undercover, they'll sniff us out a mile away, and we'll be trapped. . . .*

I sway in my seat. Nas grips my arm, and the room comes

back into focus. "Snap out of it," he growls under his breath. "I know crowds aren't your thing, but don't blow this for me. Or for yourself."

"Not my thing"? It's a little more than that. The only memory I have of my time before the Metro is being crammed into a raider cargo truck full of other terrified children and driven out of the Outerlands. It was dark, and hot, and—

A sharp flick on my ear. "Cut it out." Nas glances down to where I'm clutching my chair's cloth armrest for dear life. "You got new upholstery money? Didn't think so."

I focus on my breathing until my heart stops slamming against my chest. At the front of the room, Redding makes a fist, and the screen goes black. "Everyone clear? Excellent. Rao and Davani, we'll rendezvous at the Towers' southern gate at thirteen hundred. *Not* thirteen ten." He drills his eyes into me, and my cheeks burn. I may have graduated top of my class, but punctuality was never my strong suit. Redding's gone before I can protest any further. The Towers being off-limits is the only reason I signed up for fieldwork in the first place. If I had known for one second I could be assigned there . . . So many dark halls and tunnels . . . all those people . . .

Nas stays by my side long after everyone else has filed out of the briefing room. "A new drug in the Towers. As if those people don't have enough problems, between the gangs and overcrowding. I'll never understand how humans can be so heartless that they'd turn on their own kind," he says.

"Nas, man, I want to stop whoever's doing this. You know I do." I gulp a breath. "But the Towers? I don't know if I . . . if I can . . ."

"You can." He stares at me as if he can will me to believe it with his gaze. "Stopping Orange Haze is now the most important case in the Metro, and we've been assigned to ground zero."

I nod slowly, absorbing his words. I wanted a chance to prove myself, to show how much I believe in the world that LifeCorp has created, and now I've got one. The opportunity may not have appeared the way I expected, but it's still huge.

And it's mine to lose.

3

LIV

I'M GOING TO THE OUTERLANDS. TOMORROW.

The realization of what I've agreed to is so shocking that I almost forget to stop by Mr. Preston's library on my way out. Almost. I glance around, self-conscious, even though it's not forbidden, technically. Ever since I started here, Mr. Preston's made it clear that I'm welcome to borrow anything that looks interesting. I run my fingers over the aging spines, searching for a book to bring on the trip. Mr. Preston's car is self-driving, so that leaves me with two hours to kill.

My hand stops over a drab green paperback. *Walden; or, Life in the Woods.* Fitting. I put the book in my bag, then head to the kitchen to swipe a VitaBar or five for Kez.

I'm rummaging through the well-stocked butler's pantry, reserved for storage and the help, when Sophie bursts into the room, her pretty brown face streaked with tears and angry red splotches. She spreads her hands on the massive island counter, taking deep gulping breaths for a minute or two. I freeze. Kez thinks being a RelaProxy is a cushy gig, but honestly, their jobs are some of the hardest. It's more than just rattling off life updates. Sophie is Mr. Preston's stand-in for every argument, every piece of difficult news. Whatever she needs to get her head back on straight after a tough morning, I don't want to interrupt her.

I try to sneak out before she notices, but a VitaBar slips out of my overloaded bag and hits the ground with a *thwack*. Sophie spins around.

I wince. "Sorry."

"Liv? Have you been there this whole time?" She wipes her face frantically with her pink jumpsuit sleeve. I'm waiting for anger, for accusation. But instead, one corner of her mouth lifts in a weak smile.

"Yeah. You're not mad?" I step away from the cupboard and hand her a bar as a peace offering. Sophie and I aren't close—once RelaProxies find a patron, they typically live at their estate. So while I've been crammed in the Towers for the past ten years, she's been living it up out here, in the height of luxury. But even though she could look down at me, Sophie's always been kind.

"Not mad," she confirms. "I'm fresh out of mad." The redness in her cheeks fades to a gentler flush of pink. She's only a couple of years my senior, but the lines on her face make her seem older.

"Oh?"

"It was just supposed to be a quick coffee date. But Marco can be so . . ." She balls a fist. "Mr. Preston only wanted to know if Mrs. Preston would be interested in taking a short walk together later. Fifteen minutes at most."

"Uh-huh. What did Marco say?"

"That Mrs. Preston was needed elsewhere, and what were they paying RelaProxies for, if Mr. Preston insisted on meeting in person all the time? And that if Mr. Preston didn't focus on getting promoted, Marco'd have nothing to tell Mrs. Preston's friends' RelaProxies at brunch this weekend. Then he ended coffee ten minutes early." She lets out a yell of frustration that bounces off the chrome cabinets. "How am I supposed to tell Mr. Preston any of that? I know he'll be disappointed—that's nothing new. But he doesn't have any friends. How can I be a RelaProxy with no relationships to maintain? I'll lose my job!"

"Right. I'm sorry." There's really nothing else for me to say. Sophie's the expert here. After seeing her high level of empathy as a child, Employee Care put her on the RelaProxy track at the age of five—no factory life for her. Whereas I'd probably be two fingers short on a conveyor belt line somewhere if Silas hadn't paid for my EmoProxy chip when I was eight. There's nothing Sophie doesn't know about interpersonal dynamics, no trick she probably hasn't already tried. I, on the other hand, have approximately three friends in the entire world—three point five, if you count Silas. And one of them is a nine-year-old nuisance.

Sophie pulls out a compact and touches up her makeup. Twenty seconds later, you'd never guess she'd been crying. A butler droid sweeps into the room, his non-human identity betrayed only by the flawless precision of his steps. He bows slightly.

"Ms. Newman. Your . . . colleague Mr. Marquez has arrived." A twinge of disgust threatens to upset his symmetrical features. He frowns at a crystal pitcher of water on a nearby bar cart, picking it up to remove a smudge just as Kez rushes in. The pitcher falls from the butler's hands, toward the hardwood. Faster than I can even think of reacting, Kez plucks it from the air, mere inches to spare.

"There you go, pal." Kez gives the droid the pitcher—not a drop of water spilled—with a rough pat on the back. The silver smart lenses in Kez's eyes twinkle as he grins, indicating that his SprinterProxy mods were to thank for his agility and fast reaction time. I roll my eyes, but I can't say I'm not impressed. Even without the SprinterProxy augmentation, Kez would be fast. With it, he's superhuman. Comes in handy when you deliver things for a living . . . even the light bulbs or single packs of gum that Uppers across the Metro decide they simply *must* have in fifteen minutes or less.

"Remind me to come out to the Estates more often," Kez says. "Think I finally got the exhaust fumes out of my nose." He yawns as he rubs his neck. An embossed chrome hummingbird tattoo peeks out from his collar. His tired eyes brighten as he notices Sophie in the room.

"Sophie! Fair Duchess. Light of my life. It's been too long."

Sophie deigns to cast him a perfunctory glance. "Kez." A prim smile. "I thought I sensed the stench of unmerited confidence in the air."

Unfazed, Kez leans his forearms casually on the counter. "Tell me, Duchess. When's the last time you were held? I mean truly *held,* by someone who knows what they're doing?" He waggles his eyebrows, getting nothing but a tired sigh from Sophie in return.

"I have to go; time to check in with Mr. Preston. See you later, Liv."

She darts from the room. Kez's eyes track her the entire time. Once she's gone, he lets out a heavy breath.

"Sophie, Sophie, Sophie. Marco's a fool to make her cry like that."

"You could tell she was sad?" I ask.

"She's usually meaner to me. Keeps things exciting." He yawns again. I realize I didn't hear him come home last night. *How late was his shift?* Before I can ask, Kez's screen beeps with a warning. He's been off the clock too long. One more hour and his productivity score will take a hit; he'll lose the multiplier on his wages and go from earning two-and-a-half times each job's pay back down to one.

Kez's jaw ticks. "Let's go."

The air in the courtyard is sweet, perfumed with jasmine and honeysuckle. A SprinterProxy wearing a jet pack zooms over the trellised wall toward Mrs. Preston's house. Kez watches the Proxy wistfully. I feel for him; Silas sponsored the Proxy modifications for all of us—me, Thea, and Kez—but his budget only stretches so far. Kez will have to work for several more years in order to afford a jet pack enhancement. He catches me watching him and makes a show of shrugging. Arms outstretched, he takes a deep breath as we approach his cycle. The tension in his face softens a little.

"Nice flowers. Should we pick a few to freshen up our

place?" he asks. Getting rid of the funky smell in our apartment has been a project ever since the first night we squatted there. I gave up around the two-year mark. But four years later, Kez is still devoted to the cause.

"Aw, come on," I say. "It's not that bad, is it?"

"It smells like feet."

Eh. He's not wrong. "Yeah, but I don't mind it so much anymore."

"That's because *you* smell like feet. I've been meaning to tell you." He leans in close and takes a big whiff before pretending to gag. I shove him away, but thanks to his mods, Kez is annoyingly stable on his feet. He pops a helmet on my head before I can think of a witty rebuttal, and we start the ride to the Towers.

■ ■ ■

KEZ'S CYCLE WEAVES EFFORTLESSLY THROUGH TRAFFIC. SOMETIMES I HAVE TO shut my eyes because he cuts it so close to other vehicles, but I trust him and his mods to assess the risk better than I can. On his dashboard, a small rectangle flashes yellow-orange with bold black words in the center:

DAVID MARQUEZ—U92702-632-05

3 DELIVERIES WAITING. 81 POTENTIAL CREDITS.

START A NEW SHIFT?

"Thanks for picking me up," I say into my helmet's headset. "I know you're missing out on work for this."

The fabric on his silver jacket stretches as he shrugs. "'S not a problem. I needed a break anyway. One of the other Sprinters got pinned between an autotaxi and a tunnel wall this morning. Smashed his femur . . . part of the job, I guess." I can't see Kez's face, but I can sense his eyes shift down, the way they do when he's pretending he doesn't care about something. His posture straightens. "But listen . . ."

For a second, he sounds like Silas. I know exactly where this is going. I wait for the details: Where to go. When to be there. Who to approach.

"Silas has a job for us," Kez continues. "Tonight. This guy's missed his payments, two months running. Used to work at the river port, but apparently, he got laid off. . . ."

"Droids." I say it at the same time Kez does. "Two months? That's generous." Silas would've noticed a missed protection fee payment after the first month. He's not usually one to give second chances.

"Right? Guess the so-called Dagger of the Towers is getting dull in his old age." His shoulders bounce as he laughs, rich and deep. "Anyway, the guy's name is Jonah . . . Rodriguez, maybe? Ricardo? R-something, I'll look it up. Not sure where he lives, but I heard he sometimes hangs out in the southwest tower's Arcade."

"Can't we find another way to get Silas his money?" I ask as Mr. Preston's offer flashes in my mind. I'm not planning to tell Kez about the gig until after it's done, mostly because if he freaks me out enough, I might lose my nerve. I remind myself of the life we'll have once I return from the Outerlands, a hundred thousand credits richer. No more struggle. No more intimidating our own.

Kez's cycle slows as we exit the turnpike, the Towers looming ahead. "You ask that every time. And what do I say every time?"

"'It's not about the money.' Easy for you to say. You don't have to do the hard part."

"To whom much is given, much will be required," he says. I wonder if he can feel me rolling my eyes behind him. I'm well aware that being an EmoProxy makes me the best person for this particular job. Before my expensive modification procedure, Silas's shakedowns were . . . a lot bloodier. I came up with the idea to switch strategies, once I realized I could transmit not only happy memories but my more traumatic ones as well. Like most parents in the Metro, mine gave me up to LifeCorp's Employee Care unit at six months, the maximum allowed parental leave for Lowers before their productivity score gets dinged. The Employee Care team raised me from then on, training me for a life in the factories and warehouses as soon as I knew my shapes and colors. My time in Employee Care was anything *but* caring. But I only pull those memories out when Silas needs someone to cooperate.

Don't get it twisted: I hate—*hate*—using my chip this way. But Silas practically raised me, after I escaped from the factory. Without his generosity, I wouldn't even *be* an EmoProxy. I owe him everything, even if I hate these shakedowns. And once I get Preston's credits, I'll never have to do one again.

"Silas is just trying to keep the peace, Liv." Kez glances

back at me as we pull up to the Towers' entrance. "South-west tower. Tonight, outside the water stall." His wrist screen beeps a friendly "reminder" of how much money he could be making right now. His grip on the handlebar tightens.

One last job. Then you're free. "I'll be there." I squeeze Kez's shoulder, then join the current of people pushing through the gate into the Towers. As the buildings' darkness devours the sunlight, I breathe a sigh of relief. The Estates may be beauti-ful, but all that open space makes me feel too exposed. Here I'm safe and protected. Home.

I head east in the crowd. Someone—a *tall* someone, all limbs—bumps me with their shoulder. As his dark, clear eyes widen, I get a look at his face. It's a beautiful one, as far as faces go—strong and angular, with deep bronze skin and full, black eyelashes that I'm a little jealous of. But his jumpsuit's too clean, his movements too stiff.

A Forceman in disguise?

"I'm sor— I didn't mean to—" A flush of heat crawls up the skin above his neckline. He seems to be having trouble breathing.

A *claustrophobic* Forceman in disguise. Amateur.

"Spare me." I scowl at him, then continue walking. But something stays my steps. Silas would call it instinct. So-phie would call it *empathy*. Thea would call it my conscience. Whatever it is, it's annoying.

Help him. You get what it's like when the panic sets in, a voice inside says. Sure, I get jittery sometimes, when I think too hard about you know, life, and how literally everything we do is for LifeCorp. How it's never enough. It's not the same thing as being a Forceman who can crawl into bed in his fully furnished, LifeCorp-subsidized apartment after his shift is done. I give the guy one last glance. He's frozen in the steady stream of people, fists tight at his sides. His skin's getting clammy, and my own pricks in response.

Help him.

"Fritzing hell," I mutter to myself, and push against the current of bodies to reach the Forceman. I grab his arm.

"What—"

"You're five seconds from collapsing in the middle of the Perimeter," I say as I drag him to the side. "Nobody wants that. Stepping over a body slows down traffic."

I guide him to a quiet spot behind a junk heap. Immediately, the Forceman slumps to the ground and cradles his head in his hands. The imprint from his missing Forceman signet ring is still visible around his pinky . . . they must think we're total idiots.

As his shallow breathing slows, I wait for disgust to roil in me, but there's nothing except . . . sympathy? *Hell of a time to find your inner humanity, Liv.*

"Great, you're, uh, all set," I say. "So I'm . . . gonna go."

He says nothing, only whimpers. Doesn't he have anyone with him? A partner or something? I check my wrist screen for the time. I'm going to be late for my next client if I stay much longer. The Forceman lets out a deep shuddering breath that racks his whole body, and that annoying feeling surges in me again. *Fine.* But if I *am* going to help him, we need to move this along.

I sit beside him, a little confused. I thought the Force

equipped their officers with the latest training in psychological warfare, suspect intimidation, the works. But clearly they can't be bothered to give their people the tools to navigate their own minds.

"Right, okay," I say. "Eyes on me? Great." *Whoa.* Better than great. He's . . . Damn.

Focus!

"I want you to tell me three things you can hear," I say. His eyes drift as he listens.

"The . . . people." His voice is strained. "Their footsteps. Their voices. Their laughter." His shoulders have stopped heaving, which I only notice because at some point, I apparently put my hand on one of them. I snatch it away, mildly horrified.

"Sorry," I say. "But that's good, good job. Now two things you can, um, feel."

He considers our little patch of alley. "The gravel." He wiggles the heel of his boot against the ground. His leg shifts slightly, so that the sides of our thighs touch. His body heat radiates through the thin fabric of our jumpsuits. My stomach flips in a way that is not wholly unpleasant, but *is,* in fact, out-of-this-world insane. The Forceman must notice the same thing, because he gestures to our legs and mutters something unintelligible. Guess that's feeling number two, then.

I exhale. "And one thing you can"—*Don't say "see." Don't say "see." You're not equipped to handle those eyelashes again!*— "smell!" The dreamy expression on his face is gone in a blip.

"Oh! Uh—garbage!" He says it like he's got the winning answer on one of those old quiz shows, and I burst out laughing.

Then he's laughing too. It's a few minutes before we manage to calm down, leaning our heads back on the damp brick wall. "Thank you." His words come out breathy. "I'm not usually great in crowds, but that was . . ."

"Don't think about it. You'll only drag yourself under again. Ask me how I know."

He chuckles. "Wish I could tell my brain to cut it out sometimes, you know?"

"Wouldn't that be something?" My hood slips a little. I pull it tight over my head to cover my chip and the wires behind my ear. I don't really feel like being a technological oddity right now, and as long as I keep my hood up, he'll think I'm a regular Lower. Not that I care what some random Forceman thinks.

He shifts to face me. "I'm Adrian." Those piercing brown eyes again, and an adorable half smile that is going to be a big problem for me.

Wait, *what?* No, it absolutely will not, because he's a Forceman. And I am never going to see him again. *Damn. That's the last time I take Mean from Mr. Preston's supply.* I blink Adrian's—the Forceman's—smile out of my head and stand to go.

"Stick to the sides if you're going to be here much longer. Like I said, no one wants to trample over you. It's inconvenient." I narrow my eyes at the street and gauge the fastest way to my next client. Anything to avoid his gaze.

"I'm sorry, did I do some—"

"Your disguise sucks, by the way." And then I'm gone, into the crowd and away from a truly terrible lapse in judgment.

■ ■ ■

MY NEXT CLIENT, MAE RIVERA, IS GRINNING FROM EAR TO EAR WHEN SHE opens her front door. I guess as her dealer, I should expect nothing less. But part of me hopes that she genuinely likes me.

"Come in, mija!" She closes the door behind me, and I slip off my shoes. Mae works the night shift in a VitaBar factory, while her husband Joe's at the ports receiving shipments all day. Romantic relationships in the Metro are short-lived—hard times and logistical challenges usually make it easier to separate. But the Riveras' bond has held strong, despite their opposite schedules.

The warmth of the apartment helps me shake any lingering thoughts of whatever just happened with that Forceman, and how regrettably handsome he was. The Riveras have lived in this apartment for more than twenty years. Like everywhere else in the Towers, it's bare—most people are too exhausted at the end of the day to focus on interior design—but little touches make it feel like a home to me. A dusty chalkboard on the wall, with old notes that Mae and her husband leave for each other as they head to their respective night and day shifts. A worn photograph of the two of them in an old picture frame on the side table. The picture must be at least a decade old, given the lack of gray in Mae's hair, but the softness in her eyes hasn't changed.

And then there's the view, from the apartment's fire escape platform outside their main room. It's rare that an outdoor space hasn't been sealed off in the name of adding one more "room" for rent, even if it's just a mat on steel grating. A few potted plants sit on the fire escape, their velvety leaves begging to be touched. The vibrant green seems so out of place in the gray-beige of the Towers. And yet, here they are, reminding me that something else can grow in this place, if given the chance.

As Mrs. Rivera makes us some tea, a shock of deep, iridescent fuchsia moves between the awnings to my left, two stories up. It vanishes before I can catch it directly, but that doesn't stop me from rolling my eyes. I've only seen one person wear that color. I bring my wrist to my mouth.

"Celeste." My wrist screen beeps as it makes the call. A hundred yards away, a pair of too-big brown eyes peers out from behind a steel beam.

"Hi." Even my wrist screen's cheap speakers can capture the shyness in her voice. I smile in spite of myself.

"Hi. Whatcha doin'?"

"Watching out for you!" She says it like it's obvious. The idea of a nine-year-old kid being my sworn protector is both adorable and a little depressing. I stifle a laugh as she continues. "I know you're selling Scraps to Lowers, even though it's . . ." Her voice drops to a grave whisper. ". . . *illegal*. And there's some weird-looking guys in the alley. Stiff. Not droids, though."

More Forcemen. How many of them *are* there? I hide my annoyance. "Uh-huh. And if you can see them, what makes you think they can't see you?"

A pause. "Aw, man," she says. There's a shuffling sound

as I watch her tuck herself deeper into the awning's scaffolding, until she's out of sight. "How's this?" she asks, her voice slightly muffled now.

"Better."

"I'm scared, Liv. I don't want you to get caught."

The fear in her voice makes me doubt myself for a second. All Proxy services, including my Scraps, are reserved exclusively for Uppers, no one else. That's a LifeCorp order, issued in the name of greater productivity and prosperity for all. I only started dealing in the Towers a month ago, after I realized how much time it would take to crack Mr. Preston. It's absurdly easy; Lowers pay for the simplest things—a blade of grass blowing in the wind, the reflection of moonlight in a puddle. Things a triple shift in LifeCorp's factories won't allow them the time or energy to notice. And the best part is my dealings stay under the radar, so I get the full commission of each sale for myself, meager as a few dozen credits may be.

"I'll be fine," I say. "We can trust Mrs. Rivera. And hey, while you're watching out for me, watch out for yourself, too. 'Kay?"

"'Kay."

I'm still shaking my head when Mae brings our tea.

Minutes later, we're sitting on the Riveras' couch, synced. I smile with satisfaction as Mae's mouth opens in awe, tears welling in her eyes at the vibrant colors of the morning skyline that I captured on my commute. Watching her experience the Scrap for the first time gives me another swell of pleasure, like the echo of a well-loved song.

When it's over, she sits with her hands in her lap for a

moment. She exhales. "Thank you. I haven't seen downtown in . . . I can't remember how long."

I nod. It's an unofficial part of the gig, this listening, this processing. A twinge of impatience tickles the back of my mind. *Where's my money?*

As if on cue, Mae lifts her wrist. "I don't have much . . . will fifteen do? I know you run with the Dagger; I don't want any trouble. . . ."

Some inner part of me winces. I was so busy thinking about the boss's job, I forgot to agree to the price with Mae up front.

"Fifteen's great." Fifteen's *not* great, actually; it's barely enough for a pack of gum to cover my VitaBar breath. But soon I'll either be swimming in Preston's credits, or the raiders will turn me into a lovely area rug. I decide to consider the low price a parting gift.

When Mae stands to escort me out, it's like she's grown an inch. She stands taller. Prouder.

"Thank you, mija. Times are just . . . a little tight right now. My Joe got let go at the port. Droids, you know. He's been looking for work—" She shakes her head as she holds the door open. "Anyway, thank you. The way your Scraps make me feel—if I could afford them more often, I'd never go back to using Mean. I keep telling Joe to try it, but—men. You can't convince Jonah Rivera of anything he doesn't want to believe." She rolls her eyes.

I laugh politely. "Right. Well, have a— I'm sorry, did you say Joe—*Jonah*—lost his job?" A blast of ice courses through my body.

She nods. "Yes, it's been a couple months now. We're getting by, but . . ."

Kez's words pop back into my mind. *Joe Rivera, short for Jonah.* "*Jonah R-something.*"

Mae's husband is our mark tonight.

I close my eyes for a second and stifle a groan. Of course this would happen to me.

"Mija? ¿Qué te pasa?" Mae asks. I'm about to torture the love of her life, and she's worried about *me. Why couldn't her idiot husband make his payment like everyone else?*

"It's nothing. I'm fine." I force a smile. "Let me know when you'd like me to come by again. I'm always updating my inventory."

"Absolutely. You take care, mija."

The second she closes the door, I dart for home, calling Kez as I run.

"'Sup?" he yells over the road noises and the sound of his cycle shifting gears.

"We can't do the job tonight. Tell Silas to pick someone else to make an example of."

Kez laughs. "No thanks. I prefer my fingers unbroken. What's wrong with the mark we've got?"

"I just left his house. I know his wife. Kez . . . they're good people. We can't—"

"'Good people' make their payments. So you know where he lives? Do you know what he looks like?"

Shit. "Never met him. But I've seen a picture." My voice is thin.

"Great, we'll find him that much faster. Get in, do the job, then forget the whole thing ever happened."

"But—"

"It's not like the next person who can't pay won't have loved ones too. These shakedown jobs are hell. But they're the price of our protection. Of survival."

I say nothing, just stare at the slivers of blue sky peeking through the Towers like there's an answer somewhere in the clouds. How long will we sacrifice ourselves in the name of survival? Maybe if he knew about Preston's offer . . .

"Kez, something happened this morning. Mr. Preston gave me a job—"

"Dammit! Traffic. I gotta go," Kez says, a note of annoyance in his voice that softens when he speaks again. "I'll see you tonight?"

I squeeze my eyes shut tight. What am I doing? There's no point in telling Kez about Preston's job until the money's in hand. Until then, it might as well not exist.

"Yeah," I say. "See you tonight."

4

ADRIAN

BY THE TIME I FIND INSPECTOR REDDING AND NAS AGAIN, MY HEAD IS SPIN-
ning, and not from the crowds. I can still feel the touch of the
mystery girl's hand on my shoulder, still hear the peal of her
laughter over the ringing in my ears. Who was she? I can't
remember the last time anyone looked into my eyes like that.
Like they actually cared about *me* instead of my mission.

"Where'd you disappear to, rookie?" Nas asks with a smirk
when I arrive. "A corner somewhere to tremble?"

I wince. He's only teasing, but it's too close to the truth.

Inspector Redding clears his throat. "Focus, boys. Clues
could be anywhere." His words are sharp. He doesn't want to
be in the Towers any longer than necessary either. Now that
we're here, I realize how poor our disguises are—anyone who
looks twice at us could blow our cover easily, like the mystery
girl almost did before she took pity on me. The sooner we can
sniff out Orange Haze, the sooner we get to go home.

Nas and I face the crowd, and I tap my temple to activate
the heat map overlay. The mob of people transforms into a
floating mosaic of blue, green, and the occasional fleck of
yellow. When they were briefing us back at the Citadel, the

analytics team told us to "follow the glow," meaning to watch for a large glowing orange area on the brain activity scan. That's the telltale sign of Orange Haze.

As if on cue, something brighter pops at the edge of my vision. "There." I nod at a man several yards away. A yellow spot flares in the center of his brain.

Nas shakes his head. "Nah, that's Mean, not Haze. See how it's isolated, kidney-bean shaped?"

Redding nods. "Good, Davani." Envy flashes in me. I know I should be grateful to have one of the best junior officers on the Force as my partner. Nas works hard. Instead of training, he could do what most Forceman droids do and simply trust that the new drills are accurately uploaded to his data core. But that's not good enough for Nas; something in his personality profile makes him almost as pigheaded as I am. I'm not sure how I'm even supposed to compete. Droids are a whole new level of smart.

One thing they're not, though? Creative.

While Redding and Nas continue scanning the crowd on the ground, I look up. The Towers stretch hundreds of feet into the air, with skywalks and flimsy stairways wrapped around each building like a helix. The crowds up there are thinner, but still—

"There!" I say, way too loud for someone who's supposed to be undercover. The Inspector opens his mouth to discipline me, until he sees it, too. There's a woman, maybe five stories above us, on a fire escape landing overlooking the Towers. I can't make out her face from here, but that's not what matters. What matters is the color of her mind: an incandescent, fiery *orange*. Her entire brain burns like a lantern in the blue-green darkness of this place.

Follow the glow.

Redding's mouth hangs open for a second before he gives the order.

"Go."

Nas and I take off, approaching the building from opposite sides. People shuffle out of my way as I scramble up the labyrinth of steps and landings, the map on my neural holographic display rolling out before me as I run. I have to double back a couple of times—my map is only based on the best information we could get from satellite intel of the Towers. But things are always changing in here, halls morphing into homes, stairways appearing overnight. I make do.

We reach the apartment at the same time. I place my hands on my knees, trying to catch my breath as Nas opens the door, not a synthetic black hair on his head out of place.

"Hey, mi amor. Any luck today—" The same middle-aged woman I saw from outside freezes as she turns from her rickety balcony. "You're not my Joe."

"I'm not." Nas flashes his badge. My hands fumble in my pocket as I rush to do the same.

She comes closer, squinting at the iridescent cards to make sure they're real. "Some sort of trick, no? Forcemen in the Towers, that's . . . unheard of." As she questions us, something sparkles in her eyes, bright and inextinguishable. My breath hitches.

Nas doesn't falter. "Ma'am, we'd like to ask you some questions. You don't *have* to answer, of course. But just between us, things will go much better for you if you do."

The woman hesitates briefly at the threat, but Nas isn't going to touch her. The intelligence overlay floating in my vision tells me she—Mae Rivera—makes VitaBars for a living, and her productivity score is astronomical after decades of consistent work. She's not getting arrested; no way LifeCorp would let us take her off the production line with a score that high. She doesn't need to know that, though.

Mrs. Rivera leads us into the apartment, which is small and cluttered with knickknacks and photographs. Familiar scents hit me as we pass the kitchenette. Basil. Lemongrass. "You cook?" I ask.

She gestures to the potted plants on her balcony. "From eight p.m. to eight a.m., I have to think about those damn VitaBars. It's the last thing I want to eat when I get home, but on our budget we can't afford anything else. So I at least . . . dress them up a bit." There's that sparkle in her eye again.

As we sit in the living room, a man enters from the hall: Her husband, Jonah, my intel offers. Unlike his wife, he clocks something in me and Nas immediately. Our posture, maybe? Or maybe the way Nas watches him like he's crud gumming up the gears of a conveyor belt. I know my partner well enough to know the sneer isn't personal; he's simply a droid on a mission.

"Officers." Mr. Rivera sits next to his wife and pats her hand. "How can we help you?"

"We noticed some unusual neural activity coming from this area," I say, eyeing Mrs. Rivera carefully. Does her husband know she's using? "We have a few questions for your wife. Shouldn't take long."

Mrs. Rivera presses her lips together, but nothing else in her calm expression changes. Mr. Rivera, on the other hand, begins to sweat, hard. I check the time on my screen. We should be done by dinner.

I lean forward, my voice gentle. "Mrs. Rivera, as you know, taking illicit substances is a criminal offense. . . ."

She says nothing, only stares back with those shining eyes. If she were on Mean, the mere thought of two Forcemen in her home would be enough to make her stand at full attention. A desire for praise and validation from authority figures is one of the drug's most helpful effects. But she's . . . unfazed. Self-assured.

What is this stuff?

I clear my throat. "We don't want anyone to get hurt."

Again, nothing. Nas's gaze is hot on my face. He could jump in at any moment and save this disaster of an interrogation, but he won't. This is a test.

I open my mouth to speak a third time, but Mrs. Rivera cuts me off.

"Who decides?" she asks.

"Decides what?"

"Who decides what's 'illicit'? LifeCorp took all the other drugs off the street when they gained power."

Nas scoffs. "And you have a problem with that?"

"I didn't say that. But you want me to believe government-issued Mean is safe? When I've seen it turn people—my own husband—into mindless zombies? Seems like once a month you hear about Lowers killing each other for a few mils of that poison." She eyes the zippered case at Nas's hip. "And yet, not only is Mean legal, but as an officer of the Force, you're carrying it on you right now, are you not?"

Nas's knee is bouncing, a programmed response to a surplus of external stimuli. He's a LifeCorp machine, after all, and Mrs. Rivera's criticism of company policy is a direct threat to his maker. It's like insulting someone's mother. Mrs. Rivera must be able to feel his eyes boring into her skull, because I definitely can. Still, she remains unmoved.

"If this is about drugs, you can leave. I didn't take anything."

"Bullshit." Nas spews the word. The armchair in his grip creaks a little.

Mr. Rivera's eyes bulge at the droid's strength. "Officers, I apologize. Perhaps another time—"

"We're not leaving here until you tell us why your wife's brain is glowing like a fritzing streetlight." Nas stands, his hand twitching toward their breakable, human bodies.

Mr. Rivera's dam finally breaks. "I don't know what she took; they always leave before I get here. Mae, tell them, please!" His breathing is erratic as he clutches her arm. He *does* know something.

His wife's still unshaken, but I observe the telltale tension in Mr. Rivera's jaw.

Withdrawal.

"Listen," I say. "We understand times are hard. Everyone does what they can to survive." I meet Nas's eyes and pull a vial of Mean from my waist pack. "We're prepared to make things a little easier for you, in exchange for your cooperation."

Everyone in the Towers is at least a tiny bit hooked on

Mean, save for the children. It's a good thing: smooths the edges on their hard lives, allows them to stay focused on their jobs, keeps things humming the way LifeCorp wants. LifeCorp lets it flow on every street corner, in every Arcade, and they have to restock constantly. *Everybody* loves the drug, even if they pretend to be above it. So I can't help but note when Mrs. Rivera's expression doesn't change. It's like she doesn't even notice the vial is there, like something else has filled the Mean-shaped void in her brain. My blood runs cold as I realize how destructive Orange Haze could be. If people stop caring about Mean, LifeCorp loses control. Society will crumble, and we'll be as feral as the raiders. I can't let that happen.

"Don't," Mrs. Rivera says to her husband. Veins cord in Mr. Rivera's hands as he balls them into fists. He wants so badly to side with her. For a moment, I wish we could let him.

"Alright, then. Let's make it interesting," Nas says, irritation in his voice at Rivera's meager resistance. He pulls a vial from his own pack, tilting it slowly so the teal liquid inside makes a tinkling sound. "To be honest, I shouldn't even be giving you this. It's not publicly available yet—double-distilled, extra-concentrated . . . this vial alone would last you a month." The Riveras' harsh overhead lighting glints off of the vial's glass.

Where did he get that from?

I try to hide my surprise, but it doesn't matter because Mr. Rivera's reaction pulls our focus. He groans and clutches his wife's arm. She flinches.

"Mae. Tell them. Please." The last word is barely audible. LifeCorp's Law Enforcement Code of Ethics, section 8, subsection 3.D., states that the use of Mean to encourage civilian cooperation in high-priority investigations is perfectly legal. There's nothing wrong with what we're doing, especially if it prevents a couple of broken bones. Yet something twists inside me as Mrs. Rivera covers her husband's hand with her own.

"Joe, you're stronger than this. You—"

He sniffs. "I'm not, corazón. . . ."

This is too personal; I shift my attention to give them a moment. Outside, on the Riveras' balcony, the lemongrass bobs in the breeze. Inside, the room's gone quiet. The Riveras stare tearfully at each other, locked in a battle of wills. But the Mean will win. It always does.

"You can't expect me to stay and watch this." Mrs. Rivera wipes her eyes and presses her lips into a thin line. She stands and walks toward Nas, an inch closer than is wise. "I'm late for work. If you're not going to arrest me . . ." She cocks her head in a silent challenge. Nas's hand flexes as his eyes narrow. But he doesn't touch her.

The corners of her mouth lift in a grim smile. "Have a good evening, Officers." She heaves her bag onto her shoulders with a grunt that betrays her age. Then she's gone.

Back in the room, Mr. Rivera's gaze is fixed on the vial of Mean, his mouth slightly open.

Nas sends me a knowing glance, then leans in. "How about a little taste for now, Mr. Rivera? Don't spend it all in one place." His mouth dry with desire, Mr. Rivera nods and takes the vial. The rip of his shoulder patch, the hiss of the injector, and all is right in his world.

Nas stands and smooths his jumpsuit. I do the same, before swiping my contact information from my wrist screen, toward Mr. Rivera. "In case anything comes to mind," I say. Rivera's pupils are dilated; he's light-years away as we leave the apartment.

"Are you sure that was even Mean you gave him?" I ask Nas once we're out in the hall. "Dude's on another planet."

He shrugs. "That's what Redding said, at least. Calls it Ambrosia." I don't miss his silent boast. Redding gave *him* the Ambrosia, not me.

"Well, it'd better work," I say, slightly annoyed, while clicking on my navigational overlay. "Closest Arcade is three floors down . . . seven halls over." Nas nods, and we move out. There's only one place on earth Joe Rivera will want to be once the Mean gets its claws in properly, and that's an Arcade: a bar with chaotic sights and sounds that stimulates your brain and makes your Mean high twice as intense. One hour in there and Rivera will be putty in our hands. His desire to comply will help him remember even the tiniest details. Worst-case scenario, we can hold him for interrogation until his wife decides to cooperate. With as long as Mr. Rivera's been out of work, his productivity score must be suffering. LifeCorp won't bat an eye if we throw him in a cell for a week or two.

■ ■ ■

"WATCH YOUR STEP, ROOKIE," NAS SAYS AS WE HEAD DEEPER INTO THE TOWERS.

His voice competes with another in my head.

Two things you can feel, says the mysterious Lower girl from earlier. I do as she advised, and focus on the grit under my boots, the worn fabric of my Lower disguise against my skin. But there's a third sensation too: the faintest echo of the girl's leg touching mine as we sat against the alley wall. For the briefest moment, I felt like someone understood me . . . understood the way my mind plays tricks if I'm not careful. It's enough to bring me back to the present and remind me why my mission is so important. I'm taking down Orange Haze for her, and for everyone else in the Towers who deserves a shot at the prosperous future that LifeCorp provides.

A few dozen steps later, the hallway widens. We're in the main commons of the southwest tower. Lowers rush through the plaza, heads down. Stalls line the walls, selling various goods—jumpsuits and VitaBars, drywall, off-white paint, and putty to transform hallways and rooftops into add-on bedrooms. Everything the Lowers need to survive.

"Arcade's this way," I say.

Nas smiles and points with his chin. "And there's our man. Like clockwork."

I follow his gaze as Mr. Rivera walks down the stairs into the plaza. There's a bounce in his step, and a tightness around his eyes. As he cuts straight across the plaza, he fumbles with something in his hand—the vial of Mean from our encounter, totally empty.

"Thought you said that stuff was extra potent?" I say to Nas.

"Huh, guess he was thirsty. Anyway, I'll cover the service

entrance." He claps me on the shoulder. I nod, and we sync our comms as Nas heads for the alley, the Arcade's pulsing beat masking the sound of his steps.

Stepping into an Arcade is like falling into a fever dream. Images flash erratically on the walls: a dancing woman's seductive silhouette fades into a movie clip of a man pulling himself onto a moving train in the nick of time. People come to Arcades for mental stimulation, of any kind—doesn't matter if the clips make you laugh, gross you out, or turn you on. And based on the packed house, this place keeps its customers satisfied.

I catch sight of Rivera's balding head near the bar in the back and weave through clusters of Lowers with their eyes glued to the screens. A waitress with pale golden skin and an emerald stud in her nose approaches, balancing a tray of Mean vials stacked into a pyramid.

"You're new," she purrs. "Here, have a vial. On the house."

I glance at Rivera to make sure he hasn't moved, then accept the waitress's vial. Her full ruby lips glide into a smile.

"Cute too." She leans close so I can hear her whisper over the thundering bass. "My shift ends in twenty. If you need *anything.*"

I jiggle the vial. It's clear, not like the glittering teal of Ambrosia. "Afraid I have to decline, but I appreciate it." I hand her back the Mean. When I look for Rivera, he's gone.

"Shit. Gotta go." I take off for the bar. *Shit. Shit shit.* "Nas, you got a visual?" I spin frantically, searching for Rivera's face among the vacant expressions around me. Nada.

"Negative," Nas says over the comms.

Maybe he snuck past me, out the front again, while I was talking to the waitress? I run out the exit. My foot lands on something small and hard that almost sends me crashing to the ground as it skids under my boot.

"What the—?" I pick up the object. It's Rivera's empty vial of Mean. A single teal drop glimmers in the bottom.

"Nas, get over here quick. Sending you my location." Something moves at the edge of my vision, toward the street's end. Nas's probably a few minutes out, but I can't wait that long. I crouch, and run along the cheap plywood wall, avoiding junk and trash as I do my best to move silently.

The Arcade's pulsing beat fades as I reach the end of the wall, and I hear voices. "Where *is* she?" a man hisses to himself. I squat low and find an opening to peer through. A young man—presumably the speaker—holds a struggling Rivera, who is bound and gagged. The captor can't be more than a couple of years older than I am. Whoever he's speaking to is too close to the wall for me to make out their features. I reach for the electric blaster gun hidden in my jumpsuit, waiting for the right moment.

"Didn't you say you talked to her, Celeste?" the man continues. A small figure steps out of the shadows.

"A . . . child?" I whisper to myself. LifeCorp takes babies off their parents' hands almost as soon as they're born, to start their schooling and training and let their parents get back to work, distraction-free. Employee Care houses them in a separate facility near the factories so the parents who want to can visit after clocking out. I haven't heard a child speak since I was one myself.

"Yeah, but only for a sec; she was with a client," the child—Celeste—says. "Mrs. Rivera, I think she said?"

Mr. Rivera reacts slowly through the Mean-induced stupor. "Mae! Please don't hurt my Mae!"

"Shut up." The man kicks the writhing Rivera in the gut. I wince, but then I put the pieces together. Whoever they're waiting for serves Mae Rivera as their client. But Lowers aren't clients; they *have* clients. Unless whoever's serving Mae Rivera is serving her illegally . . .

Which means we're about to meet the dealer of Orange Haze, in the flesh.

Movement behind me. The unmistakable cold kiss of a blaster's muzzle brushes the back of my neck. My blood goes cold.

"Watch your six, rookie."

I could cry, I'm so relieved at the sound of Nas's voice. But he's made his point; we're too exposed here. Staying low, we follow the plywood wall under some scaffolding and duck behind some decaying VitaBar crates. "Did you hear—" I begin in a whisper.

"Yeah. Pair of lucky fritzers, we are, right?" Ambition shines in his eyes, mirroring mine. Redding's going to piss himself with happiness. I can see it now: The praise, the promotions. A decoration ceremony, a parade in our honor. All we have to do is wait for the culprit to show.

So we wait. Rivera's cries weaken to whimpers. Celeste practices cartwheels. The young man checks the time on his screen every thirty seconds. Based on the vein throbbing in his neck, he's contemplating murder. And not of Rivera.

"Liv," he barks at his wrist screen after another ten minutes.

Then, only a few yards from where we're hiding, another wrist screen buzzes in the shadows.

"Liv Newman, mercenary for hire," a voice says in a sing-song. "How may I direct your call?"

She steps into the light, and I do a double take. I know this girl. Barely an hour ago, she helped me talk myself out of a panic attack, helped me remember my mission and my purpose on the Force. She made me feel less alone.

Mystery girl is the one dealing Orange Haze?

"It's her," I say. Out loud. Which isn't where I meant to say it.

"It's who?" Nas whispers. "You gonna puke, rookie? You look like you're gonna puke."

I move my jaw to speak, but no words come.

Nas gives me a few more seconds. "Well, if you *are* gonna puke, do it *that way,* please." I barely register what he's saying. The anger's too loud. She made me trust her. She made me *like* her. I thought I was doing this to help her. But it turns out she's the biggest threat of all.

She tricked me.

"You're late," the young man says.

"Well, I'm here," Newman says coolly. Then, softer, "I hate this, Kez." Her voice trembles. Another trick, probably.

"I know." There's a flash of sadness in Kez's eyes, but it's gone in an instant. "Just do the thing, then we can leave."

She nods back. "Celeste, get out of here. I'll count to twenty," she says flatly, without turning. The numbers echo in Newman's cold monotone as the girl takes off running. By ten, she's halfway down the alley. But then she doubles back, her steps silent, and climbs a fire escape that gives her a vantage point of the whole scene. Nas and I shift so we stay hidden.

"Move in on my count," I say, reaching for my weapon.

Nas stays my hand. "Wait."

"*Wait?*"

"Yes, rookie. Think. If we take her in now, she's back in the Towers by midnight."

"But—she—" My face falls. Nas is right; at this point, our evidence is circumstantial at best. We need to see her give Rivera the Orange Haze if we want the charges to stick. I lower my weapon and watch in disgust.

Newman's accomplice pulls out a knife, and Rivera flinches as the cold metal grazes his throat.

"Pair with her," Kez says.

"What?" Nas, Rivera, and I say at the same time. Newman pulls down her hood, and I gasp at the large chip protruding at the base of her neck. She's . . . an EmoProxy? I think back to our meeting in the Towers earlier, when she was wearing gray, not amber, her hood pulled tight.

Another trick.

But how will pairing with Rivera do anything to harm him? Unless . . .

"Ask me how I know," she'd said, when I was telling her about the heaviness in my head.

Newman's friend presses the blade harder. Rivera does as he's told, lifting his ring finger to his temple. Liv Newman does the same, then turns from them, eyes squeezed shut. There's a thick pause in the air. And then—

LIV

Begin Scrap replay:

You are nothing. You don't matter, and you will never matter, do you understand? Good.

Oh, tears now? Nobody cares. You are alone. Alone, alone, alone. Cry all you want. Nobody will come for you because nobody cares about you. Why would they? Anyone who ever cared has forgotten you. Your parents have forgotten you. Because you aren't worth remembering. You aren't worth anything. Until we decide you are.

Nobody. Cares. They're happier without you, and you will always be alone.

It's what you deserve—

"RUN!" KEZ SAYS. THEN HE'S YANKING MY ARM, AND WE'RE BOLTING, AND there's glass breaking and blood. So much blood. The connection with Rivera is severed unwillingly, slicing through my mind. The pain eclipses everything.

"Put your hands up!"

I turn. The boy from this afternoon. I remember kind eyes and shared laughter in an alley.

Not kind now. Not laughing now.

"Dammit Liv, run!" Kez's voice sounds like he's under-water. I run.

"What happened?"

He doesn't answer me. Maybe he can't hear me over his own pounding heart. Maybe my question never left my mind.

My legs burn. My lungs burn. *Where is Celeste?*

The boy with the kind eyes. I wish he hadn't seen me like that.

Why do I wish that, when I know what he is?

I want to rest, but Kez says we have to run some more. Everything blurs, until it's dark.

Quiet.

Silas will be pleased. Kez says I should clean off, but I just want to rest.

I just want to rest.

ART NOT FINAL   *Creating a World of Value*

METRO OFFICE OF LAW ENFORCEMENT

I N C I D E N T   R E P O R T

Record No: 2364-BOS-00423

Filing Officer: Adrian Rao, Badge #BOS-009827

Date: October 13, 2364

Time: 7:30 PM

Place of Occurrence: Southwest Tower Arcade, Fenway Towers, Borough of Boston

Weapons Used: (1) neurochip (2) glass bottle (self-inflicted)

Relationship between Victim and Perpetrator:

☐ Related

☐ Acquainted

☐ Strangers

☑ Unknown

Detail of Event: At the above date and time, Jonah Rivera was walking from southwest tower Arcade in Fenway Towers ("the Towers") back to his home, when he was accosted and detained by a teenaged male and female child. Male suspect (referred to as "Kez") physically assaulted Rivera, before being joined by a teenaged female EmoProxy identified as LIV NEWMAN. Newman and Kez proceeded to force Rivera to sync with Newman, who then seemed to transmit disturbing sentiments to Rivera using her neurochip.

Subsequently, Rivera assaulted himself with above weapon in an effort to cease the transmission. Officers gave chase, at which point the sync was severed. Newman and her accomplices escaped. Rivera was transported to Mercy North hospital for treatment of his non-life-threatening injuries.

TO ALL UNITS, METRO-WIDE: BE ON THE LOOKOUT FOR LIV NEWMAN.
SUSPECT IS CONSIDERED ARMED AND DANGEROUS.

6

ADRIAN

"DOCS ARE WORKING ON GETTING RIVERA SEDATED. AND STABLE," NAS'S VOICE says in my comms. After we lost track of Newman and her associates, we returned to find Rivera a bloodied mess. He'd been yelling at Newman to get out of his mind, and when that didn't work, he found a glass bottle and beat himself over the head with it until it shattered. I can still hear his broken voice echoing in the alley:

I'm alone. I'm worthless.

"Any sign of them?" Nas continues in my ear.

I scan this stretch of the Towers' Perimeter for the millionth time. "Not yet. I'll ping you if I find anything." We end the call.

Three minutes. I hate that we left Rivera alone for so long. Hate that Nas convinced me to think of a man's torture as evidence, instead of what it was on the surface: suffering that we could have stopped. I hate myself for having Newman in my grasp hours ago and letting her play me for a fool. I hate her.

I hate *her*.

Newman. The liar. Whatever you want to call her. She is the only reason any of this happened. Even without the threat that Orange Haze poses to LifeCorp, Newman's a danger to society. Anyone who can destroy a person's mind like that, with no remorse, has to be taken off the streets. Something surges in me, white-hot, and clear as Mean.

A mission. A calling. A purpose.

Find Liv Newman and lock her up so she'll never hurt anyone. Ever again.

Someone shifts in the crowd, and across the walkway, there's a burst of color. The little girl from the attack—Celeste—perches on a stool at a food counter, one knee up as she drinks the soup directly from her bowl. I scan the surroundings to make sure she's alone, bracing myself for the confinement of the crowd before moving in. I don't summon the mysterious Lower girl's voice this time. Now that I know what she truly is, I'm back on my own.

The stool next to Celeste is empty, and she barely registers my presence as she slurps and shovels her food: a VitaBar submerged in broth. She makes random grunts of satisfaction as she eats, drops of broth splashing onto the cuffs of her fuchsia jacket. There's something so pure about her enjoyment, how a simple meal has her lost in her own world of pleasure, and I find myself smiling.

"Can't sit here without ordering," the man behind the counter grumbles over a bushy beard covered in a hairnet. Raised scars cover his dark brown forearms. Celeste glances my way midbite. She gasps. If I had any doubt she'd recognize me from the chase, it's gone now.

Celeste's muscles tense—she's ready to run.

"I'm not going to hurt you; I just have some questions. My

name is Adrian." *Don't blow my cover,* I plead with my eyes. She doesn't say anything, but she's still curled up like a frightened mouse. How can I put her at ease?

The cook hands me a menu. I address him. "One bowl of—" A quick scan tells me my options are limited.

MENU

VITABAR IN BROTH	50
~~VITABAR STIRFRY~~	~~80~~ **Sold Out**
~~CURRIED VITABAR~~	~~80~~ **Sold Out**
~~VITABAR AU GRATIN~~	~~100~~ **Sold Out**

FREE VITAMUFFIN FOR PRODUCTIVITY SCORES OVER 2000! LIMITED SUPPLY. OFFER **SOLD OUT**

"One bowl," I finally say.

It's then that I notice how tightly Celeste is gripping her dish, how her other hand shakes as it clenches the spoon. I'm familiar with that death grip. She's not focused on her food out of hunger. She's focused so she can block out everything else in her head. The brutality she witnessed. I soften my posture, adjust my interrogation strategy to allow space for the question that matters most.

"Are you alright?" I ask softly.

Celeste shifts in her seat, hugging her raised knee a little tighter. "I will be. I closed my eyes." She says this like it makes everything okay, like she's not a little kid with an imagination big enough to visualize anything that might be happening on the other side of her eyelids. "I didn't see anything," she continues. "But I heard . . ."

Her shaky voice trails off. My food arrives. My stomach roils at the scent of the incoming dish, but I taste a spoonful under the cook's watchful stare. Needs salt and a pinch of red pepper at the very least. "Here." I slide it to Celeste, who gulps it down happily, then flick fifty credits the cook's way.

"You're not like the other one," Celeste says, finally relaxed. I don't have time to unpack that before she continues. "You won't hurt Liv, will you?" Her almost-black eyes are sparkling and wet. For a moment, I wonder if the Forcemen have ever considered training children to be interrogators. With eyes like that, I'd tell this kid almost anything she wants to know. Almost.

"No." It's not technically a lie; as long as Newman comes willingly, no one has to get hurt.

"Because she's not a bad person, you know? She only wanted to make Silas happy. He's not as scary when he's happy. And she just wanted that lady, Mrs. Rivera, to be happy too. Besides, Uppers use Scraps all the time and nobody says anything."

My mind spins at that last part. What do EmoProxy Scraps have to do with this? I'm working to connect the dots when Celeste moves on to another topic.

"You live outside the Towers, right? Have you ever seen a movie? Because I have. Liv was watching one for a client, and she thought I was asleep, but . . ." She continues while I revel in the time to think. I've never questioned why only Uppers are allowed to take Scraps, always assumed it's because they're the only ones who need them. All the Lowers need is a hit of Mean to be productive and an Arcade to squeeze out as much of the thrill as possible. Even if what Celeste is saying is true—if the new drug we've been chasing is actually some renegade EmoProxy's Scraps—I still get why LifeCorp wants Orange Haze gone.

Mrs. Rivera's defiance, that burst of disrespect in her eyes—we can't let that spread. In one person it's dangerous enough. But at full scale? You get violence, people throwing away LifeCorp's order for whatever rules suit them best that day. It doesn't matter that the Scraps aren't an actual drug. Used improperly, they're as big a threat to our peace and prosperity as any unsanctioned needle or pipe.

Celeste's hands flail wildly now, her eyes bright with wonder. ". . . and then they kiss! Which I didn't care for, really. I liked the other parts, though. They never showed us movies or anything like that in Employee Care. It's way more fun here. There's less rules."

"Sure," I say, half listening. I'm already thinking about Redding's reaction to my discovery about Orange Haze, and what it will mean for my career. If we can figure out what makes Newman so special compared to other EmoProxies, we can eliminate the chances of anything like Orange Haze happening ever again. I'll be a hero; they'll name a fritzing street after me.

"I won't tell Silas I talked to you," Celeste says. "I don't want anyone else to get hurt." That pulls me back to the conversation. It hadn't even occurred to me that Celeste might rat me out. I imagine Nas's voice in my head: *Nice move, rookie. Getting your cover blown by a kid is a new low, even for you.*

"I appreciate that. I really do." I pause. "And I *have* seen a movie before." I've spent more nights alone, off-duty, in my apartment in front of a screen than I'd care to admit.

"Really?" Her gap-toothed grin is infectious.

"Really. About this guy who had to save his city from people who wanted to destroy it. There wasn't anything special about him necessarily, but he was smart and used what he had to do what he could."

"I'm smart too," she says confidently. "With machines and stuff like that."

I can see why Newman has a soft spot for the kid. "Well, stick with it and maybe you'll be a RepairProxy someday. A lot of older-gen machines are breaking down in the Estates lately—cars, service drones. They could use someone like you to keep things running." Celeste's smile goes supernova, and I can't help but smile back. It's not too late for her to get her life back on track. I just have to get the obstacles out of her path.

"Here." I raise my wrist and transfer a few thousand credits her way. Not like I need them anyway; LifeCorp covers my rent and rations . . . I only really spend money on my plants. "So you can start saving up for your modifications."

Her mouth hangs open in shock. "But—"

"I insist. And here's my number if you need anything." I swipe her my contact info. "Take care of yourself, Celeste. You've got a bright future ahead. Don't let anyone stand in your way." As I stand and slip back into the crowd, I feel hopeful. I can make a difference in Celeste's future, the same way LifeCorp made a difference in mine. The chaos of Orange Haze may be a scourge on our society, but I can at least tip the balance back toward order, one life at a time.

LIV

A jet pack, I want to answer. *A time machine. A new life.*

"No." I fiddle with the tattered blanket on my floor mattress. "Good night."

"Night, Liv." Kez's lips press together, but then he turns to go, one hand gripping the door's frame so hard that the muscles in his hand cord. He never lets on how much the jobs bother him, especially not when he's trying to make me feel better about "helping." But in the moments after it's done, there's always a difference in how he moves. A little too rigid, a little too tight. Like his body tracks all the horror he's witnessed, even if he can convince his brain it's no big deal.

At last, Kez steps into the hall, and I'm left alone to think about the job. Why did that fritzing Forceman have to be there? Adrian. And why, out of all the horrific things that happened tonight—what I did to Rivera, his violent reaction, the searing pain of severing our pairing incorrectly—is Adrian's face the part I can't stop thinking about? The way he looked at me, like . . . I let him down somehow?

I push the questions aside for now. I've learned over the

years that my mind is especially worked up after a job. Usually, I just need to be a little gentler with my thoughts for a week or so, until the storm passes. But that's only because I always—*always*—archive the memory of the job for a few weeks. To be safe, I also archive the memory I used, of my first day at Employee Care, scared and alone. Memory archiving is part of the EmoProxy package, originally designed as a solution for storing high-resolution Scraps. I select a memory, and my neurochip places it in storage far away in the cloud, set with a timer that gradually fuses the memory back into my normal memory bank when I'm ready. For a while, I can forget my old trauma. And memory archiving is good business sense too: a thought like that accidentally surfacing, overpowering a happy Scrap during a session with a client, would ruin me financially. So I have to be careful.

Tonight, I'm not careful.

I'm so exhausted, so distracted by the memory of the job—of Adrian—that I fall asleep without bothering to archive. And that is why I wake up, three hours later, drenched in sweat, jaw throbbing, my teeth aching where I've been grinding them together. Like a faithful bloodhound, my brain sniffed out the memory I used for the job and began gnawing on it like a gristly bone. Suddenly, I'm six again, sitting on a LifeCorp warehouse floor while my Employee Care "teacher" (LifeCorp speak for "line manager") chews me out for missing a step in the packaging process.

"Everyone has forgotten about you," she begins in my mind. *"Not because of time, but because you aren't worth—"*

No.

I bolt from bed as quickly as my blurred vision allows and take off running through the Towers' narrow hallways. Eventually my legs give out, and I collapse shivering in the drafty night air of a long-forgotten stairwell. I'm done. I can't do Silas's dirty work anymore, no matter how beneficial he claims it will be for us. This can't be how the rest of my life plays out, or any of our lives—sacrificing our humanity for a few hundred credits, inflicting our trauma on one another so we can make it through the day. In the morning, I'm leaving for Mr. Preston's, and the Outerlands. No matter what waits for me there, I *have* to come back with that Scrap of the stars. I *have* to pull myself—and everyone I care about—out of this never-ending cycle.

A light patter of footsteps running down the stairs stops my train of thought. One of my closest friends, Thea, appears before me on the landing, the undertone of her tawny skin a pallid gray. "I've been looking everywhere for you," she says, sweeping her stick-straight black hair into a quick bun and fanning her neck. She's wearing her navy blue CareProxy uniform, and it looks like Celeste convinced her to put some of her homemade glitter eye shadow on the lids of her hooded eyes.

Thea's chin trembles as she clocks the terror on my face. "You forgot to archive?" The rims of her pupils glow dark blue for a second, indicating that she's using her CareProxy modifications—in this case, her body's ability to produce oxytocin on demand—to reduce her cortisol levels.

"Guess I should start writing this stuff down," I say. "A mercenary's manual: Drink water. Get lots of rest. Archive your memories so you can pretend you're not a horrible person."

"You're *not* a horrible person," Thea says immediately.

"Yeah, right. 'Violence . . . the last refuge of the incompetent.' Asimov." The stairwell devours my voice, making it sound thin and childlike.

She grimaces, then takes a small step forward, hands raised like she's approaching a wounded bird. When I don't move away, she gently wraps her soft, sturdy arms around me. I breathe in, smelling diaper cream and fingerpaint, the scents of Upper childhood that have seeped into her clothing after years of caring for privileged children around the clock. The hug is such a simple thing, but it cracks me open like I've fallen on the jagged rocks of the Bay. I don't deserve this gentleness, this grace. Thea's been out of work for a few weeks, but she's a natural CareProxy, trying to remind me that I'm still human. I'm not so sure she's right.

"Maybe it's a good thing, not burying your feelings all the time," she says. I laugh at the irony: an EmoProxy who denies her own emotions. Too busy feeling things for other people to process my own shit.

"You had a hard start in life," Thea continues. "You can't keep burying those feelings forever."

"Says who?" As far as I'm concerned, the future is the only thing that matters. Why would I waste time rehashing the past?

Thea sighs, holding my gaze for a few seconds before she— wisely—decides that I'm too exhausted for a heart-to-heart right now. Resigned, she slides an injectable of crystal-clear Mean from her coat pocket and hands it to me. My heart flips. Thea's easily one of my favorite people on the planet, and in this moment, she skyrockets to the top spot.

"Bless you," I sigh as I release the drug into the meat of my shoulder. In seconds, the world has a brightness it didn't before, and I have a new, bold confidence to go with it. I'm myself again.

"I thought about turning myself in," I confess as I roll my head in slow circles. I pocket the empty vial.

"That's not something a horrible person would do. A horrible person would revel in the torture." She wipes a tear from my cheek with her thumb. "But this doesn't seem like reveling to me. I know if you had a choice, this is the last thing you'd be doing."

If I had a choice. That's what I'm trying to do by going to the Outerlands tomorrow: give all of us a choice. I want so badly to tell Thea about Preston's offer. But "high risk, high reward" isn't really her thing, and I don't have the energy to argue with her about the dangers right now.

"You didn't come to see how I was doing, did you?"

"He wants to see you," Thea admits softly. She doesn't even have to say Silas's name. With a sigh, I head down the stairs, but Thea scans my tearstained face, my grimy clothes, then grabs my arm.

"Not so fast." Thea's almost three inches shorter than me, but her tone commands authority. She guides me in the opposite direction, up toward my apartment. "The man can wait while you take a shower."

■ ■ ■

THE TELLTALE AROMA OF THE SOUTHWEST TOWER'S ARCADE HITS ME BEFORE I turn the corner: an acrid, cloying synthetic blend that enhances patrons' highs. Electronic beats thump under my feet as I step inside. I shade my eyes against the flashing strobe lights and neon shapes. Pictures and video clips play on every surface—the walls, the floor, the bar's countertop—flashing to the next thing on the playlist with jarring abruptness. Pouty lips near a lover's ear, racing cars on a winding road, kaleidoscopic shapes against blindingly bright backgrounds. Not that the customers are actually watching the screens; their neurochips are all wirelessly synced to a hub in the utility closet that transmits images straight to their brain, in higher resolution than any projector ever could. The surrounding projections are mostly to lure people in from outside, seducing them with these oversaturated snippets as a welcome distraction from their monotonous realities.

Cocktail waitress droids flit between the customers, the triangular chrome barrels around their slim waists loaded with vials of sparkling, clear Mean. It's almost four in the morning, but a dozen customers still wander the rooms, their glassy red-rimmed eyes switching in and out of focus. As if they're droids on a timer, their expressions shift in sync with the visuals around us. Arcades are the closest most Lowers get to anything resembling a Scrap. But instead of my expertly crafted experiences, they're getting quick hits of lust, glee, and exhilaration—just enough to get them amped up and back to work.

Kez is already waiting for me in Silas's private room, where the boss conducts most of his business. Silas is laughing at something Kez said and rubbing his salt-and-pepper goatee in amusement. The scene brings me back to one of my strongest memories from childhood: I was eight. Kez found me shivering in a dumpster and brought me to meet the famed Silas Bekele for the first time. The boss had already started to build a reputation for himself by then, an erratic thirty-five-year-old newcomer from Atlanta, determined to carve out a territory for himself in the Towers' dog-eat-dog underground scene. And carve he did. Hence his nickname: the Dagger.

I had never seen an Arcade before; based on all the lights, I thought it was a place for kids until the owner slapped my hand away from a projector. By the time I got to Silas, I was nearly in tears, afraid he was going to cut out my tongue or sell one of my kidneys. But instead of hurting me, Silas knelt before me and pulled out an apple—a *real* apple—and an ancient-looking children's book, written over three hundred years ago. *The Phantom Tollbooth*.

"What's it about?" I asked as I held the book reverently.

"Being smart when it counts."

I couldn't believe it. We sat on the ground together, and I ate while he read. Ten minutes later, I was seated on his lap, giggling as he gave the performance of his life, pitching his voice high and low to fit the story's characters. Ever since then, I've loved to read. Of course, paper books are almost impossible to find in the Towers—Lowers don't have time to read, and even Uppers prefer movies or television. But Silas still tracks down the worn editions for me—his two most recent gifts were *Station Eleven* and the complete Legendborn series—and leaves them on my doorstep a few times a month. He's convinced that my love for reading makes me a better EmoProxy, and he may be right. Reading helps me imagine what it might be like to laugh harder, scream louder, love deeper. To live fully for myself, and no one else, at least in my dreams.

Seeing Silas sitting kinglike in that old armchair now makes me smile, even as the memories of earlier this evening hover on the edges of my mind. He appraises me carefully behind half-moon glasses.

"All right there, Livvy? Tough night, I know. Never heard of a mark reacting like that before." A frown wrinkles his rich brown skin. "But at least it sends a message. Might spare others the same fate?" The question hangs heavy in the air, like the artificial smoke that surrounds us. *Will it?* I'm not so sure. But I stand a little straighter, the shivering child inside me not wanting to let him down, not wanting him to think I can't handle any assignment I'm given.

"I'm alright," I say. "Just tired."

Unconvinced, he sits back with a sigh. "Sometimes I forget how young you are. Well, this won't take long. Please, sit."

Kez squeezes my arm as I join them. Silas flicks a hand toward a cocktail waitress in the corner, who brings us a round of chilled Mean. I don't usually partake so heavily in a single day, but I have no regrets as the euphoria of this third hit sweeps my dark thoughts to the furthest corners of my mind.

"Sector Eleven's at their breaking point." Silas says. "The boss over there is getting greedy, watering down their Mean to stockpile for his own uses." His voice is laced with more

than a hint of disdain. Silas has had his eyes on the next territory to the south for almost as long as I've known him. About
six months ago, I woke up to an empty apartment. Silas had
taken Kez along with a few strongmen to intimidate the leader
of the Eleventh into swearing allegiance. I knew better than
to ask how it went when they returned. Kez's bruised face and
the blood seeping through the bandage on Silas's shoulder
told me everything I needed to know.

"We move at the end of the week," Silas says.

My mouth drops open. "Five days? What about what happened last time?"

"That was different. With the diluted Mean, folks in the
Eleventh aren't quite as loyal as they used to be. I think we'll
find them much more . . . amenable to our offer now." He
smirks. "And for everyone else, there's you, and your remark-
able talents." Pride twinkles in his eyes.

I close my eyes and exhale silently. I haven't even gotten
the sound of Rivera's pleading out of my head yet, and Silas is
already focused on the next job. There has to be another way.
There is. Get Preston's credits. When I open my eyes, Silas is
watching me, concerned. I want to tell him about the Outerlands offer, but the secret isn't mine to share. If LifeCorp
found out Preston was encouraging someone to go beyond
the Metro, he could lose his job.

Beside me, Kez bounces his knee with the excitement of
Silas's plan. "Congrats, Boss. You've been waiting a long time
for this."

Silas smiles, brilliant white against chestnut brown. "Con-
gratulations to *you*." He pointedly eyes us both. "I'll never be

able to pull this off without you two. And once we've taken the Eleventh, our territory will be too much for any one man to handle. Even me. I'll need someone to watch the Towers and the rest of Sector Ten for me while I stabilize our new domain. *Two* someones."

The room goes still as his meaning slowly drips into the air, no sound but the electronic music pumping behind the door. Kez wipes his sweating palms on his pants, leans forward. The two of us have talked about something like this happening, late at night, when the Mean in our veins made the impossible feel inevitable. But hearing the words from Silas's lips now, I don't feel the same thrill I once did. Silas deserves more than this constant pressure to angle for power. We all do. And when I bring that Scrap back, we'll have a shot at *real* opportunity. We won't even care about the Eleventh anymore.

"So what do you say? Still our little crew against the world?"

"Yes! Hell yes!" Kez almost jumps out of his seat. I smile. At Kez's excitement, and also because I know that something even better waits for all of us, on the other side of tomorrow night.

Freedom.

■ ■ ■

KEZ GETS DISPATCHED TO DELIVER A DOZEN CREDITS' WORTH OF TOILETRIES across town a few minutes later, and I walk out with him. He's so excited about Silas's decision that he practically floats out of the Arcade, even though he can't have gotten more than four hours of sleep in the last couple of days.

"See you," I barely manage to get out before he's off. I watch him until the last silver flash of his jumpsuit disappears into the crowd of the morning commute. A knot tightens in my stomach. I won't see Kez again until I'm back from the Outerlands. For all I know, this could be goodbye forever.

But I won't let it be. My crew is counting on me, even if they don't know it yet.

Forty minutes later, I'm almost to Mr. Preston's estate when my wrist screen buzzes. Celeste's bright, gap-toothed smile appears.

"Morni—"

"Do you think chrome or copper?" Celeste's words all run together. "Not real copper, of course, but—"

"Whoa, whoa. Slow down. What are we talking about?" I veer toward the shade of the courtyard's walls and squint at the screen.

She beams at me. "I've been thinking a lot about my future, and I've decided to become . . . a RepairProxy!"

"Your future? A wha—?" The words escape me, even though I *should* be thrilled. RepairProxies are in high demand, with cheap LifeCorp electronics breaking down constantly. From holoscreens to autonomous cars, people are finally realizing it might be cheaper to repair things than to upgrade them. Celeste would never want for a job. But she's still only nine, and the mods mean replacing her forearms with robotic attachments. I think about her delicate kid arms, her bioluminescent pink nail polish (a chip-resistant formula of her own invention, of course). All of it, gone—just so she can make an Upper's life a little more convenient.

"Why . . . why would you do that?" My throat is tight, and the words come out too quiet.

Celeste has two sample plates of metal in her hand, and she's holding them both against her right forearm. "The chrome is nice," she rambles on. "But my skin's already sort of coppery, so I thought that would be kind of cool too. Like— my arm, but shinier? But how cool would the chrome fingers look coming through the RepairProxy gloves? Like, chrome on black? *So* good."

Icy dread sluices down my insides. "Celeste, where are you right now?"

"The hospital. I wanted to surprise you, but then I couldn't pick a color. You can't tell Kez and Thea, though. I want to show them myself. They're gonna flip!"

The ground wobbles under my feet. I lean against the wall. Celeste and I have talked about her becoming a Proxy a few times before, but it always felt like a "someday" conversation. As in someday when we have five thousand credits to spare for the attachments. "How—but . . . where did you even get the credits?"

She smiles. "I'll never tell. And the doctor says she'll give me a discount. Since my arms are so small, you know."

"Celeste, you . . ." The words thicken in my throat. "You can't do this."

"Why not? You're a Proxy. All you guys are. I want to help. If I can pull my weight, maybe you won't have to risk the side jobs anymore."

"You aren't even old enough to consent!"

"Silas said he'd sign for me."

"Of course he did." That's Silas, always pushing us up the ladder, never questioning the destination. I ball my hand into a fist.

"But even if he didn't, I'd find a way," she continues with proud defiance. "Adrian said to not let anyone get in the way of my future."

"Adrian?" My eyes bulge wide at the familiar name. "Celeste. Please tell me you're not about to take life advice from a *Forceman*? When did you even talk to him? Wait . . . is *that* where you got the credits?" I'm going to kill him. I swear I'm going to kill him.

"So what if it is? They're mine now, and I can do whatever I want with them." Celeste's voice goes high and squeaky, like she might cry. "This is what I want. I want to be useful."

"You *are* useful, you—" I groan as the first fat teardrop spills down her cheek. "When is your surgery?"

"Day after tomorrow, first thing in the morning." She sniffs and wipes her eyes roughly with her sleeve. "Liv? I really want you there."

The fear in Celeste's voice reminds me that she's just a kid. Arguing with her will only make her dig her heels in more. "Of course, sweet girl." I calm the tremor in my voice, and she relaxes. "Gotta go. See you at home, okay?"

"See you."

As soon as Celeste ends the call, I slam a fist against the brick wall behind me. "Dammit!" On the other end of the courtyard, the Prestons' help staff stop and stare. I'm sure they'll talk about me later. I don't care.

I need Preston's credits, to get us out of the cramped

Towers permanently, and into a life of our choosing. Without that money, there will always be another reason for Celeste to go through with the surgery, even if I can delay her this time. Another tool she can't afford in order to make her gadgets. Another Forceman putting so-called dreams in her head that are nothing but a front for LifeCorp's control. There is no equilibrium in the life of a Lower. No peace. Only a constant striving for . . . what, exactly? The best most of us can expect is a job that will provide enough security to keep us fed, housed, and clothed for the rest of our lives. But the cost of that security is high, and LifeCorp and its Forcemen will never stop demanding their literal pound of flesh.

Celeste's beautiful hands. Kez's sleep. Thea's time. Sophie's personal life.

My innocence.

How many more pieces of ourselves will we have to lose?

I sprint through the courtyard and into Mr. Preston's estate, even though my chest is so tight I can barely breathe. There's no time to waste. Because now I don't have until the end of the week to bring Mr. Preston his Scrap. I have two days.

ADRIAN

THE FORCE'S DIRECTOR OF ANALYTICS, MARIE GRAYSON, IS WAITING FOR NAS and me at her desk when we enter. She's one of those people who just *looks* smart, like she's got four different lines of thought all running in her head at once. By the time we reach her, her shrewd brown eyes are focused on our fraying Lower jumpsuits. In comparison, Marie looks sharp, her deep brown skin contrasting nicely against the cream of her freshly pressed uniform. Her eyeliner is so precise I wonder if it's tattooed on.

"You're the rookies assigned to the Towers, right? Orange Haze?" She tucks a few strands of her graying black bob behind her ear, before they immediately come loose again. Without waiting for confirmation, she swivels back to her computer screen. "Got a name for me?"

"Liv Newman," Nas and I both say at the same time.

Marie enters the name in a series of staccato keyboard strokes, and the screen splits into quadrants. One of them shows the suspect's stats—

AGE: 18
HEIGHT: 5'5"
PRODUCTIVITY SCORE: 1260

Decent, but not enough to save her from arrest.

ADDITIONAL INFORMATION: NO KNOWN ALIASES.
NO KNOWN OFFENSES.

No criminal record. But we'll change that soon enough.

Liv's bio says that she was raised in Employee Care, but her record in the factories ends about ten years ago. An eight-year-old girl in the Towers on her own? No wonder Celeste sees her as a role model. I know Employee Care isn't exactly a privileged upbringing, but was Newman's experience really so bad that she decided to take her chances on the streets?

The other screens show pixelated surveillance footage, playing in looped clips. One—captured by a drone, judging from the viewpoint—shows Newman sitting on the roof of the western Tower, facing east. As the time lapse continues, the footage shifts from green-and-black night vision to the brightness of dawn. I stare at her hunched form, wait for her to do something else to incriminate herself. But she simply sits there, watching the sunrise. I imagine I see her shoulders—the same ones that grazed mine yesterday afternoon—lift in a sigh as the day breaks. But I chock it up to poor resolution.

Marie lets out a low whistle. "Database is turning up hits from all over the Towers. Even a couple in the Estates. And that's only the past seventy-two hours. Your girl gets around, doesn't she?"

"Yeah, well . . . I'm sure her clientele keeps her very busy," I grumble, still watching the footage of Liv at sunrise as the loop restarts. A horrible thought suddenly occurs to me, that one of these surveillance tapes might have footage of my, uh— encounter—with Newman. I'd be fritzed if word got out that I met her, that we spoke. Or that I can't stop thinking about the way her face lit up when she laughed, or the way she bit her lip before she smiled—

But that's ridiculous. Thinking Newman is beautiful doesn't make me an accomplice; she's objectively attractive. That's just plain science—shapes and ratios.

"Right?" I blurt out.

"You say something, rookie?" Nas asks. He and Marie are hunched together over the screens, and now they're both staring at me.

I swallow. "Um, sorry. Nothing. It's nothing."

Slowly, Nas peels his eyes from my face and points at a panel on the computer screen closest to him. "There's the kid from the hit last night," he says. Sure enough, Celeste is walking hand-in-hand with our suspect. Newman stops to adjust the girl's puff pigtails, and Celeste tries in vain to squirm away. The smallest bit of guilt flashes in my chest. The two are obviously close, and I worry about how lost Celeste will be once we lock Newman up. *Lost, but better off,* I remind myself. *Let her find a better role model.*

With a hard blink, I ground myself back in the moment.

"So if this footage is all from the past few days, where's New-man now?"

More keyboard clacking. "There's typically a lag for the visual surveillance so the cataloging software has time to do its thing. But we can see where she was about forty minutes ago. Latest ping had her . . ." Marie's typing slows, and she leans in to decipher the wall of coordinate data on the screen. "That can't be right." She's talking only to herself now, which means there's a problem even *her* mind can't compute. Which means we're about to be fritzed.

"What is it?" I squint at the jumble of numbers and letters. She opens her mouth to speak, closes it again. Beside us, Nas is perfectly still, only his eyes moving as he scans the data for processing. When he's done, he lets out an almost human groan of frustration.

"She . . . left the borough?" Marie's confident tone evaporates.

Alarms blare in my head. "Call External Relations. We can extradite t—"

"No." Nas runs a hand over his chin, already forming a plan for a problem I don't fully understand. I feel a familiar pinch of envy at the speed of his mind. "She's not in another jurisdiction. She's . . . well, technically, she's in *no* jurisdiction, I guess."

The realization dawns on me. "She ran to the Outerlands?" All this time we had a BOLO alert on Newman for every conceivable corner of the Metro, we never thought to secure the Metro itself. But *no one* ever leaves. Why would you? LifeCorp promises everything you'd ever want, if you're willing to work for it.

A new window pops up on Marie's screen, and she expands it to its full size. Staring back at us in high resolution is Liv Newman's face at the Metro border checkpoint. She nods, glassy-eyed, at the droid border agent as he asks her a series of checklist questions that all amount to "Don't come crying to us when the raiders tear you a new one, okay?"

The blank stare she gives says she's not listening, like she doesn't even care. The dead expression is a far cry from the bright face I met in the alley, and the ache of betrayal washes over me again. *This* is who Liv Newman really is. Not the helpful Lower who came to my rescue, or the big-sister figure who dotes on Celeste. Those are all masks she wears. Lies.

This is the true Liv. The one who turned Joe Rivera into a walking ghost without so much as a frown. No wonder she's fleeing to the raiders; she might actually fit in with them.

"Nas, alert all units," I say, heading for the exit. "We need everyone at that checkpoint, now!" The other analysts swivel their heads at the shouting.

Marie stands, disappointment crinkling the lines around her eyes. "Rao, I already told you: there's a lag with the visuals. This is from almost an hour ago."

Nas pats my shoulder like I'm a little kid whose fish just died. "Sorry, man."

Newman's cold, unfeeling eyes are still on the screen, and every time I catch a glimpse of them, I want to break something. She may not be in the Metro anymore, but she's still out there. Heartless. Dangerous. And Joe Rivera's still up the street at Mercy North, with no one to answer for his broken mind.

That's not justice.

"Marie, send me the coordinates for that checkpoint, and any other drone surveillance footage for a car traveling that route in the past hour."

To Marie's credit, she doesn't ask questions, and the data's in my chip mere seconds later. Nas is the one who furrows his brow.

"Adrian, stop. Are you nuts?" He chases after me as I bolt toward the Citadel's garage.

"You and I both know that if an Upper had been attacked in that alley, half the Outerlands would've been turned upside down by now, jurisdictions be damned. The Lowers deserve our protection, same as those in the Estates. Don't they?" I pause. Nas's frown tells me he knows something's up. He deserves the full explanation of my history with Newman, why I *need* to bring her in. Maybe someday I'll have the gears to tell him. Right now, there's no time.

The garage attendant approaches us. "I need a car, a fast one," I tell her. "Quiet, too."

Nas puts a hand on my shoulder. "Just—stop and think. This is the Outerlands. No comms, no backup. You'll be a sitting duck out there. And if the raiders get their hands on a Forceman—"

"You saw what she did to the Riveras—broke one, turned the other into a rebel. We need to bring her in and ensure nothing like that ever happens again." I shrug his hand off, resolve hardening in my chest like concrete. Nas thinks I've lost it. But what I'm fighting for is worth the risk. Yes, I feel duped by Newman. Beyond that, though, as long as she's free, LifeCorp is under threat. She's cleverer than anyone is giving her credit for. She'll find her way back into the Metro and deal Orange Haze again. The peace and prosperity we've fought so hard to maintain isn't safe, as long as Liv Newman is out there with the key to anarchy.

"We're not ordinary citizens, Nas. We're officers of the *Force.*" I check my blaster, making sure it's charged. "LifeCorp trained us at the Academy, gave us a badge and the privilege of using our position to defend this borough. We're the only things standing between the order of the Metro and the raiders' lawlessness."

Exasperated, Nas looks to the ceiling. "You're going no matter what I say, aren't you?"

"Bet your shiny chrome ass I am."

The garage attendant returns, holding a set of keys. I reach for them, but Nas is faster. "Then I'm driving," he says over his shoulder as he heads toward the vehicles. "You have below-average reaction time for a human, and that's saying something."

I smile at his back. This feels right, two partners setting out to defend the home we love. Newman committed a crime against LifeCorp; she needs to pay for it.

Order must be restored.

LIV

THIS IS BY FAR THE STUPIDEST THING I'VE EVER DONE.

It's also the nicest car I've ever been in, but I'm too nervous to enjoy the premium leather upholstery in Mr. Preston's two-seater, or even to pull out the book I grabbed from his library yesterday. I should've let Kez know I wouldn't be back tonight so he and Celeste wouldn't worry. But I was barely thinking straight enough to hear Mr. Preston as he spouted his effusive thanks. Getting that Scrap of the stars before Celeste's surgery was the only thing on my mind.

The journey into the Outerlands is disorienting. For the first twenty miles, there's enough evidence of LifeCorp's influence that I at least feel anchored to something—an old billboard touting the company warehouses as a great place to work, an out-of-commission delivery drone station. But then the paved smoothness of the turnpike gives way to nothing but overgrown grasses and shrubs. I watch the wind rustle their leaves and wonder what they feel like, how soft they might be . . .

I'm jolted awake when the dashboard display tells me I've been asleep for two hours. Two hours of obliviousness against the raiders who call the Outerlands home, or even a mechanical malfunction, with no one out here to call for help. *Great job, Liv—barely four hours and you've already made yourself easy prey.*

With a yawn, I stretch and take in my surroundings through the window. I guess *forest* is the technical term for it, but I've never seen trees like this. *Forest* is the meticulously spaced columns of drone-grown oaks that LifeCorp set up west of the Metro, with companion plants placed perfectly between rows, to ensure a steady supply of lumber, paper, and other goods for the Metro's growing population. *Forest* is the LifeCorp droids who test the soil's nutrient content, adjust the rainfall projections, and prune any branch that dares to lose its way. *Forest,* as the Employee Care teachers taught us, is a testament to LifeCorp's concern for its citizens—the ingenuity to control nature itself in order to provide for its own.

This is not a forest. This is chaos, and it's magnificent.

Enormous gray-brown giants stretch upward, haphazardly spaced, so that I can't see my way out in any direction. The trees' branches grasp desperately for the sky, like lovers' hands outstretched. Their leaves are the colors of the sun itself—a blinding combination of fiery oranges and yellows. On the ground below, there are no trail markers, no carefully laid paths for people or droids. Only a deep layer of leaves from seasons past and shrubs that have rooted faithfully in the rich decay.

Towering over the bushes, the trees seem almost protective of the smaller plants. Thoughts of Celeste twist my stomach. She's the reason I'm out here, leaving the familiarity of the Metro to change all our lives. I'm going to succeed, for her. Get the Scrap and make it back before her modification so she knows that she has options, and that there's more to life than being someone's Proxy.

When the woods become too dense for the car to wind through, I park and step outside. The forest is louder than I expect. Wind rushes gently through the branches, accompanying the birdsong overhead. From the sound of it, there's a river nearby. The crisp, earthy air runs down my throat as I inhale. When I take another breath, something surges in my chest, as untamed as the trees that surround me. I tamp it down. This yearning would make an excellent Scrap, but I need to get to the Prestons' cabin before nightfall in a couple of hours. My screen's comms don't work out here—not enough connectivity—but I downloaded Mr. Preston's map of these few square miles before I lost signal. I pull it up and see the icon for his cabin pulsing a few miles to the northwest.

As I head out on foot, the woods change. The brown skeletons of the shrubs are exposed, their leaves torn off. And someone—some*thing*—has scraped away the side of a tree trunk in rough, powerful gouges. I stop in front of the shredded tree's bark and rub my fingers against the deep grooves. It's too haphazard to be a human design, even one made with the primitive tools the raiders are probably working with. No, this isn't manmade. It's from an animal—a big, angry one. I pick up the pace and make a note to find a weapon at the cabin, just in case.

When the cabin finally emerges through the trees, I almost miss it. I was expecting something in line with the Prestons' home in the Estates—an enormous compound smack in the middle of the forest. But the beacon on my screen tells me this smaller cream-colored house with a brick chimney is my destination, so I proceed. Through the trees on either side of the house, I catch glimpses of the lake Preston said would be here. I've got less than an hour until sunset, so instead of exploring the house, I decide to head down the winding path to the water and plan out my Scrap. If I'm going to "be open to the awe" like Mr. Preston wants, I need to get out of my own head and fully take in the moment.

As soon as I set foot on the pier, I know finding the awe won't be a problem. On one end of the lake, the sky is a deep azure, until it fades slowly into the burnt orange of the day's end. The setting sun casts glittering golden ripples across the water, which echo the fiery hues of the trees. An ache swells from deep in my chest. Has the illustrator of the dull blue oval on my map actually ever *seen* a lake? Because I have some notes.

The sense of wonder starts to cool as the sunset dims, but I'm still thrilled. If this scene is already stirring my emotions, I can only imagine how amazing Preston's Scrap will be. A sky full of stars. An account full of credits. A future full of potential.

After what feels like an eternity, the sun finally makes its descent into the western end of the lake, pulling the crimson and orange light with it. I'm jittery with excitement, but nerves and awe don't mix. I close my eyes and inhale slowly to center myself. My emotions become a blank canvas. With a long breath out, I open my eyes and take in . . .

Nothing.

Well, almost nothing. There are a few bright pinpricks in the sky here and there, but it's not even that different from the view from the Towers, honestly. I search the sky frantically from one end of the lake to the other. Am I missing something? Maybe there's a sudden blanket of clouds that will pass over, revealing the magnificence that Mr. Preston told me he remembered from his trips here? I wait. I scan. Still nothing.

My heart pounds against my chest in wild, desperate beats. This can't be happening. I *can't* fail. Everyone's counting on me: Celeste, Thea, Kez. Even Silas. This job is the only chance we have at breaking out of the roles LifeCorp has assigned us. Think. *Think.* Celeste's surgery isn't until the day after tomorrow. I could try again tomorrow night, risk a day out here on my own with the raiders and animals and who knows what else. It would be worth it, for the perfect Scrap. But even as the plan takes shape, I know there's no point. The Metro's light swallows the darkness, making it impossible to see the stars. One night won't change that.

It's hopeless. This trip, and all my dreaming. There's not going to be a swanky New York City apartment, or a cozy bookstore of my own, or a cat-bot Celeste whispers her secrets to before bed each night. I won't be able to stop Celeste from destroying her body for pay, won't be able to stop Silas's plan to take Sector Eleven by force, or my part in it. I can't save anyone. I can't even save myself. We're all trapped, pawns spilled out onto a board we didn't create and can't change.

My wrist screen chirps.

WARNING: 36 HOURS SINCE LAST RECORDED SCRAP.

PRODUCTIVITY SCORE WILL DECLINE IN 12 HOURS.

RECORD NEW SCRAP?

I clench my fists, my nails digging half-moons into the flesh of my clammy hands, and scream.

The sound echoes across the lake, until it's like the lake is screaming right back at me. It's the scream I should have let out when I unleashed one of my worst memories on Jonah Rivera, and when I saw Celeste's eagerness to alter herself forever because of some Forceman's "kind" gesture. It's the scream I should have been letting out this entire time.

When there's nothing left in me, I sink to my knees on the pier and clutch my head in my hands. My fingers slide against the smooth wires of my chip, which gives me an idea. I may be trapped, but there is one way to escape. At least for a while.

"Nero, requesting one hundred percent memory archive. Initiate."

I'm used to selectively archiving parts of my memory after one of Silas's jobs. But tonight has made it clear that that's not enough. Like the wild vines that wind through this forest, LifeCorp's tendrils are woven into every aspect of my life. I only need to escape for a little bit . . . but I need to escape it all. Absolutely everything.

My screen pings with a wall of text that amounts to *Are you nuts?* "Give me a break," I mutter as I flip through the legalese. A short rest, then I'll be myself again. Twenty-four hours should do it. I set my preferences and slide the memory loss percentage down to 90 percent. The remaining 10 percent will allow me to remember my name, my executive functioning—the stuff that makes me, me, and not a bumbling child trapped in a teenager's body. I also add a note about finding the stars, should they appear. But until this time tomorrow, I want to forget the rest: the Forcemen, Proxies, the Mean, Silas's jobs, and the Metro itself.

The prompt blinks at me to confirm my settings: time, date, yadda yadda yadda.

"Confirm."

As soon as the word leaves my lips, I spot the biggest fritz-up of my life. In the Metro, all the data could come rushing down from the cloud as soon as the day's up. But we're not *in* the Metro. Out here, there's none of LifeCorp's infrastructure to ensure instant connectivity. Which means, according to the display on my wrist screen, the full restoration of my memory will take . . .

A week?!

I can't have my memory wiped for that long. I need to get home. Need to save Celeste and stop Silas and Kez from walking into a death trap in Sector Eleven without me. My pulse pounds in my ears. I scramble to cancel the command as the completion bar crawls across the scre—

■ ■ ■

WOW, WHAT A GORGEOUS NIGHT. I THINK I'LL GO FOR A SWIM.

ADRIAN

"I FEEL LIKE I NEED TO STATE, FOR THE RECORD, THAT THIS IS A HORRIBLE IDEA," Nas shouts as the decaying pylons of the turnpike zoom past us.

"You already said that, when we reached the first mile marker," I say, rolling my shoulders against the creeping uncertainty. "And before that, when we went through the checkpoint."

"It was true then, and it's true now." He leans the cycle into a bend in the road. In the end, the garage attendant couldn't bring herself to sign off on a patroller outside the Metro's boundary, in case the vehicle was hijacked by raiders. We were barely able to negotiate the decommissioned cycle and rickety sidecar we're riding now, which greeted us with more maintenance alerts than I even knew were possible when we started it up. But it beats a hundred-mile walk.

To Nas's credit, every mile deeper into the Outerlands has me questioning myself too. There's something about the way the reassuring, dependable gray and chrome of the turnpike and surrounding buildings gradually gives way to an onslaught of bright green overgrowth. The farther we go, the less recognizable everything is, which only makes me think about the ultimate conclusion of our path: a place where even the faintest sense of the Metro's peace and stability goes quiet.

I refocus. For now, Nas is still with me, though he'll have to stop several miles short of the last signal from Arthur Preston's car. Redding approved our mission only so long as Nas stayed within the bounds of the Neuralink network in case the Citadel needed to call him back to the Metro for another mission. After twenty-four hours, regardless of my status, he's to report back to the Metro. Unexpendable, Redding called him. I'm choosing not to think too hard about what that says about me. I glance at my wrist.

"Five exits to go—oh." As we crest a small hill, the turnpike disappears into a sinkhole. Nas skids the cycle to a stop before we run out of road.

I swallow. "Or this exit works too." Slowly, we veer onto an eastbound side road. I eye the afternoon sun nervously over my shoulder as it dips closer to the horizon. If I don't find Newman before nightfall, this mission becomes considerably harder. All Forcemen go through survival training, but it's been years since I've had to think about building my own shelter or starting a fire.

"Not getting cold feet, are you, rookie?" Nas asks as twigs crack under the cycle's tires.

"What? No. Why would you—"

"I can feel your leg bouncing."

Get it together, Adrian. "I'm fine. Just ready to get out there."

Nas brings the cycle to a slow roll, then kills the engine.

"Well, here's your chance," he says, pointing north. "The Metro's network signal ends ten yards that way. This is where I leave you."

He says the last part with a mocking gravity, but the moment still feels heavy. Nas guides the cycle into a thick patch of brush and waves me over to help him cover it with fallen branches.

"Okay, let's go over the plan, yeah?" he says. "I'll power down out of sight. You follow the signal, find Newman. As soon as you've got her, ping me on my auxiliary channels. I'll start back up and head your way."

I nod. "And you're sure Redding will let you come back out, even if it goes past your twenty-four-hour curfew? Wouldn't want to risk such an *unexpendable* resource as yourself."

"He'll let me." Nas stands, and his serious tone stops my eyes midroll. "And if he doesn't, I'm coming anyway. You're not alone out here, even when it might feel like it."

My voice gets stuck in my throat. I can barely manage an audible "thanks, man" before Nas stalks toward a crumbling overpass and nestles himself against a cracked pylon. Every time I start to think of Nas as my competition, harping on all the ways we're different, he reminds me that we're partners. A team.

Nas lets out a breath like he's settling into bed after a hard day's work. "Don't do anything stupid, Adrian."

"Too late." We chuckle. "Leave your background sensors on, will you? Who knows what's lurking out here." *Or who.*

He sighs flippantly. "Yes, Mother. See you in a few hours." We give each other a nod, and then his eyelids shudder closed and he's gone, leaning against the cratered cement blocks like he's nuzzling a pillow. I roll my shoulders back, give Nas a final salute, and set my sights north.

The woods engulf me like a yawning mouth, and I don't have to check to know that Nas's overpass is long gone after just a few minutes. A shiver runs through me. I can't remember the last time I was truly alone like this, and I can't decide what's worse: complete solitude in this seemingly unending wilderness, or the Towers' constant press of bodies. Again, my traitorous mind connects the memory of my claustrophobia to Newman's comforting words, how easy she was to be with. Talking with her in those brief moments felt like . . . coming home. Like something in me recognized something in her and said *ah, there you are, finally.*

I bet making people feel safe like that is part of her game.

A creature chitters in the tree beside me. I jump, then chide myself when the guilty squirrel appears. "Breathe, man. She doesn't know you're coming; you've got the advantage." The sound of my own voice distracts from the rush of blood pumping in my ears. As I talk to myself, I twist the silver Forceman signet ring on my pinky. Nas and I figured it made good sense to stay in disguise in the Outerlands—anyone we run into is likely to have Forcemen ranked number one on their shit list. But I can easily hide this ring if it comes down to it, and it's a comforting reminder of my mission.

I trudge through the brush, trying to ignore the setting sun and the moon slowly rising overhead. "Did you hear the one about the store that sold sentient drones?" I ask out loud. "They couldn't stop them from flying off the shelves!

"Why did the droid get upset? Because everyone was pushing his buttons.

"What's the difference between a surveillance drone and particle physics? One goes way over your head, and the other— *Shit.*"

I feel it before I hear the squelch, sliding under my boot with a disturbing slickness. A glance down confirms my suspicions: a massive pile of animal dung, steam still swirling in the beam of my flashlight. Perfect. My wrist screen tells me I'm still several miles from the signal on Preston's car, but tracking animal scent through the woods is a surefire way to become prey instead of predator, so I adjust my course. There's a small lake half a mile away; I'll rinse off there and double back to the car. Odds are Newman's somewhere between the two, anyway. Even the cold-blooded can't survive without water.

The last wisps of sunlight fade from the sky, taking the day's warmth with them. I shiver against the chill and flip on the heattech embedded in my underclothes. With night vision on, the woods transform from warm brown and yellow to an eerie pale green. My breath is shaky, but the sound fades into the chorus of loon cries and cricket song that follows me to the lake. I climb a small hill, and the woods opens up to the water, gently lapping against a marshy shore. I'm almost out of the tree line when my training kicks in: a natural water source is prime territory for anyone who lives in this forest, raiders and animals alike. But a heat scan of the shore tells me there's no one in my immediate vicinity, save a few bullfrogs I hear in the grasses. With caution, I proceed.

The dung washes away easily enough, with the help of a twig to fish out the bits between the treads of my boots. I'm nearly satisfied that the musky smell is gone when I notice ripples in the water. At the same time, a gentle splash from somewhere in the darkness sends my heartbeat into the stratosphere.

Something's out there.

Too quickly, I shove my foot into my boot and topple into the water. I manage to stand before I'm fully submerged, but my jumpsuit is soaked from the chest down. *Just fritzing perfect.* I switch from night vision to thermal optics. And then I see it, clear as day: a bright orange mass, gliding across the lake. I squint at the unintelligible blob drifting closer—an animal of some kind? But then it raises an appendage, and I panic. It is, unmistakably, a human arm.

I scramble out of the water, desperate to get to the high ground of the pier in case the person charges. Whether it's a raider or Newman, equal footing is a death sentence. Nas's voice echoes in my head, reminding me to check my blind spots, so I whirl around as I creep backward toward the end of the dock.

Nothing.

Breathing a sigh of relief, I scan the water. But the lake is empty. There isn't even a hint of orange blurred under the surface. Whoever was there, they're gone.

"Hello."

I jump and make a sound that Nas would never let me live down if he were here. The voice came from almost directly below me, from a blaze of orange in the shape of a woman's head and shoulders. Slowly, I reach for my wrist, switching my heat vision off and my headlamp on. Bobbing in the water, Liv Newman grimaces against the bright light, but as her eyes adjust, she looks up at me again, a surprising openness in her features.

"Hello," she says again. If I didn't know better, I'd say she sounded friendly. It's dark out, but my headlamp is on its close proximity setting, so I know she can see my face. Not to mention my blaster. I should use my weapon now, I'm aware. But somewhere along the path from my brain to my hand, the signal is lost. Newman's watching me with those clear brown eyes that almost lured me in back at the Towers. No malice in her expression, or even suspicion.

Something's way off here. I assess the situation and search my brain for my Academy training, but there wasn't anything in the handbook about being stranded in the wilderness with a suspect who *should* be out for your blood but is instead greeting you like you're two strangers passing in a T station. I am woefully unprepared for this, so I do the only thing that comes to mind.

I reply. "Hello."

Liv Newman's smile shines like moonlight on the water.

LIV

I LIKE THE SOUND OF HIS VOICE. IT'S STRONG, BUT NOT TOO DEEP, A TENOR that complements the soprano of the chirping crickets and the deep bass of the bullfrogs.

And most importantly, it's human.

"It's nice to see another person; I was beginning to wonder if I was alone out here," I say as I tread water. I gesture to the ladder on the side of the dock. "Could you help me up?"

Confusion flashes across the boy's face. "I mean, I know how to climb a ladder," I say. "But it's a little slippery and the rails have rusted, is all. I could wade to shore, I guess. . . ." My wince is uncontrollable as I consider the slimy pondweed a few yards away. A piece grazed my toe in the lake earlier, and I swear my soul left my body. He doesn't need to know that, though.

The boy opens his mouth and closes it as his eyes shift from side to side. I'm working up the courage to swim to shore when he slowly crouches and extends a hand, his features tight. I breathe a sigh of relief and step onto the ladder. When I clasp his hand, the furrow in his brow deepens, but he says nothing.

"Th-thank you," I manage once I'm up on the dock, my teeth chattering.

"Yeah, well . . . not like I was going to let you drown . . . ?" he mutters, more to himself than to me. My fingers touch something hard on his hand.

"Oh! That's pretty." I admire the silver ring on his pinky. The boy's features harden into a scowl, in agonizing slow motion.

"Very funny."

"What is?"

He stares at me with stunned confusion. I shiver, and that's when we both realize I'm only in a bra and underwear. My rescuer releases my hand and jumps two yards away in a single bound.

"Just a second!" I rush to the pile of my clothes at the edge of the pier. He pivots to face away from me and says something I can't quite make out. I lean in. "Sorry?"

The boy fidgets with something jingling at his side. "I said your und—your under—"

"I'm only in my underwear, I know. I'm hurrying. Guess I'm still a little surprised someone else is out here." I pause halfway into one pant leg. Why *is* he out here? And why *am* I? Alone with him, at that?

"I can't—while you're—" His words fade into an exasperated sigh. He peeks over his shoulder to see that I'm dressed in my gray jumpsuit—the same as his, I note—then turns back around. But he holds his arms up in front of him, like he's attempting to herd me to the end of the dock. What's he protecting? My gaze trails the shoreline until I notice the small cabin peeking out from the cover of the trees. *Ah.*

"Your home is lovely," I say, pointing behind him.

He drops his hands. "My . . . what?" Even when he's glowering at me, I can't help but notice how handsome he is. Smooth bronze skin, a strong jaw with full lips. Eyes I'm already getting lost in. But those eyes are staring at *me* like I'm a few trees short of a forest, so I quickly course correct.

"Uh, uh—I mean *my* home. Is lovely." It must belong to one of us, right?

Wrong. The boy disappears somewhere inside himself, scratching the back of his neck as he whispers words I'm sure I'm not supposed to hear. "Okay . . . okay. What the fritz is happening?"

Don't leave. Don't leave. His alarm makes me painfully aware of how vulnerable I am. In my head, I search frantically for pieces of myself, but little comes to mind. I know my name, how old I am, how to discern right from wrong. I know that I'm me. But everything else—where I've come from, where I'm meant to be, who I'm meant to be with—is gone. My mind is an attic that's been scrubbed clean.

"Look, I'm sorry if we're . . . supposed to know each other." I freeze. "Oh, shit. Do we *know* know each other? Like, intimately?" If we were dating, him being here would make sense. But the more I talk, the farther his mouth hangs open.

"No." He stretches the word into three syllables.

"No! Of course, no. Because you're—" A gorgeous bronze statue. "And I'm—" A lunatic alone in the woods at night. "I'm

Liv. Newman. And I'm sorry for being weird, I'm . . . piecing some stuff together right now."

". . . Right." His tone darkens. "Whatever that means." He huffs, and a lock of his thick black curls briefly takes flight. But as he moves his head, I notice something missing. "Where is your . . . ?" I reach for a word to describe the large metal node at the base of my skull, but I can't think of one. He tilts his head, waiting. *Don't freak him out any more, or he'll leave, and you'll be alone again.*

"You're serious, aren't you?" he asks. "You don't remember anything?"

His question makes me certain something is very, very wrong. I glance up in panic, searching for an explanation. The stars glimmer back at us, calming me and calling to me simultaneously.

"Huh . . ."

"What is it now?" the boy asks.

"The stars. I think I'm supposed to . . . see them?"

"What? Why?"

I open my mouth to explain, but the answer is gone as quickly as it arrives. The wind picks up, sending a chill through the thin fabric of my clothes. The boy is unfazed, but he notes my discomfort. His shoulders rise and fall in a resigned sigh, even as the suspicion never leaves his eyes.

"Come on." He gestures to the cabin, annoyed. "Let's get inside."

12

ADRIAN

THIS IS INSANITY.

I should be carting Newman off toward a lengthy sentence in a virtual prison pod. We should be halfway to Nas's overpass, even walking in the dark, with her in handcuffs. I should be doing my fritzing job. But instead, I'm sitting in the window of the Prestons' cabin's breakfast nook, my head in my hands, as the sound of a shower runs halfway down the home's single hallway. In my defense, I did case the house as Newman and I entered, and I have a handle on all the viable exits and a line of sight to anywhere she might run. Short of being inside her mind, there's no way for me to know for sure if this memory loss thing is legit, but the least I can do is watch her closely until I can decide if I'm being played. Again.

"You're under arrest," I mutter at the green plaid cushion under my feet. Of course, the words come easily now, the same way they have hundreds of times over years of training. But when it was time to put all those drills into practice for my first field arrest, I blew it. Just stood there, stammering on the pier like an idiot. Defeated by the sight of a girl's bare stomach. But what was I supposed to do, tackle her in her underwear?

For the tenth time since I left him, I wish I could ping Nas for advice. But he'd only laugh and give me shit for not being able to bring a helpless teenage girl into custody on my own. He wouldn't understand exactly *why* I can't do it. Every assignment I've been on, every scenario I've trained for, the suspect at least had knowledge of their crimes. Even if they were lying, there was always that barely perceptible sliver under the surface—they knew their deception was part of the game. But Newman's personality shift feels like more than a simple lie. I've received extensive training on every class of Metro citizen, so I'm familiar with EmoProxies' memory archiving capabilities. But would Newman really be foolish enough to wipe her entire memory, out here in the wild? And if so, why?

Stop playing psychoanalyst and arrest her already, I imagine Nas saying. But every time I picture her floating helpless in the lake, I can't.

"Pathetic," I whisper to myself.

The shower stops. My ears prick at the shuffling noises coming from the bathroom, and I sit up a little straighter. She could be fashioning some sort of weapon out of the shower curtain rod or concocting a bomb from household cleaners under the sink. *Dammit, rookie. Should have been more thorough.*

The door opens, and Newman steps out in black leggings and an oversized pale blue sweater, a hand towel draped across her shoulders to catch the drips from her still-wet curly hair. She's holding an object in each of her hands, one of which is roughly the same size and shape as a knife, in the dim warm light of the hall. I jump out of the booth and scan the room for any sort of weapon I can use to defend myself. The kitchen is only a few yards away. I sidestep awkwardly toward the silverware drawer as Newman comes closer. This is it, the showdown I've been waiting for. My hands fumble behind me for the knob as she approaches, determination on her face, and reveals her possessions:

A wide-toothed comb. And some hair mousse.

"Found these in the cabinet." She smiles. "Lucky, right? And feel this sweater. It's so soft. There's a drawerful of them." Half of her hair is in a plaited pigtail, the other half still up in a messy, wet bun. She puts the comb and tub of mousse down, and steps into my space. My body tenses, ready for an attack. But Newman stretches out the cuff of her top expectantly, and I lift a shaking hand to the fabric. She's right, the sweater is indescribably soft. And warm from the heat of her skin. Up close, she smells like citrus and honey. I watch as a stray drop of water slides its way from her temple down her jaw, leaving a trail a slightly darker brown than her chestnut skin. My fingers graze hers as I pull away. Does she really not remember me? Because I remember *so much* of her. The way her hand felt in mine as she pulled me through the crowd . . .

"Yes. Very soft." If she notices my voice crack, she doesn't acknowledge it as she plops down on an armchair in the adjoining living room area. Casually, she takes down the unbraided half of her hair and runs the mousse through her curls with her fingers. She's relaxed. Calm. It's the perfect time for an interrogation.

"Nice place, huh? Kez would get a kick out of these curtains." I have no idea what Kez would think of these curtains; I'm only 80 percent sure I got the guy's name right. But it doesn't matter because Liv's expression never waivers.

"Who's that?" she asks.

"Just . . . some guy I know." Damn. I switch tactics. At the Academy, they taught us that people have different physical cues when they're recalling facts versus when they're making things up. If I can establish Liv's baseline actions for creative thought, I'll be able to catch her in a lie.

"If you could be any kind of tree, what would you be?" I blurt out. Newman glances at me like I've sprouted branches myself. But then she pauses, looking up and to the right. *Got her.*

"Hmm. I don't know the name of it, but down by the lake there was one big one, with these long, drooping branches that dipped into the water. That tiny point of contact between the little green leaves and the lake felt so delicate. Tender, almost."

"A willow," I say softly.

"How about you?"

"Oh! Uh—a pine."

"Why?"

I'm surprised at how easily the answer comes. "They're the tallest. Like the protectors of the other trees." Newman seems genuinely interested in my response. But now it's time for me to regain control.

"How did you get out here?" I wait for her eyes to swing up and to the right, like before. But instead, they widen with alarm.

"Out here? Is this not where I usually am?"

If this is an act, she's very, very good. "No, but don't worry; you're only a few hours from home."

THE DIVIDING SKY

"Home . . ." Her stomach rumbles loudly. Newman giggles. "Oops, excuse me."

My mind can't make sense of the enormous gap between this casual domestic behavior and the suffering I know she's capable of inflicting. It's like if a lion walked up to you and put its head in your lap. But her embarrassed smile, and the way her feet are tucked under her on the armchair . . . she's adorable, actually.

What? No. *No.* Time for a distraction. Anything.

"Let's eat!" I shout, so suddenly that Newman jumps a little in the armchair. I unzip my pack on the counter, but my enthusiasm sours at the sight of the VitaBars stored there. It feels like a crime to eat these, when the Prestons' cabin boasts a full-size kitchen that puts my kitchenette to shame. But there's nothing to cook.

"What's the matter?" Newman asks, catching my fallen expression.

I let my eyes wander the kitchen aimlessly. "Just . . . hang on a second." Nestled between two wooden cabinets is a silver door I initially assumed was an oven, until I caught the faint lettering etched on the handle: *Cryo-fridge by LifeCorp.*

"No way," I say. I've heard of these appliances only the megarich can afford, that can store fresh food for years without spoiling. These days, all the food in the Metro is nonperishable— way cheaper to transport, and easier to eat while commuting to work. I hold my breath as I give the handle a hard tug.

Sitting on the shelf inside is a carton of eggs, a half-gallon of milk, and a package of bacon. I've had shelf-stable bacon substitute before, as part of my rations from the Citadel's commissary, but something tells me this is going to be better than the flavored shoe leather I'm used to.

"What is it?" Hair freshly braided, Liv joins me in the kitchen and squats to peer inside the fridge. A tendril of her hair comes loose, dangling like an ebony version of the willow branches she loves so much. Even though I'm well aware of our bizarre situation, I can't contain my excitement for the stash I've discovered. I give her a smile that only bacon can summon.

"Breakfast for dinner."

■ ■ ■

THIRTY MINUTES LATER, NEWMAN'S SEATED AT THE DINETTE AS I BRING OVER two plates of bacon and eggs. The cabin smells like heaven on earth. Well, actually it smells like real-life, nonsynthetic bacon and eggs, which I now know is pretty much the same thing.

Newman's reading a book at the table as moths tap against the bay window trying to reach the warm light inside. The scene feels . . . almost normal. Except every few minutes I remember who Newman and I actually are to each other, and what I should be doing. Nas is out there, waiting for me. And the sooner we're back with Newman, the sooner I'll save our society and be rewarded.

But on the other hand, it's not smart to be walking through the woods at night. And also, bacon.

"What's that?" I ask Newman as I set the plates down. She closes the novel to show me the cover. *Walden.*

"It was the only thing in my bag," she says. I take in its thin, yellowing pages. Must have cost someone a fortune. I bet she stole it from some antique vendor—or normal-Newman did, anyway.

"Hmm. It's yours?" She shakes her head and reads an inscription on the inside cover. "'To Arthur, until we meet again. "I went to the woods because I wished to live deliberately. . . .' Love always, R.'"

Arthur. Of course. Preston aided Newman's escape by giving her a car; why not give her something to pass the time? Lucky for him, his tenure and senior position at LifeCorp make him practically untouchable, but I still wish we'd stopped to question him before we left. Did he tell Newman to archive her memory?

Supposedly. Supposedly to archive her memory.

Newman carefully sets her book to one side and picks up a piece of bacon. She takes a small bite, and her eyes go wide.

"What, is it bad?" Quickly, I taste my own food.

She shakes her head. "No! It's—"

"Incredible," I say as the flavor hits me. Salty and greasy perfection. And the texture! Crunchy and tender all at once. Beats the hell out of bacon substitute.

"Can everyone cook as well as you where you're from?"

Heat rushes to my cheeks. "Nah. It's . . . kind of my thing, actually." I shouldn't care what she thinks, I know. Tell it to my ego.

We eat in silence, except for little noises of enjoyment coming from Newman's side of the table. I watch her slyly between bites, until I can't focus on my own meal anymore. I've never had the chance to see someone enjoy a meal I prepared, let alone someone who's enjoying it as much as she is. It's usually just me eating at my kitchen counter. A thrill rolls through my chest with every appreciative murmur, every savoring lick of her lips. I don't realize I'm leaning toward her until my chest hits the edge of the table.

"Aren't you going to eat?" Newman asks, lifting her last piece of bacon.

"Huh? Oh, sure." My eggs are cold now, but still delicious.

"You never told me your name," she says, still chewing. What do I say? I take another bite, giving myself time to think. If she doesn't remember anything, then there's no reason to lie, really. At least, not about this.

"It's, uh, Adrian. Adrian Rao."

She nods, like she's pleased to have one less missing puzzle piece in her understanding of the world. "And who are we to each other, Adrian Rao?"

The question, coupled with the sound of my name on her lips, makes my head spin. I can't even begin to answer her with even a shred of honesty. But the way I've been treating her, it's clear we're not strangers. She won't buy it if I tell her we only just met.

"I'm your bodyguard. Mr. Preston—the man that owns the house—sent me, to protect you from the dangers of the woods." Definitely not the most convincing lie I've ever told, but she doesn't seem to notice.

"Protect me. Like the pines." She stiffens in her seat. "What dangers?"

"Oh, a myriad of wild animals, not to mention the raiders that would eat you alive . . ." Every one of us grew up with frightening stories of the people beyond the border. But Newman stares back at me, blank. How much of her memory did she erase? Does she even know what the Metro is? Or LifeCorp? Hell, does she even know she's a Proxy?

"Why would they do that? Hurt me?" I've got her attention now. Her eyes shine bright as she waits for more answers. But it's late, and I don't feel like explaining all of political history from the last century to someone who could remember everything by noon. So I simplify.

"Because they can," I say with a shrug. "Don't take it personally, they're not a fan of bodyguards either."

Again, Newman nods with understanding. Something inside me twinges with guilt at explaining the world in such half-truths. But she's beginning to trust me; the lies will be worth it once we eliminate the threat of Orange Haze.

"Alright," she says, "we'll leave tomorrow."

We will? "Of course. . . . Remind me where?" Now we're getting somewhere. What assignment is so important that it survived Newman's memory loss?

She glances toward the windows behind the breakfast nook. Her eyes are glassy, almost like she's under some kind of spell. "I need to see the stars. More than are here. A sky full of them."

"Why?"

Her face falls. "I'm not sure. . . . Maybe seeing them will help me remember?"

She hugs her knees to her chest, still watching the sky. One thought rises above the rest as I consider the sad girl in front of me:

This might end up being the easiest arrest of my entire career.

I've got orienteering training. As her "bodyguard," I can convince Newman that I should be in charge of navigation and slowly lead her from wherever she thinks we're going, back to Nas. By the time her memory returns, I'll have backup. If Newman were in her right mind, I'd have no issues slapping some cuffs on her and using any means necessary to get her to Nas and the cycle. But since she's . . . different right now, I'd rather resort to more peaceful methods. There's more than one way to dismantle a drone, as the saying goes. Either way, justice will rule the day.

"Sounds like a plan. We'll leave first thing in the morning."

Her face blooms into a smile. "And, Adrian?"

"Yes?"

Her fingers trace a line from her ear cuff, along the wires, to the chrome chip protruding from her skull. As soon as her fingers touch the metal, she winces. "Tomorrow, can you tell me what this is? When I was alone in the lake, I assumed everyone had one, but then I met you, and . . ." A frown pulls at the corners of her full lips.

If Nas were here, he'd smack me on the head. I can hear him now: *You're seriously falling for this? That she doesn't know you have a chip too? That she doesn't know exactly why she's different?*

I don't know what I believe. But for now, the plan seems to be working, so I play along.

"Yes. Tomorrow, I will tell you."

13

LIV

THERE'S ONLY ONE BED IN THE SMALL CABIN, SO I DECIDE TO SLEEP IN THE kitchen. The booth is spacious enough for me to make a decently comfortable setup out of the extra pillows and heavy blankets we find in the back closet. Plus, the oversized windows give me a perfect view of the night sky. Even though I have no idea why I'm drawn to them, the stars are the only thing giving me a sense of certainty right now. They tell me there's a reason I'm out here, alone and confused. That I have a purpose, and maybe even some people who are counting on me to achieve it.

My bodyguard—Adrian—watches me set up my nest. Then he makes the extremely odd choice to pull the pillows and comforter off of the plush mattress in the bedroom and sleep on the dinette floor. I don't get it, but I don't know him well enough to argue. Which is too bad, because up until now, being around Adrian has made me feel safe. But this choice, to forgo the bed and stay close to me, without explanation, makes something in me prickle a little. Like the dangers he talked about earlier are maybe worse than he let on.

He's still there on the floor when I wake up the next

morning, his brow permanently furrowed, arms crossed tightly, even in sleep. I sit up, drawn to the window by birdsong. It's my first good view of where we are, surrounded by dense forest on all sides except for the path that leads to the lake. A thick mist creeps along the ground, only thinning slightly as it retreats from the water. Above the mist, the tree trunks still hold a tinge of blue-gray as the sun pushes back the darkness.

On the floor behind me, Adrian stirs.

"'Autumn came, with wind and gold,'" I say.

"Mm?" He yawns.

"It's from the book." I wave the copy of *Walden* in the air, still facing the window. "We should find a map. It would be easy to get turned around out there."

He grunts his approval. I sense him stand and pad over to the kitchen. When I finally pull myself away from the natural magnificence outside, he's rummaging through the cabinets, growing more and more frantic.

"Come on, come on." He crouches to check a cabinet he already searched, in vain.

"Something I can help with?" I join him in the kitchen. My sweater's too big, and it slips off my shoulder. "What do you need?"

"Coffee." Adrian stands to look at me, before blinking at my exposed skin. "Definitely coffee."

I nod. "Absolutely." No idea what we're talking about, but I'm tired of him knowing more than me, about . . . well, everything.

He lifts one brow. "You've had coffee before?"

"Yep."

"Describe it, then." Adrian folds his arms, lips quirking in a smile.

"Well, it's, um . . ." I look around the kitchen. "Something you eat. Probably."

He laughs. "It's okay, not many people know about coffee. Back home, it's mostly just a . . . bodyguard thing. But anyway, it's a hot brown beverage. Best with cream and a little sugar. Elixir of the gods."

"Wow, that sounds wonderful!"

"It is. We practically live off the stuff. Bodyguards, I mean. But there isn't any here." He groans and drags a hand over his face. "It's fine, I'll be fine. Let's check for supplies."

He makes a list, and we split it. We start with clothes, taking the warmest and least bulky sweaters from the main hall closet. It's only after removing those that I notice a panel against the closet's back wall. While Adrian is checking inventory in the kitchen, I press the large square, which gives with a satisfying click. I slide open the panel to reveal . . . the jackpot.

"Is any of this useful?" I ask a few minutes later as I drop an enormous mound of items on the kitchen floor.

Adrian's eyes go wide. "Camping backpacks, sleeping bags, a lantern . . . where did you find this stuff?"

I hand him a soft sweater like my own, a gray-green to my pale blue. He pulls it on. "I have my secrets," I say proudly. "There's more." I hold up a finger before I dash back to the closet. I return with a heaping armful of food items. Canned beans, VitaBars, water purifying tablets. I spill it all onto the counter. Adrian picks up one of the VitaBars.

"What's that?" I ask.

"Food, technically."

"Like bacon?"

He winces. "Yes and no. But this should all be plenty; it won't take long to make it back to—uh, the stars."

I gasp. "You know where they are?"

"I do." He pulls a folded paper out of his back pocket. "Found this map in the bookshelf. Here's the cabin . . ." He points to a red dot. ". . . and here's where the stars should be visible." Slowly, he drags his finger to a blue triangle a few inches away. *Mount Barton,* the label reads. "High enough to get good visibility, and far from the light pollution of the Metro."

That word—*Metro*—blares in my chest. It means something to me; I know it does. But I have one goal right now, and I can't lose sight of it. I tuck the word into a drawer in my mind for safekeeping; I'll pull it out when the time is right.

"It's not a straight shot," Adrian continues. "There's a river we'll need to get across, and some rougher terrain we'll have to go around. The path will meander a bit. But I can lead the way."

Hearing the confidence in his voice, and seeing our route laid out so clearly—it makes everything seem possible, and a thrill runs through me. Adrian's really going to take me to the stars. Maybe once I see them, I'll understand more about why I'm out here on my own.

No, not on my own. With him. My bodyguard. My protector.

An item shifts in my pocket as I lean over the map again.

"Oh, right! I almost forgot." I waggle my eyebrows in a look of peak mischief. "You're not the only one hiding secrets in their pockets."

He glances at my waist. "Wh—?" I pull out my treasure: a slim, tubular packet of—

"Coffee." He gives me a smile that's wide and unrestrained, and something in me flutters.

"I like your smile," I blurt out. *Real smooth, Liv.* I may not know a lot right now, but I *know* I can do better than that. For his part, Adrian appears to have swallowed a worm. He blinks at me several times, then focuses intently on opening the packet I gave him.

While my bodyguard makes his beloved elixir, I check our stock against the list and start loading up the backpacks. Halfway through, I notice something's missing. I turn to Adrian, surprised to see him studying me. Caught off guard, he swallows his coffee too quickly.

"Something wrong?" he sputters. *How long was he watching me?*

"Shouldn't we have something to defend ourselves with? You said the woods are dangerous." I spin to the kitchen's rear wall and open a drawer. "How about these?" I ask, brandishing two large knives.

Slowly, Adrian rests his mug on the counter. "Good idea. I can carry them."

He reaches for the weapons but stops when I put my hand on his arm. "We should each have one, don't you think?" I ask. "What if we get split up?"

Adrian falters for a second; then that confident mask is back on. "Well, do you know how to use it?" he asks smugly.

I shrug. "It's a knife. Pretty self-explanatory."

"Not how to stab someone. How to use a knife. Where to stick it, for different purposes. To kill, to incapacitate, to intimidate."

"No, but—"

"I do. I've trained for years so that I know exactly what weapon to use and when." His bravado softens as he lowers his voice. "It's my job to see that you're safe. And I promise: we won't get split up."

Warmth floods my insides as I regard his face. My past is a blank space. But Adrian's vow gives me the slightest belief in a future. I hand over the knives.

"Fine. But I'm taking the bacon, then. You don't get to carry both."

Relieved, he grins. "Wouldn't dream of it."

■ ■ ■

THE MIST IS MOSTLY BURNED OFF BY THE TIME WE HEAD OUT, REVEALING AN endless phalanx of trees dappled by the late-morning sun. Adrian gets his bearings, and we're off. Soon the house is lost to the woods. Now it's only him and me. He shows me all the different ways he judges our course—moss growing on bark, the small shifts in our shadows over the length of an hour. He lets me walk in front. I settle into our pace, following the only guidepost I need: the sound of Adrian's voice, steady and strong. Helping me find my way to the stars. To myself. What will I discover once we arrive?

Which reminds me: Adrian said he'd answer some of my questions today. I slow down so we can walk side by side.

"So, what is it?" I ask over the sound of our steps. "This thing on—in—my head."

"Oh, right. It's, ah. It gives you special abilities. You can do things the rest of us can't do."

Vague much? I wait for him to go on, but he doesn't. "Such as?"

"Like . . . feel things. Notice things and have feelings about them."

"You don't have feelings about things?" I arch a brow.

"Eh, kinda—"

"You seem to feel pretty strongly about coffee."

His laughter joins the tittering birdsong. "I have feelings. But yours are more magnified, like turning the saturation up on a—well, I guess you wouldn't know what that means. They're just stronger when you want them to be."

His explanation sounds like nonsense: a device in my brain that makes my emotions more powerful? I try to summon the sensation, stare up at a hawk perched on a branch high overhead, and attempt to feel something at its majesty. But nothing comes. The hawk flies away, and all I feel now is disappointment. Whoever sent me on this mission, I hope I don't let them down.

We walk a bit longer. When I've turned over the answer to my last question enough times in my head, I ask another.

"Why?"

"Why what?" Adrian checks the position of the sun, then veers right. Is he being obtuse on purpose?

"Why do I have this ability to feel? What's the point?"

I can't see his face, but he makes a hemming sound. I feel like a child who's pestering him with ignorant questions, and I'm about to tell him to forget I asked, when he responds.

"You can also . . . capture and share those feelings with others. Look." He lifts a shock of his coils to reveal a slight bump in his skull. "I have what you have. A smaller one, that can receive your signal."

Without thinking, I lift my hand to the raised skin at the base of his skull. My fingers bury themselves in his hair, to feel the hard metal beneath, barely bigger than a grain of rice. A sharp intake of air passes through Adrian's lips.

"Sorry, did I hurt you?" I ask.

"No." His voice is gravelly as he watches me, his face only a few inches from mine. I marvel at the metal he's revealed, but also the softness of his curls. This close, I can also see the early signs of stubble on his chin. The many contradictions of Adrian Rao. Rough and smooth. Warm and cold.

"So." He swallows. "You're not the only one with a chip."

"I'm not alone?"

"Not alone." Pain shines through his dark brown eyes. Because of me?

"Adrian . . ." I slip my hand out of his hair. "Do you know why I can't remember anything?"

"I'm not positive," he says, scanning the trees for some invisible enemy. "But I think you might have done it to yourself."

To myself? "But why? What happened to me that I don't

want to remember?" I feel a pang of sadness for the girl I really am, that she—*I*—would be so desperate to forget so much of her life. "Or maybe I did something. . . . Something I wanted to forget."

Tension ripples through Adrian's shoulders. "Let's just get you to the stars." There's more he wants to say, but he presses his lips together into a tight line and starts walking.

Just like that, he's back to cold again.

The forest comes alive as the day goes on. Every once in a while, the wind carries the sound of flowing water, but for the most part it's me, Adrian, and the trees. We eat on the go for lunch—brown-green squares called VitaBars that come in several flavors: chicken, beef, fruit, or vegetable. Honestly, I don't think they're half bad, but judging by Adrian's face as he barely keeps them down, you'd think they were manure wrapped in river sludge.

"Nope. Can't do it." Adrian gags, still half a bar to go. He analyzes the wrapper, like he's searching for clues as to why it was so gross. "Zesty chicken, my ass. And *that's* the new and improved flavor? How the hell do Lowers eat this stuff?"

"Lowers?" My ears perk up at the new term. A chance to learn something. "Are those the people you protect?"

"Yes, among others."

I look up through the trees. Another hawk—or maybe the same one from before?—coasts on the wind. "What's it like there? In the Metro. Is it different from here?"

He scoffs. "A bit, yeah. Let's see . . . it's louder. Busier. People get more done."

"And you like it there?"

"Yes." His answer comes too quickly, like I poked a bruise.

"Do you think I liked it there?"

"I . . . hm. I assume so."

The hawk flies out of sight. I frown, half listening. "Why?"

"Because everyone does."

I catch a glimpse of the hawk again through the canopy, and forge ahead so I don't lose track of it. As soon as I start walking, Adrian's close behind. I slow down, and so does he. *Interesting.* I pretend not to notice, then speed up faster than before. He lurches to keep up, and I have to stop myself from laughing. Adrian plays it off casually, but I can feel his attention on me, even as his eyes roam the woods. The fourth time I rush ahead, he loses his balance and almost trips over a fallen branch. I don't turn my face in time to hide my smile.

Adrian's mouth falls open. "You're doing it on purpose!"

"Should've finished your VitaBar. Maybe then you'd have the energy to keep up."

He chuckles. "Funny," he mutters to himself. "Didn't think you'd be so damn funny."

"Is there a particular reason you insist on being no more than four feet behind me at all times?" A curl sticks to the sweat on my forehead. I push it back defiantly.

Meanwhile, Adrian's barely out of breath. "You mean beside the alluring scent of bacon trailing from your pack?"

"Ha, ha. Seriously, why?"

"What kind of bodyguard would I be if I didn't keep you close?"

Around us, the birdsong has stopped. My hawk has disappeared again, but thousands of miles beyond where it flew, there's a faint shimmer of something, a speck of metal gliding across the heavens.

Satellite.

Almost as quickly as the new word hits me, the pain comes. A buzzing, electric pain that radiates from this thing—*neurochip*—in my head, through my skull like a chain saw. Shards of meaning make themselves known with every bolt of lightning, some as clear as words, others in waves of raw emotion. I glance at the sky, and suddenly I *know* we're not going north, the same way I know the symbol on Adrian's ring means something very, very bad. I crouch on the ground, clutching my head in my hands and growling in pain.

"What's happening? Are you—" He moves to comfort me.

"Don't touch me!" I don't even know if the words are intelligible, and I don't care. I just need the screaming in my head to stop stop stop stop stop—

Silence. The pain is gone, and I'm not whole, but I'm not as broken as I was before. I even have a name for what I did to myself: *memory archiving.* I just wish I knew why I did it.

One by one, the birds start their chorus anew.

"What happened?" Adrian asks softly, still squatting in front of me. He stands and extends a hand. I eye it warily, then decide to stand on my own.

"I'm not sure. I—" He's studying me carefully, so I have to be smart here. "I must need water or something."

He nods, unhooks his canteen. "Here, I've still got a little left." He checks the map while I sip, watching him closely over the bottle. "There should be a river this way." He changes course, away from what I now know is south, toward the east. He doesn't ask for his canteen back.

I start walking in front of him, the same way we were a few minutes ago, except now everything has changed. Now I'm in the woods with a total stranger who says he's here to protect me, but who's lying to me about where we're going. I have no idea where we are, or how to defend myself.

All I know is that I need to escape.

14

LIV

THE RIVER'S MELODIC BABBLING IS MUSIC TO MY EARS. ONE, BECAUSE IT soothes the ringing in my head that set in after the satellite transmission. And two, because it's the key to getting the hell away from Adrian.

As the water comes into view, I assess my surroundings. The river is wide and clear, with smooth round stones on the bank. The side we're on is a gentle slope to the water's edge, but the eastern bank is a steep cliff. Which means the only direction for me to run is back the way we came. That's fine; I remember the terrain well enough. I can hide in the woods until another satellite comes around, and then another. As many as it takes for me to remember myself and get a handle on what's going on. And because Adrian insisted on carrying the weapons, I've got most of the food. If I can find a good enough hiding spot, I can outlast him. But for right now, the plan is to play it cool, maintain his trust. Until the time is right.

Adrian sets his pack down with a grunt and kneels at the riverbank to fill his canteen. I do the same.

"You okay?" I ask, my voice sweet. "You don't—"

"I'm fine," he says tersely. "Pack's heavy, that's all." He

doesn't lift his eyes from the water. This isn't good. I need his defenses down so I can slip through the cracks.

"I bet," I say as I walk behind him. "Here." I kneel, and tentatively place my hands on his warm shoulders. My thumbs knead into the tight muscles there, and though he initially tenses at my touch, Adrian soon sinks down to sit on the ground. I'm not sure what I'm doing, but my hands seem to know the way, walking curved lines along the length of his upper back, working out his weariness in deliberate circles. I grip tighter, and he lets out a soft groan that beckons something animalistic in me. Suddenly, I'm aware that my breathing has quickened, that I can feel my heart beating *everywhere* in my body, and that this plan has evolved from clever strategy into something much more dangerous.

I pull my hands away.

"I'm, uh, going for a swim," I say.

"Hmm?" He sounds far away, and the rasp in his voice matches my own.

I clear my throat. "Yeah. Might help me cool down—for my headache, that is. And I'm sure I smell awful."

"You smell good. Uh, fine, I mean. Average." His ears burn red.

"Could I change, please?"

"Sure." Adrian's eyes are still half dazed when they meet mine. I gesture a few yards away.

"Could you . . ."

"Oh! Of course." As he stands, I regain the last of my senses. The second his back is turned, I silently grab my pack and get ready to run. There's a small cave I identified a few dozen yards upriver, a perfect hiding spot until he heads back through the woods, searching for me.

It's a good plan. So why do I feel a pang of guilt as I glance back at him one last time, standing there patiently like a total gentleman?

"You're not alone."

I shake my head. I'm not sure who Adrian is, but if he were such a gentleman, the satellite transmission wouldn't have set alarm bells off in my skull at the sight of him. Before I head for the cave, I grab the two knives tucked into the side of his pack and slide them into my own. I don't plan to use the knives on Adrian, I only need *him* not to have them. Then I'm gone, darting along the narrowing bank and into the enclosure before he notices I've left.

A wall of stench hits me as I enter the cave, an acrid smell of earth and musk. Some animal has clearly made this place its home recently, and I receive the territorial claim made by the odor, loud and clear. I don't want to be here any longer than I have to. I peek around the cave wall, waiting for Adrian to turn around, notice I've disappeared, and run frantically into the woods.

But that's not what he does, at least not at first. His eyes find the empty air where I stood before; then his gaze shifts quickly to the water. When that search also turns up empty, he yells my name. There's frustration in his tone. But something else, too: worry, genuine concern.

"Newman!" Adrian spins in erratic half-circles as he cries. The more he calls my name, the more afraid he sounds, the less I remember exactly why I thought this boy was so intimidating that I had to leave him. When he does finally head back into the tree line, it's not with the angry determination I expected. He seems to be chastising himself for letting me out of his sight. I don't follow him as he heads into the brush. But I do feel sorry about the way we parted.

I hop out of the cave, my thighs already twitching from holding a crouch for so long. I'm not sure how much time I'll have to create distance between me and Adrian; who knows if he'll double back at some point? I decide the best path is to follow the river northwest, making a wide arc around the path we took from the cabin.

The river picks up after half a mile or so, and my pants and shoes are soaked. I stay as close to the water as possible, where I can walk on the smooth pebbles instead of the muddy riverbank that would betray my steps. As the river arcs west, I tread more carefully. If Adrian decides to track me north instead of retracing our route, this is where we're most likely to cross paths. Thinking about Adrian reminds me of the cabin, and it dawns on me that this river must feed into the lake where we met. If I can find a spot where the northern bank is less steep and get myself on the other side of the river, when it opens up to the lake, I'll be one step farther from Adrian's pursuit and one step closer to Mount Barton and the stars.

After another half mile, I see my chance. The opposite bank slopes gently, and a fallen log slows the river's flow so that it appears nearly still. A perfect place to fade into the trees.

Even though the river is calmer here, it's still a couple of feet deep. Quickly, I pull off my shoes and socks and tie them to the top of my pack. I roll my pants legs up above my knees.

Tiny fish dart away as I step into the cool water. But as I approach the middle of the river, they get more curious, and then daring, like they're playing a game with each other to see who can nibble my toes the most times. I laugh at their tickles.

Before I know it, I'm on the other side. I sit to put my shoes back on, and a branch snaps behind me. My head whips in the direction of the noise.

"Adrian?" I ask. But that makes no sense; Adrian wouldn't be coming from this side of the river. I scramble to get my shoes on faster, but fear makes my fingers clumsy, and I can't get the wet socks over my feet. Another branch cracks, loudly, and then something shifts in the brush. Whatever's coming is big. I fumble for a knife from my pack, but I cut myself on the blade as I pull it out and drop the weapon on instinct. With a *thunk,* it lands in the river and disappears beneath the surface.

Shit.

Deep grunting comes from up the hill. The threat is getting closer. Slowly, carefully, I reach for the second knife, gripping it tightly despite the pain from my cut. I hold the weapon awkwardly in front of me, eyes scanning the tree line for wherever the danger might appear. My blood pounds in my ears until it's louder than my trembling breath. I switch the knife to my other hand, hoping it will feel more natural there, but it doesn't help.

One final crack of wood, almost directly ahead of me on the slope. The creature emerges, like a beast from a fairy tale.

And I scream.

ADRIAN

PATHETIC.

Honestly, I should just stay out here. There's no point in going back to the Citadel. Even if I never tell anybody what happened—how I had Newman in my grasp and she pulled one over on me like it was my first day on the job—I'll still carry the shame of this moment with me for the rest of my career. Who just collapses shrieking in a forest?

Even worse: Who falls for it?

And if the story *does* leak—if my colleagues find out that the rookie from the Outerlands let LifeCorp down in such an embarrassing way . . .

It's over.

Every minute I spend running through these woods makes me sick to my stomach. I can't look at a tree without picturing Newman's face against the backdrop of gold and amber leaves, how she made herself seem so helpless.

Maybe if you hadn't pretended to sleep all night because you were afraid she'd run, you wouldn't have been so out of it when she actually did.

I double back the way we came from the cabin for about

a mile, then head north. Newman doesn't have a map, but maybe she can navigate better than she let on. I won't underestimate her again. The birds overhead sing happily, only quieting when the shadow of a circling hawk passes over the forest. It feels like they're laughing at me, watching me search in vain for the escaped suspect that was mine alone to lose.

"Gah!" I slam my fist against a tree. The delayed, throbbing pain is welcome. Anything to distract me from watching my dreams of victory slip through my fingers. I decide to search for one more hour before heading back to the overpass where I left Nas. I'll hitch a ride with him to the Citadel and turn in my badge. After that, who knows? Maybe that guy who sells the bowls of VitaBar slop in the Towers is hiring.

I expand my radius, and something stops me in my tracks. It's not a sound, not exactly—the birds are too noisy to hear much else. But there's an undertone, like the suggestion of something I should be able to hear, creating a dissonance with the birdsong that makes my skin prick.

"Shut up. Shut up!" I shout. For a second, the birds are silent. In that moment, the sound breaks through and confirms what the hairs on the back of my neck already knew.

She's in trouble.

I bolt toward the screams, which soon give way to her gasping cries for help, and the crash of something enormous barreling through the forest behind her. Newman springs from the trees. When she sees me, her eyes are white with terror.

"Help!" she shrieks as she runs, stumbling over a root. Seconds later, the beast appears. A wild boar, at least as tall as my rib cage, is trampling everything in its path to get to her. Its mouth foams as it closes the distance.

Growing up, you'd hear stories of the wild animals that reclaimed the Outerlands when almost all the population left for the security of the Metro. But no textbook ever explained the ice-cold paralysis I'm feeling. None of the glossy photos I saw made me piss my pants. I can barely recall my own name, let alone what I should do in a situation like this. Which is why I'm grateful as hell when Newman returns to grab me by the arm, and yanks hard in the other direction.

"Hell is wrong with you? Run!" She pulls harder this time, and it jostles me out of my trance as the boar closes in. We run faster than I've ever had to move in my life, the boar's wet grunts growing louder with every pounding step. Newman whimpers and drags a sleeve across her eyes.

"Don't cry," I say, panting. "You gotta be able to see." *If you can't see, you'll fall. And if you fall, you're dead.* Probably better to leave that part out for her sake. I glance back at the animal, which is slowing but still in pursuit. *Think, Adrian. Protect her.*

"There!" I point to a large tree a few yards ahead. "It can't climb. If we can get up there, we're safe."

She nods, and we veer right. Newman seems to be having as much success coordinating her limbs as I am controlling my bladder, because she's moving frantically but not making headway up the trunk. The way she's sobbing, I wonder if she can even see the tree.

The boar is seconds away. We're out of time.

"Go!" I grab her by her waist and shove her as hard as I

can toward the branch overhead. Miraculously, she clambers on and stays put. I face the advancing boar, say a prayer, and shoot it with my blaster. The beast is stunned for a second, but it must weigh six hundred pounds, easy. The shock's not enough. I reach for my knives.

My *missing* knives.

"Oh shit. Adrian!" I tear my eyes away from the beast to see Liv clawing at something in her waistband. A knife emerges, and she drops it down to me. A number of questions come to mind, like how she ended up with my knife, and why she only has one, and why the fritz she hasn't been trying to stab the boar this entire time. But all that is second to our immediate survival. I pick up the knife and jam it as hard as I can into the stunned boar's armpit. The animal's warbled shriek ends with gurgling gasps that let me know I've hit my target. But death doesn't come quickly, or without a fight. As it struggles for breath, the boar thrashes wildly. I feel the warm blood on my sweater before the searing pain of the wound itself. It's not deep, but it will need some attention to prevent infection.

The boar drops, then collapses under the tree, sending a whorl of dried leaves out from underneath. Liv starts climbing down.

"Wait. Stay there until we're sure." I step up to the beast, its side heaving with quick, shallow pants. This close up, with no real threat of danger, I have a chance to appreciate how magnificent it is. I mean, I wouldn't exactly call the creature beautiful. But there *is* a kind of beauty in its power, its strength. The way it's relied on itself, and nothing else, to survive in these woods.

With a quick stroke, I end the animal's suffering.

■ ■ ■

THE BOAR'S FLESH CRACKLES ON OUR FIRE. WE WON'T LEAVE IT LIT FOR long—even hidden in this cave by the river, the flames make us too exposed—but the fire is a welcome respite from the chilled night air. The smell of cooking meat fills the cave, and I wish I had my spices. This would be a hell of a feast with some thyme, a bit of chili powder, maybe a pinch of oregano. But for now, I'm just grateful it's not a VitaBar, and that we're alive to enjoy it at all. My stomach growls loudly, and Newman gives me a look.

"What?" I say. "I'm hungry. Fighting for your life is hard work."

"Uh-huh. Here." She reaches into her pack and pulls out one of the cans we took from Preston's cabin. "Baked beans." She loops her thumb through the tab on the lid and pulls.

"I think you're supposed to heat—" Quicker than I can talk, she digs into the cold beans with a spoon. "Or that . . . is fine too. How are they?" I ask as she swallows.

"Delicious!" I'm not ready when she smiles. My breath hitches as I'm caught in the crosshairs of its dazzling warmth. The firelight already made her eyes shine bright, but now they're stunning. A dimple appears in the smoothness of her brown cheek. Heat rises from somewhere deep inside me. Did she have dimples yesterday?

Shit, this is bad.

Newman holds out the can. "Try some." She scoots to my side, and her knee grazes mine. For a second, my whole body goes fuzzy. Does she really not remember the last time we sat

like this? Do I even want her to? To my disappointment, Newman pulls her leg away, and the sensation ends. I blink away
whatever it is I'm definitely not feeling and taste the beans.

"Very good. Would be even better warm." I eye her pointedly. With a laugh, she shrugs.

"Next time. Wait! Put the bacon in it, in little pieces!"

"That's . . . actually brilliant." So I do.

Exhausted from the day's events, we slip into silence. In
the wake of the attack, everything seems more saturated. The
texture of the wooden spoon in my hands is enhanced, the
embers' fiery glow more vivid. My wound chafes sharply
against the makeshift bandage Newman tied around my rib
cage. In the distance, crickets play a symphony. The rush of
simply being alive has eclipsed everything else, for the moment, and I don't want to ruin it. But there are questions that
demand answers.

I shift the cooking meat over the fire. "Why did you run?"

"Why aren't you taking me north?" she blurts out at the
same time.

I meet her gaze slowly, waiting for her to pounce. But
there's no sign of threat, only patient expectation. "How did
you know?"

"I remember the map from the cabin." Hesitation flickers
on her face. Or are the flames playing tricks on me? "The river
should've been on our other side. Why did you lie?"

Of all the scenarios I planned for, having to defend myself
to an insulted but oblivious suspect was not on my list. I run
through everything I've told Liv about who I am so far, and
cobble together an answer. "Alright, fine. The truth is, I got

nervous. I don't know a whole lot about what's up north . . . more of this, I'm willing to bet." I gesture to the boar. "I don't know if I can protect you up there. But south, there's a whole world of people. So many people—"

"Like the Lowers you mentioned earlier. Do you lie to them too?"

You don't know the half of it. I say nothing.

Liv shifts on the ground. "I'm sorry, that was unfair. Just . . . promise you're really here to keep me safe."

"I promise," I say, hoping she can't see me wince in the low firelight. She's a criminal, and this conversation—this whole plan—is simply a means to an end. So why does it feel like my stomach's twisting into pieces? "I won't let anything happen to you." Without Newman, there is no justice for Rivera, or LifeCorp. It *is* my job to protect her . . . until I can turn her in. That's the only reason I care.

Isn't it?

When the pork is done, I top it with some watercress I found and portion some out for each of us. We're both exhausted and hungry, and we don't say much as we eat. Newman finishes quickly and pulls out her book. A tendril of curls falls from behind her ear as she reads, but she's too engrossed in the pages to notice.

What's going on inside her head? I start to wonder if her memory's returned, but she doesn't seem to be her old self yet. A wild boar attack would've been the perfect time for Newman's violent nature to kick into action. But instead, she ran for her life, and practically forgot about the weapon she had. You can't fake poor survival instincts.

"You never call me by my name. My first name," Newman says out of nowhere. Her voice is soft below the fire's crackle, but I can still hear an edge of accusation.

I dramatically scan the cave from one end to the other. "Who else would I be talking to?" The joke works to lighten the mood. She tries unsuccessfully to hide a smile, and I feel like I could fight that boar with my bare hands.

"Okay, fair," she says, placing the book on the ground. "But right now, my name is, like, one of the few things I know about myself. It would be nice to hear someone else say it, is all."

Shadows dance across her face as she watches me, hopeful. Three letters, one syllable; it would be over in a second. But I can't bring myself to say the word. "Noted," I reply. She recovers from the disappointment quickly, but even after she turns back to her book, the pain doesn't leave her eyes. My throat aches at the way she clutches the pages a little tighter than she needs to, like she's willing herself to concentrate. Why does her sadness bother me so much?

Easy. Because there *is* a difference between this girl— Liv—and Newman. Newman deserves a long stint in Verch, LifeCorp's virtual reality prison. But Liv? Liv barely even knows what the Metro is. She's as deserving of happiness as any other law-abiding citizen. If her memories stayed away forever, if she never changed back, then—

Someone has to pay for what happened to Rivera, imaginary Nas reminds me.

Fine. There's no way around it: Liv Newman's ultimate destiny is behind bars. But maybe not yet. She seems determined to see the stars in a sky devoid of the Metro's comforting light. Maybe seeing a part of the world without LifeCorp's influence makes the Orange Haze stronger? Maybe I really can take her to Mount Barton and figure out how she makes the Scraps that threaten law and order. Then I won't just be bringing in a single criminal, I'll be stopping any other EmoProxy from undermining our society ever again. I'll shield the Metro from the world's chaos, the way it shielded me.

Imaginary Nas opens his mouth to speak, but I shut him up. It's been over a day since I left him; surely Redding's called him back by now. We've got time for one short detour. Especially if it means saving more Metro citizens.

I thumb my signet ring as I watch her, then pull the map out of my pack. "Here. From now on, you lead us . . . Liv."

Her head doesn't lift until that last word. Eyes never leaving my face, she reaches to take the map from my hand. When she returns to her book, a smile plays at the edges of her mouth.

And we begin again.

16

LIV

I WAKE IN PAIN. SOMETHING IS VERY, VERY WRONG.

"Adrian?" I gasp as I grope for him in the dark. I'm on fire, and it feels like the cave—no, the world—is spinning around me. I can't tell if I'm reaching toward him or the sky. Or into the flames themselves. *God, it's so hot.*

"Adrian!"

He hears my rasping croaks after the third or fourth try. "What is it? Another boar?" He leaps up, scanning the cave entrance.

"No, it's me. I—" Bile rises in my throat too quickly to explain. I throw up on the cave wall. "Ugh, sorry. The meat must have been off."

"We both ate it, though. . . ." He pauses, staring at my trembling hands, then up at my clammy face. "Oh, shit. Oh, shit."

"What?" I ask the two Adrians blurring together in front of me. I collapse back onto my bedroll as my body switches from blistering heat to debilitating chills. Adrian scrambles for his canteen, but also checks his pack for something else.

"I'm so sorry, I didn't bring any—"

"W-water?"

"What? Oh, right, here." He hands me the canteen. I drop it through shaky fingers. "Shit," he says again.

"S-said that already," I mutter as he lifts the canteen to my mouth. My stomach spasms wildly as the water goes down. Adrian rests the back of his hand against my forehead, grimacing at my fever.

"Liv, if this is what I think it is, you're going to go through hell for a while."

"A while?" I clutch the earth so I don't fall off.

"A day, at least."

I sit up. Big mistake. More boar bits end up on the cave wall. "A *day*? Adrian, what's happening to me? What is this?"

His deep brown eyes watch me sadly. "Mean withdrawal."

■ ■ ■

MY DREAMS ARE FULL OF TERRORS—NEON BOARS WITH JAGGED TUSKS, CUTting through the woods and leaving lightning in their wake. Trees with haunted eyes and sunken, familiar faces. Each time, I wake with gritted teeth, swallowing my screams. Each time, Adrian is there. He makes a broth out of the boar's bones, lifting the dish to my chattering mouth when I'm shaking too badly to hold it on my own. I wish I had that kind of patience with myself. All I feel is anger and frustration, at this body I don't understand, which seems hell-bent on sabotaging my trip to see the stars—the only thing in the world I know I need.

"Close your eyes," Adrian says when he catches me quietly

seething as I clutch my stomach, on the second day of withdrawal. "You should be resting right now."

"If I sleep any more, I'll calcify." I don't mention my nightmares. I crane my neck to check the sky outside. "Besides it's, what, midafternoon? We're losing daylight. We should go; I'm feeling better, really, I . . ." The world blurs as I strain to stand. Adrian's arms wrap around my waist, firm but gentle. The cave stops swirling as he slowly lowers me back to the ground.

"Rest." There's an edge to his voice. "Can't find the stars if you don't get better."

"Rest." I surrender. His arms are still around my middle as he sits behind me. His chest is warm. Sturdy. "Are you going to let me go?" I ask.

"Depends. Are you going to stand up again?" His breath tickles my neck. I'm lightheaded, and I'm not sure I can blame the fever entirely.

"I make no promises." But the fight's already leaving me. I nestle into his chest to chase the sudden chill from my bones. Our breaths synchronize. A soft wind rushes through the trees outside. "Do you know any songs?" I ask after a while.

"Hmm?" He pulls a lock of my hair off my sweaty cheek and tucks it back into my braid.

"I think music would help me sleep. But I just realized I can't think of a single melody. Do you know any?"

His body stiffens for a second, but then he starts to hum. I feel it before I hear it, resonating deep in his chest, against my back. The pulses in my vision soften as the lilting notes surround me.

"That's nice," I murmur. "What's it about?"

"Shaving cream," he says, not bothering to hide the amusement in his voice. "An old commercial jingle. Sorry, it was the first thing I thought of."

"No, I like it. Don't stop."

He sings again. I focus on the deep timbre of his voice and drift into a peaceful sleep.

■ ■ ■

WHEN I WAKE THE NEXT MORNING, IT'S LIKE A STORM HAS PASSED. I'M WEAK on my feet after two days of illness, but stable. I tell Adrian I'm ready to move on, and he starts to shift things around in our packs, until he's carrying almost double his share of the load. He doesn't look much better than I feel: dark circles have formed under his eyes, and after days in the woods, his stubble's even thicker. Did he sleep at all? Knots of guilt form in my gut. He shouldn't suffer because of me . . . my addiction. Adrian said I was having withdrawal from something called Mean. But what is it, and is it common back in the Metro? Or is there something uniquely wrong with me that I'd want to take some kind of drug? I consider asking, but I'm afraid of the answer.

The northern side of the river is a whole new world. The trees are farther apart here, leaving more space for dappled sunlight to break through to the forest floor. A carpet of pale white flowers stretches across the ground, as far as I can see. Against the dark earth, they resemble tiny stars. I smile.

"What's up?" Adrian asks, shaking the chilled river water from his shins and rolling his pants legs down.

"It's like . . . my body is tired, but my mind's never felt

sharper. Clearer. I see connections in things. Like this—" I gesture to the small white flowers. "Stars below, to lead us to the stars above." Our gazes lock for a second before I turn away, sheepish. *Geez, am I always this corny?* When I bring myself to face him again, Adrian's stooped to tie his boots, and the backs of his ears are slightly redder.

The map says we can reach Mount Barton in five days, and from there, it's a two-day climb. I check it more than I probably need to, my thumbs wearing thin the old, folded paper with every consultation. But it's more than a map. It's a lifeline, a way for me to pull myself out of a free fall and anchor myself to this world. Every hill and river bend we pass that I can corroborate with the map is confirmation that I know where I am and where I'm going. That I'm not as helpless as I feel.

The forest eventually opens up to a small field of wildflowers that takes my breath away. The white star flowers are still there, but now they're joined by pale violets and fuchsias. Taller flowers with delicate golden buds bob gently in the breeze. I gasp with delight and take Adrian's hand before I have time to think about it. My lingering headache loosens its grip a little.

Adrian blinks at my hand but doesn't let go. "We should go around it," he says. "We're too exposed here."

"Oh." My face falls, and I drop his hand.

He frowns. "*Or* . . . we could go through it . . . if you think you're fast enough?" he says. His offer sounds nonchalant, but there's a mischief in his eyes that makes my stomach flip.

I grin wide and adjust my pack on my shoulders, and we

take off as fast as we can through the field, which isn't very fast, considering he's injured from the boar and I'm still a bit wobbly. I start slow, but it feels too good, like a salve for my pain. Butterflies erupt into the sky as we carve our path through the flowers. I catch a glimpse of Adrian's wild grin, bright as the sun's rays. Joy spills out of me, first in giggles, then as squeals and hearty laughter. By the time we reach the other side of the field, we're both out of breath, chests heaving.

"That was . . . ," I begin, but I can't find the words. I recall our conversation two days ago and touch my neurochip.

"Do you know how this works? Could you . . . show me?"

Adrian's still catching his breath. "What?" he pants. "No. We shouldn't do that."

His tone is suddenly sharp, and it puts me on guard. "Is it dangerous?"

"Yes. No. I mean, I don't know. But . . ."

I step closer. "I want to share it with you. What I'm feeling." My eyes widen at how intimate that sounds. I backtrack. "To see if I even can, I mean."

We regard each other for a long time. Adrian seems to wrestle with something in his head. *Please, I need this. I need to know what I can do.*

"All right," he says at last. "When you see the prompt, tap twice." He lifts his hand to his temple, and I do the same. As he taps a sequence on his warm brown skin, a sense of familiarity wafts through me, barely out of reach. *I know this.* Like magic, words appear, floating in the air.

ADRIAN RAO WOULD LIKE TO PAIR. ACCEPT?

Suddenly, I'm less sure. "What will it feel like?" I ask.

He swallows, but his voice is still raspy. "I . . . I've never done this before."

My finger hovers beside my temple. What, exactly, happens when we pair? What parts of my mind does he gain access to? I can sense him watching me as I read the prompt in the air over and over again. The floating words offer no answers, so I peer beyond them, to his face. His jaw is taut with concern, and his deep brown eyes study me back.

"We don't have to—" he begins. A pang of disappointment hits as he inches away, and that's reason enough to squash my reluctance.

I tap to accept our pairing, and Adrian's step falters.

"Whoa," he says.

"What's it like?"

His hands are out like he's trying to steady himself on a rickety bridge. "It's like—huh—like there's someone else in my head with me. Another layer. I know these feelings aren't mine, but if I don't resist, I react to them. It's . . . good. Like two people sharing a coat." He laughs nervously.

"Okay," I say. "Stay here."

"What are you doing?" He hisses as I step out into the clearing again. "Liv! Li—" My name dies on his lips as I let the emotions overwhelm me. I take in the field of flowers, the wonder at each tiny blossom, the dizzying delight of their scent. I pluck a daisy and hold it up to the sky, focusing on the simple grandeur of the sunlight dancing through its petals. The chill from the river water melts away as warmth fills my body. Footsteps sound behind me, and the sight of Adrian approaching pushes that warmth to near burning. His lips are slightly parted, delight and confusion swirling on his features.

"All good things are wild and free."—Henry David Thoreau.

"Liv. Your eyes . . ."

I touch my cheek. "What about my eyes? Are they doing something weird?"

"No, they're beautiful. Glowing. Like sunlight." Gently, he pulls my hand from my face. "This is what you feel, all the time?" His words are so soft that the wind nearly carries them away.

"If I really stop and notice things. Yes," I say, watching a hawk swoop overhead, a small animal trapped in its talons. That too provokes a strong sensation in me, but a more complicated one this time. Awe and pity swirl together until I can't feel one without the tinge of the other. "You . . . don't feel things like this?"

He shakes his head, his eyes focused on the middle distance between us. "I've never . . . I didn't know *anyone* c-could . . ." Even though I know nothing about the world he comes from—the world we apparently *both* come from—something in his reaction makes me a little sad for him. He deserves more than a flattened life. He deserves to take in the total beauty of the world, to laugh until he's breathless every day. I want to give him that.

"What's this?" Adrian's voice pulls me from my thoughts, and I find him staring at me, searching my face. With a jolt, I realize I'm broadcasting the melancholy affection I feel for him straight into his own mind.

"Nothing!" I fumble for my screen and jam the button to

disconnect our bond. The longing lifts from him like a fog, replaced by his own curiosity at my frenzied response. He bends to catch my downward gaze.

"Definitely not nothing. Liv, what was that? Like a sadness, and a—"

"Let's keep moving. You were right, we're definitely too exposed here." I skirt around him, back into the woods.

17

ADRIAN

I CAN'T GET HER MIND OUT OF MY MIND.

Good thing Liv has the map, because I'm so mixed up, I can't make sense of anything right now. I follow her deeper into the woods for the rest of the afternoon, but my thoughts never leave that field. The first time running through the flowers was fun, but once we paired . . . the way I felt when Liv noticed the flowers—*really* noticed them—was something else entirely. The whole time, my own emotions were struggling to keep up. Her mind was doing somersaults around mine. I've never felt anything that strongly, didn't even know it was possible.

Now I'm noticing everything—shadows fading in and out as the clouds block the sun overhead, the birds' songs blending into one another like streams feeding into a river, the way the wind makes the curly wisps of Liv's hair dance around the edges of her face. When she stops to say something to me, it's like the world is moving in slow motion. It's brighter and more intense than anything I've ever seen before.

"Adrian? Did you hear me?" Liv waves a hand in front of

my face. I take in the smoothness of her fingers, remember how they felt against mine.

"Adrian!"

"Uh-huh?" Even as I ask, I'm still distracted by her eyes. No longer ringed with amber like when she used her abilities. Bright and fluid, like molten bronze.

Follow the glow, the Citadel's analytics team told me. How right they were.

Liv pulls those same mesmerizing eyes away from me now, toward the clouds. "I was saying, it looks like it might rain."

I trail the path of her gaze to a marbled graying sky. "It does." I assess the clouds and the ominous breeze. Liv's holding the map, and as I lean over her to check it, I catch a whiff of her hair. Honey and citrus, from whatever she raided from the Prestons' cabinet the other night. And fresh air. She notices me pause, and I have to blink the smell out of my brain before I can concentrate again. *What is happening to me?*

I point to the map. "Here. There should be some cover on the other side of these foothills. We can settle in until the storm passes."

She nods, and we adjust course. As we approach the hills, the breeze transforms. The dizzying scent of honey washes over me with every gust of wind. It's enough to make me forget the coming storm, to distract me from anything but the two of us.

I've never been a heavy user of Mean; always felt like it dulled my sense of taste. This, though, whatever pairing with Liv did to me . . . I want more—like, I *really* want more. But I don't *need* more. Not like the way Liv's body fell apart after only a few days without a vial of Mean. I shiver now as I remember her feverish and trembling in the cave. With each helpless whimper, I imagined standing in front of a wall full of Mean and smashing every last vial to bits for what it did to her.

What would Nas think if he heard me say that? Or Redding?

"Oh, felt a drop." Liv picks up her pace, checking her forearm for raindrops every few steps. Around us, the woods have changed, now dotted with ancient pine trees. The higher branches make it easier for us to see our way to the hill, a few dozen yards ahead. Liv's staring down the target, pushing through the deep brush, when she steps on a pinecone.

Crunch.

My senses are still heightened, and the sound hurls me back to the last time I heard a noise like that in her presence. Liv's oblivious to the connection, but I'm back in the alley, hearing Rivera smash the bottle on his head until it shatters, his shoes grinding the shards to dust as he stumbles blind. Because of her.

Crunch.

Or I'm watching Celeste break up the dehydrated VitaBar in its broth as she papers over her horrible memories of Liv and Kez, and pushes them deep, deep beneath the waters of her mind.

Crunch.

I even think of Mrs. Rivera, who seemed happy enough, but whose newly emboldened attitude is sure to eventually cost her job, and maybe worse if she insults the wrong Forceman. With Jonah already unemployed, that could make life in the Towers worse for them. The girl in front of me has caused so much unnecessary pain. And I pity her now because, what, we held hands, and she smells nice? None of that changes what has to happen, for there to be any true justice in the world. The second she sees those stars, we're on our way back to the Metro, and order will be restored.

Crunch.

We reach the top of the hill and crouch low to stay out of sight. Liv points to a carved-out piece of earth a few yards below. "Let's tuck in there for the night."

I eye the hollow, then her, following the elegant line of her chin, down her neck, to the curve of smooth brown skin where her collarbone dips . . .

Enough. I've gotten *way* off track from my mission, and it ends now.

"No." I clench my jaw. "Let's press on. We've got an hour, at least." Liv frowns at me, and I move past her, pretending not to notice.

"Adrian, do you see the sky? It's going to pour any minute."

I spin on her. "Hey, I gave you the map. Can I at least get a say in when we stop?" Her eyes are wide with surprise, and a little bit of hurt. Remorse pricks at me, but it's no match for the certainty growing in my gut:

I can't let myself get to know Liv Newman any more.

Every moment we spend talking, or synced, is a step away from completing my mission, away from order, and toward who knows what. Even this—stealing sideways glances at her as we walk in silence—is hardly acceptable behavior for a Force-man and his suspect. If we can carry on, even for another hour, it's one less hour she has to crawl under my skin and make me doubt myself.

"Adrian . . ."

Her voice sends a shiver up my arm.

"One more hour." I'm not sure if I'm talking to her or to myself. "We just need to push through."

18

ADRIAN

"I'M NOT GOING TO SAY ANYTHING, BUT YOU KNOW WHAT I *COULD* SAY, RIGHT?" Liv wipes a lock of soaking wet hair from her soaking wet face with her soaking wet sleeve. Water droplets fly from her lips as she speaks. "Because there's a *lot* I could say right now." Rain pounds the ground like bullets, and she almost has to yell for me to hear her.

"Message received," I shout back. With a grunt, I shove my shoulder into the thick branch that—I'm pretty sure—will support the hastily made lean-to I've built. The branch slides against me in the mud, but I force it behind a raised root. The ground underneath the lean-to is damp, but not as wet as everything outside of it. Thankfully, I had a few minutes between when the first few raindrops fell—after Liv sent an unimpressed arched eyebrow in my direction—and when it started raining in earnest. That gave us time to put together the top of the structure and cover it with enough brush to make a decent shelter.

"Better late than never, I guess." Liv heaves her pack onto her shoulder and ducks into the lean-to. The second she's seated, she peels off her jacket and starts riffling through her pack for something to eat.

"Want some?" She holds out a VitaBar that claims to taste like spaghetti Bolognese.

"No thanks." I don't even bother to hide my disgust as she takes a huge bite. Seeing I'm still watching her, Liv closes her eyes in mock rapture.

"Oh," she moans. "That's even better than bacon."

"Hilarious." I turn my attention back to the lean-to's covering and try to ignore her fake sounds of pleasure still echoing in my head. *Try* being the operative word there.

Get it together, man. She is your suspect.

She squints up at me. "You coming in? You're getting soaked."

I turn too quickly and slip on a leaf. Liv moves to help me, but I hold up a hand. "No, no. That one's yours. I'm going to make my own."

Liv laughs. "What? That's ridiculous; it'll take you hours to build another. And everything's wet anyway. There's plenty of room." She scoots over and pats the patch of earth beside her. Even though I'm only a few feet away, I can barely see the lean-to through the raindrops that gather on my eyelashes. My clothes are drenched, and I have to ball my fists to stop myself from shivering in the cold. But I'll be damned if I'm going to let her wear down the last few shreds of my resolve.

"I'll make my own; won't take long."

"Hello, my name's Adrian, and I enjoy catching pneumonia in my spare time." She deepens her voice for effect.

I ruffle with indignation. "I don't sound like that."

"You sound *exactly* like that."

For the next hour, we play an agonizing game in total si-lence. Liv reads her book and pretends not to watch me from the comfort of her lean-to. And I pretend not to notice her not-watching me, as I struggle to wrap small, pliant twigs around larger branches to make the second lean-to's roof. I keep my back turned whenever possible, partly so I can't see her, and partly so she can't see my growing frustration as the hard rain helps the twigs unwind themselves into a tangled mess.

"Fritzing—ugh!" I slam the disaster onto the ground. My wounded side screams; I tore the healing flesh open again. My back is still to Liv, but I can hear her shift to the left a little, making room for me. This act of assumption, that she knows me well enough to know what my next move will be, only pushes me further from her. I grit my teeth against the pain and scan the trees around us, until I find one with branches low enough that they might offer some shelter from the down-pour. When I finish trudging over to the wide oak and man-age to settle in against its damp trunk, Liv is staring at me in disbelief, mouth hanging open.

"What is your problem? I know I don't smell the freshest right now, but in my defense, neither do you." She's half jok-ing, an attempt to disarm me. A chuckle escapes against my will, but I quickly mask it by clearing my throat.

"It's not that bad."

She narrows her eyes, studying me for too long. Then, to my horror, she moves to crawl out of the lean-to. "At least take this blanket."

I shoot my hands out. "No! You use it. It's no good to either of us dripping wet."

"Neither are you. You said it was your job to protect me. How are you going to do that if you can't feel your toes?"

". . . How do you know I can't feel my toes?"

"Educated guess."

Liv takes advantage of my lack of protest to deliver her final blow: a self-satisfied smirk that lights up her face. If I *could* feel my toes, I bet they'd be buzzing with—*something*, the same way every other part of me is. I'll deal with the buzzing later, because in addition to being beautiful—again, not my opinion, just an objective fact—Liv's also right: I can't do my job if I catch my death in this rain. I need to be alive to bring her in.

I assess the lean-to as I approach. It's decently big; if Liv tucks herself into the back wall, I may be able to stick to the opening and avoid any sort of contact.

I peel off my damp sweater. Liv has a dry one waiting for me by the time I duck inside, and it feels like a hug as I pull it over my clammy skin. Liv nods once, like my being inside the lean-to has set the world back in order, and lies down to sleep as thunder rolls above.

"'There was never yet such a storm but it was aeolian music to a healthy and innocent ear,'" she sighs.

"Hmm. Book?"

"Book," she confirms. True to my plan, I scoot forward until I'm right at the edge of the lean-to's coverage. There's about three inches of space between my body and Liv's, and I stay aware of each and every one of them, adjusting my hips or legs as she does hers. The rain is a mercy, muting the sound of her soft snores. Before I close my eyes, I notice *Walden* near Liv's feet, getting spattered with rain. Only a few stray drops here and there, but by morning the book will be soaked. Creeping slowly so I don't wake her, I grab the book and place it between the two of us. Much better. The extra space means there's more like five inches between me and Liv now, and when I lie down again the front of my body is barely under the lean-to at all. But the book's important to Liv, so I'm happy.

Twenty-two minutes of pelting raindrops later, there's a loud crash of thunder, and Liv stirs.

"What are you doing?" she asks.

"Sleeping." Rainwater sputters off my lips as I speak.

"Drowning is more like it." I sense her shift behind me, hear her tuck the book into her pack. "Here, scooch."

"Scooch?" I glance over my shoulder.

Liv holds her arm up as she lies on her side. "Yeah, come here." Her tone is casual. Meanwhile every possible alarm bell is ringing in my head. Snuggling overnight with a suspect is absolutely not permitted under the LifeCorp Law Enforcement Code of Ethics. Voices—Nas's imaginary one, and my own—scream at me to get out of the lean-to as quickly as possible. It's only a little rain, nothing that—

"Seriously, Adrian, I don't bite." She reaches forward, enough to wrap her arm around my middle and bring my back to her front.

And everything goes still.

No more yelling, no more sirens in my head. Just me, and Liv, and the rain. She's soft and warm, and she falls asleep almost instantly. My breathing slows to match the rise and fall of her chest on my back. Something jolts me, and I realize her fingers are grazing the bare skin on my stomach where my sweater's ridden up. In my mind, I know the touch should be cool, as she's still warming up from the rain. But every time her finger brushes my skin, it's searing, hot as a poker. Like it's branding me, binding me to her in a way that I didn't ask for but can't bring myself to pull away from. I don't know who I'm becoming, or what being around Liv is doing to me. But my last thought before I fall asleep is that I don't want it to stop. I don't want any of this to stop.

My first thought when I wake up is that there's a blaster in my face.

19

LIV

"LIV. LIV, WAKE UP." ADRIAN'S HAND RESTS ON MY SHOULDER, SHAKING ME gently. I groan and nestle deeper into the blanket's warmth. The rain has quieted, but it's chilly outside my woolly cocoon. Adrian jostles my shoulder again.

"Liv." His voice is more insistent this time.

"Ten more minutes won't hurt."

"It might," says another man's voice, deep and harsh. I bolt upright so quickly that my head hits the top of the lean-to. That gets a laugh out of the stranger, and three or four other men I can also hear. Adrian's staring at me with wide, apologetic eyes. All I can see of the men are their worn leather boots, and the drooping muzzle of a long-range blaster. Icy dread spreads in my gut. These are the raiders Adrian warned me about.

"Wakey, wakey," the man with the blaster—their leader, I assume—says. "Out you come."

We step into the damp dawn as the men call out jokes. I tremble with fear as much as cold, and Adrian wraps his arm around me.

"Ah, little brisk, isn't it? But I bet you two couldn't feel a thing in your little love nest there," one of the men jokes crudely.

"What, with *him*?" another says, gesturing to Adrian. "He couldn't do much, there's hardly anything to him!"

"It's not about muscle, Harcourt. It's about *finesse*."

"That's enough," their leader clips. He's tall, and handsomer than I'd like to admit, with amber skin and a wide nose. The sleeves of his linen shirt are rolled up to his forearms, and though he's lean, his muscles are well defined. He can't be much older than twenty. When he sees me, his full lips break into a devilish grin. My heart stops cold as he takes a step toward me. Adrian's grip on my shoulder tightens, and he moves to step between us. The man gives him a single cold glare that stuns him midstride.

"I wouldn't, if I were you." He almost sounds bored, but the intensity in his eyes conveys the threat. Adrian takes his hand off my shoulder, and the sudden coolness makes me shiver. The man continues to stare him down. Why? I'm confused until I hear something behind me click. Adrian's taken his blaster out of the holster, and he hands it over silently.

The handsome raider steps closer. His eyes rake over my body dispassionately, until they catch on something. "Quit shaking. I need to see . . ." Carefully, he lifts my damp braids to reveal the neurochip underneath. My skin prickles at his delicate touch. One side of his mouth ticks up. "Well, hot damn," he whispers to himself. Then, loudly to his men: "Grab their packs. We're taking them back to the village."

"Are you going to kill us?" I ask him, my voice shrill.

"Why? Because that's what you two would do, right? Shoot

first, then spread lies to cover your tracks? That's your kind's answer for everything," he sneers.

What's he talking about? I search for answers in the four men's faces but find only hatred.

The head raider's eyes narrow with disdain. "No, we're not going to kill you."

One man, older than his leader by at least a decade, makes a whining sound. "But, Noah, Icarus said they were food!"

"Icarus said they *had* food," the handsome one—Noah—says, and the older man pouts as he retracts his switchblade. Noah steps back and addresses us both. "A boar, was it? And . . . this poor excuse for sustenance?" He holds out a hand to one of his men, who tosses him an empty can of beans. *Shit.* We were so stupid, not to cover our tracks.

"How long have you been watching us?" Adrian asks.

The man shrugs. "Oh, I don't know. How long have you been here? These are our woods. Nothing goes on that we don't know about. And this"—he cocks his head, admiring my chip again—"is definitely something we ought to know about."

■ ■ ■

THE RAIDERS BIND OUR WRISTS WITH ROPE, WHICH THEY ALSO LOOP AROUND our waists. Then they thread another rope between those, so that we're linked together. Unless Adrian and I run single file, there's no way we'll make it more than ten feet into the woods before a tree snags us.

Three of the four raiders walk behind us, chatting and

teasing each other. Noah walks in front, silent. Only four new people, but it makes the woods seem as vast and unknowable as they did a few days ago. When I thought I was alone in the world, seeing Adrian on the pier was surreal, like a dream. But this is a nightmare.

"Nice blasters. Who'd you steal them from?" Adrian asks. There's an unfamiliar bass in his voice.

"Wouldn't you like to know," Noah responds. "They do work well, though. I'd be happy to provide a demonstration if you'd like—"

"Stop!" I shout as Noah lifts the muzzle toward Adrian's chest. "Adrian. Please."

"Stand down, pup," Noah says coolly. Muscles cord in Adrian's neck as he stares the raider down. But after what feels like an eternity, he finally falls back to my side.

"I'm sorry," he says to me as we march on.

"Don't be. We should be showing them we're not afraid."

He shakes his head. "Not that. I was supposed to protect you. I let you down."

"You *never* let me down. Adrian. Hey . . ." No matter how I try, Adrian keeps his gaze locked on the leaves under our feet. So I grab his hand and lace my fingers through his. He still won't look at me, but as he releases a shuddering breath, his hand squeezes mine. Even in the middle of this danger, the simple act sends my heart racing.

"You trusted me," Adrian mumbles.

"I still do." Damn these restraints. I'd give anything to hug him right now, to make sure he understands that I'm not angry or disappointed. I don't blame him for getting caught. It's as much my fault as his that we came this way, and just like we traveled together, we'll escape together. I won't let these raiders hurt us.

We walk in silence another hour, until the woods come to an abrupt stop. A river of stone splits the forest, extending east and west toward each horizon. The feel of the even road under my feet is jarring after the soft forest floor. Unease ripples over me at how exposed we are, without the cover of the trees to protect us. Then I remember who we're with; the worst has already happened.

Around the bend, the northern side of the woods gives way to some kind of community. Squat beige buildings edged with stone cover an enormous plot of land. They're the first buildings I've seen other than the cabin, but I accept it as one more revelation of many. What really takes my breath away, what makes me gasp so loudly that Noah notices and laughs at me, are the people.

There are hundreds of them, young and old, walking alone or in groups, their complexions ranging from lightest brown to the darkest umber. At first glance, I think they're all wearing the same gray jumpsuit I had at the lake. But then a pop of vibrant green jumps out at me, a strip of patterned fabric that a woman has added to the jumpsuit's pants, transforming them into a skirt. A man passing by has cut the jacket of his jumpsuit so that his bare stomach is exposed, through strands of dangling red glass beads. The monotony of the gray jumpsuit is challenged everywhere I turn, with emerald fringe, gold buttons, or cerulean embroidery. Stripes and prints that even the most audacious forest bird's plumage could never mimic. The expression on Adrian's face tells me he's never seen anything like it either.

"Waste not, want not," says Noah as he catches me staring.

"But . . . you and your men. You wear the normal jumpsuits," Adrian says.

"Sure, when we're patrolling. I'm not going to risk snagging my good clothes on a stray branch. You know how expensive kente is?" He pauses, checks himself. "Ah, but of course you don't. Everything's 'free' in the Metro."

Everyone pauses to stare as we walk by, and it's always the same. First, their focus is on the six of us. Then on me. Until, at last, they settle on the wires behind my ear, leading to the chip on the back of my head. *They know what I am.*

My insides quake, but I force my shoulders back and distract myself by marveling at the ornate stone fountains between the buildings. No water runs in them. Instead, the basins are filled with soil, and crops of fruits and vegetables grow in neat, carefully labeled rows. Adrian's drawn to the smallest basins, at the top, which have an assortment of plants with labels like *borage, fairywand,* and *feverfew.* Overhead, tattered banners hang on light poles, flapping in the wind. I squint at the faded script and make out what must be—or must have been—the name of this place: The Shops at Barton.

Barton. As in Mount Barton. I gasp. We must be close to the stars.

Noah turns toward me, maintaining his pace but walking backward now. "It's not polite to stare, Feeler."

Feeler. It's an unfamiliar word, but suddenly my blood runs hot, and the tips of my ears are on fire. My body remembers the insult, even if I don't. Adrian balls his hands into fists. "Don't you dare call her that."

"*You* are not in a position to be making any sort of threat right now. Take a cue from your girlfriend and stay quiet."

"We're not—" Adrian and I both begin, but Noah holds up a hand and we go silent. Before we can object any further, his back is turned again.

"Hey, Noah." The youngest of Noah's crew, a scrawny teen, ambles up to his leader, "What do you think the boss will do with them?"

"The boss will do as the boss pleases," Noah says. "Harcourt, you may get your wish after all."

"Do you think?" The older raider who wanted to eat us speaks up from the back. Adrian's face reflects my fear. All I know of the raiders is what he's told me. Would they really eat us?

"No, Harcourt. I'm joking," Noah says over his shoulder, and my insides uncoil themselves. "And you're coming up on four years with us now. This isn't the wild; you need to cut that cannibal shit out."

My mind races, trying to forge an escape plan out of all this new information. The raiders—*these* raiders, at least—have some sense of morality, it seems. They've built a seemingly thriving society. If we can convince them that we're not a threat, that we'd even be willing to share what we've got, maybe they'll let us go.

Noah's steps slow, and I get the sense that we're nearing the end of our journey. Heart pounding, I take an extra step toward him.

"We mean you no harm," I say. "You're welcome to anything in our packs. Clothes, toiletries, beans. No, you didn't like the beans. . . ." I rack my brain for what else might be valuable. "Have you heard of bacon? We have some; it's delicious. Maybe he'd like to try it."

Noah frowns. "He who?"

"Icarus."

His step stutters. "Icarus?"

I scowl. Is he being dense on purpose? "Icarus? Your boss?"

There's silence for a moment; then laughter erupts from the men. Harcourt turns red. Noah wipes tears from his eyes. I'll take their amusement over glares and threats any day, but I still bristle at being mocked.

"I'm sorry, did I say something funny?" I glower.

"Why don't you ask the boss?" Noah says, shoulders still bouncing. He gestures toward a storefront with an ivy-covered awning. Adrian squeezes my hand. With one reassuring glance back at him, I step inside.

20

ADRIAN

NOAH SWINGS THE DOOR OPEN AND LETS LIV AND ME ENTER BEFORE HE AND his team follow. I pretend to trip over the threshold, and lower my arms just long enough to send a beacon signal to Nas using my wrist screen. It's a long shot—if Redding called him back, then Nas has probably been home for days now. The Citadel is way too far from here to receive the short-range signal. But the last time I saw him, Nas told me to remember I wasn't on my own out here. That we were a team. I pray we still are.

The room we step into is dimly lit, despite the window in the back. When my eyes finally adjust, I see a matronly woman behind a large wooden desk, scribbling on one of many stacks of papers before her. Unlike the clothing of the raiders outside, there's hardly any trace of a Lower jumpsuit in her outfit, except for the dark gray trim around her loose linen shirt. Her skin is a light beige, and she has an aquiline nose and wide brown eyes that are sharp despite her apparent age. Her hair—black with a prominent streak of gray—is woven into a long, thick braid that disappears into her lap.

"All right then," she says. I'm not even sure she's talking

to us, until her eyes flick up from her work for the briefest of seconds. "Why don't you tell me who you are, and what business you have in our woods?" As we approach, I notice the large leather pads on each of her shoulders. The raiders have the most bizarre fashion sense.

"I'm Adrian, this is Liv. We came—that is, we escaped—from the Metro about a week ago. I work the line in a VitaBar factory, by trade." I slipped my signet ring off when I woke Liv in the lean-to, and now it burns a hole in my boot. "And Liv is . . . well, you can see for yourself what she is." I can't even bring myself to turn Liv's way, I'm so ashamed. I hate myself for getting her into this situation.

"That I can," the woman says. Liv's face is blank as the woman looks her up and down. Behind me, a young boy pulls my Lower jumpsuit out of my pack, along with a VitaBar.

"Ugh! How do y'all eat this crap?" he asks.

I play along. "Right? You think one's bad, try eating them for eighteen years straight. There's not enough Mean in the world to make that shit go down smooth."

The men laugh, and even Noah cracks a smile. But I keep my focus on the woman, who's now staring straight at Liv. And she's not laughing.

"Mm-hmm. And how did you two meet?" the woman asks.

"She worked for my—"

"Didn't ask you, young man." She hasn't taken her eyes off Liv's face. My insides twist with nerves. If the raiders find out she's wiped her memory, it'll raise questions—about her, and about my alias. Does Liv know enough to lie?

"I worked for his boss," Liv says calmly. "At the factory." Nothing more than a very good guess, but her confidence helps sell it.

"And how was that? Selling your life to those *LieCorp* cronies?" The woman stands and walks to Liv until their faces are mere inches apart, glaring at Liv as if she's personally responsible for whatever hardships the raiders have chosen to endure out here. The room goes still as everyone waits for Liv's response. Whatever she says next seals our fate, and she knows it. She wets her lips and takes a quiet breath.

"If I enjoyed it, I'd still be there, wouldn't I?"

Slowly, the woman's stern expression thaws. "Thirty-two years. That's how long we've been in the Outerlands, and how long I've been waiting for a Proxy to wake up and see their life in the Metro for what it is. Sure, everyone in the Metro is trapped by LifeCorp's shackles, chrome-plated though they may be. But I've always thought Proxies in particular bear the burden of making LifeCorp's whole operation run smoothly, at great personal cost." She smiles. "And here you are. Now, normally I'd say we're at full capacity. Winter's around the corner, and our own folk will be coming in from the wild for shelter. Plus, LifeCorp's getting smarter. We've had a few run-ins with people masquerading as Metro refugees. Run-ins that have ended badly for both sides, but considerably worse for them. But with that chip, you just bought yourself a ticket to stay a few days."

"What about Adrian?" Liv's eyes find mine. Guilt winds through me. The only reason I'm with Liv is to make sure she gets locked up, possibly forever. But she's only thinking about how to protect me.

The woman glances between the two of us. I can almost see the gears turning in her head. "The boy is also valuable, in his own way."

Hell is that supposed to mean? I open my mouth to speak, but a sudden stab of pain from my wound sucks the breath out of me. I play it off as speechlessness—no need for anyone here to know about my injury. Suddenly, the room darkens. A hawk's cry pierces the air, and the large raptor lands on the windowsill, sunlight glinting on its tawny wings. The bird twitches its head from side to side as it regards us. Liv and I jump back, but no one else seems surprised.

What the fritz?

"Ah, there's my smart boy!" The harshness melts from the woman's voice as the hawk flies to her, settling to a comfortable perch on her shoulder pad. She reaches into a pouch at her hip and gives him something to eat. "See who's joined us today, Icky? Your friends from the river." She smooths the feathers above his beak tenderly. I gape, before realization strikes.

"Hang on. 'Icky'? *This* is Icarus, the one who knew we had food? This *bird* was spying on us?" The woman doesn't dignify my question with a response as she coos to her pet. Noah offers an amused smile. The bird watches me, his head twitching with unnerving speed. He chirps, then takes flight again, this time landing on a mat in the corner of the room. The mat's worn brown leather is scored into a dozen squares, each engraved with a different symbol and word. I make out a few from where I stand: *river, food, intruder.* Icarus hops spryly from one to another, as the woman nods.

"What did he say?" Liv asks as Icarus lands on another square I can't see from here.

The woman purses her lips. "He said your friend here is in trouble." Gravely, she lifts her eyes to me, and I feel like I've been pinned by a laser. "How long has it hurt like that?"

I stiffen. "Don't know what you're talking about." Even as I lie, a bead of feverish sweat drips down my temple. I pull my right arm slightly closer, instinctively protecting my wound.

"Oh no?" She raises her eyebrows, then juts her chin toward Noah, who swiftly moves in to hook my arms from behind. I jerk helplessly as he tightens his hold. Another henchman has his arms around Liv's waist.

"Get your hands off her!" I yell as she flails wildly.

The woman steps toward me. This is it. They've found us out, and we're as good as dead. But the determination in the woman's eyes isn't tinged with menace. She lifts my shirt to reveal the makeshift bandage, which is seeping a pungent yellow-brown pus.

"I'll ask again," she says. "How long?"

I clench my jaw in defeat. "Didn't get bad until last night."

"What?" Liv whispers.

"Liv. I—" Pain cuts my words short as the woman's hand pulses around the wound. I grimace and hiss behind gritted teeth as the woman clucks her tongue.

"Your friend's hurt bad, sugar," she says to Liv. "The infection hasn't spread too far yet, but it will. The good news is, it's nothing that can't be cured with a few days of antibiotics, which you won't find for hundreds of miles but we happen to have. So now we ask ourselves: What's a fair trade? Before you speak"—she raises a hand to Liv's open mouth—"you should know that we have a healthy stock of food and other essential supplies. Trade with other settlements even brings in some luxuries now and then. Bet you've never had chocolate, eh? So I want something only you can give . . . for something only I can give."

The gears in Liv's head turn. The guilt is unbearable. Whatever she's thinking of giving these people—any part of herself, for my sake—is too much. All I've done since I met her is lie to her, and now she's going to sacrifice something, for me? Liv meets my eye. I shake my head silently.

Don't. I'm not worth it.

Calmly, Liv addresses the man restraining her. "Let me go, please." His gaze sweeps to the woman in charge, who nods. Then Liv steps forward, hand at her temple. "Would you like to pair?"

The woman smiles. "With what, exactly?" She lifts her thick braid off her neck. A silver gash streaks across her hairline, exactly where her chip would be.

I stare at the scar in disbelief. "You had it . . . removed?" I've never heard of anyone removing their chip. Not only is it illegal; the chip is wired into your nervous system, making removal extremely painful. Why would anyone do that?

"I could care less if LieCorp's trackers don't work this far out. In the Haven, we are *free*. They have no right to me, or my body. If Dr. Poulos had refused to do the surgery, I would have clawed it out myself." My shock only deepens. I've never heard anyone refer to the chip as anything but a blessing. Is that how Liv felt, before she wiped her memory?

Is that *why* she wiped her memory?

The woman goes on. "I think we're getting warmer, though. Walk with me, Liv. Harcourt, take this young man to Doc Poulos right away. Noah, go get your strings and meet us in the square."

Noah nods and walks briskly out of the building. Harcourt nudges me gruffly toward the door. I reach for Liv as I pass her; to reassure her, or maybe reassure myself. But before I can feel the softness of her shoulder, Harcourt shoves me again. A glance at the jagged silver mark creeping around his skull tells me he's had his chip removed too. What have we gotten ourselves into?

The last thing I hear before we leave is the old woman talking to Liv as Icarus flies out the window. "By the way," the woman says, "you may call me Reem. Welcome to the Haven."

21

LIV

REEM AND I AMBLE SLOWLY DOWN THE HAVEN'S WALKWAYS. I GLANCE SIDE-
ways at her every few steps. Mostly because I'm worried her
friendly demeanor is a trick and she's still planning to eat us,
but also because it helps distract me from the dozens of raiders who gawk openly at the sight of me. For her part, Reem
seems completely unbothered. But then, she's not the one
with the huge chunk of metal poking out of her skull.

"Before I explain what I'd like you to do, you should know
that I wasn't lying about our plentiful supplies. We do alright
for ourselves." She smiles politely at a line of food vendors
standing behind carts and trucks that are generating the most
wonderful smells—smoking meats and buttery sweetness,
even Adrian's precious coffee.

"I don't doubt it," I say, eyeing a stand that sells something
called a kebab.

Reem's gaze cools. "That being said, not every season is
a bounty. Winter will be here soon. The trade convoys will
come half as often, and that's if the weather's on our side. The
cold here is brutal, the generators fail on occasion. And unlike
Icky's feathered friends, we don't have the luxury of heading

south for the winter. People need something to hold on to, until warmer days. Personally, I find there's nothing like a good party." She smiles.

"Party?" I ask, still working to figure out where I come into her plans.

We turn onto the main square, and she gestures to the decorations being hung by a team of men and women. There are bright streamers and bouncing balloons, and a banner over the center of the square reads THIRTY-SECOND ANNUAL FOUNDING REVELRY—TOMORROW NIGHT, 7 PM.

Reem nods. "Every year we celebrate the day our people chose to make a new place for ourselves."

"That's lovely," I say, and it is, but I can't help feeling like we're circling the point. "Ms. Reem—"

"Reem."

"Right. What exactly do you need from me?"

At that moment, Noah arrives, a black oblong case at his side. "I'm here, Boss. Where do you want me?" He sets the case on a decorative boulder next to a bush of bright pink flowers and pulls out a violin.

"You can stand up there." Reem points to a nearby cement pylon supporting a light pole, and Noah nods, rosining his bow. "Liv, you'll be at ground level, with the people," she continues. "That will make it easier to see their requests."

Okay, now I'm totally lost. "Requests?"

"Are you familiar with Sacchetti's study on emotional memory?" she asks. I shake my head. "No, ma'am." *Memory's not really my strong suit,* I add silently.

"It's fascinating," Reem continues. "When subjects were asked to remember a series of details, the average person could only recall about sixty percent of the data. But when that fact was paired with some other sense—smell, touch, sound"—she gestures to Noah, who's tuning his instrument— "then the recall percentage doubled. And when the associated sound was replayed, the subjects were able to recall those feelings. The brain is a machine; it takes input like any other. What better input than to have you two translate joy directly into song?"

"You want me to pair with Noah?" I ask, incredulous.

She nods. "We have artists and photographers capturing happy moments, of course. But music is unique in its connection to the mind."

Noah hasn't reacted this entire time. When I paired with Adrian, it felt so intimate. I almost can't imagine that experience with anyone else. I turn to Noah. "Did you know about this?"

"Nope."

"And you're just . . . okay with it?"

He gives a small shrug. "I've been part of worse plans."

Reem goes on. "The people will bring their most joy-filled items to you and tell you about them. They may even let you sample them so you experience the sensation for yourself. Noah, it will be your job to translate those feelings into something audible, for all to enjoy."

A dazzling white smile spreads across Noah's face. "Sounds like a hell of a concert, Boss."

"I can't pair with him. I barely even know him! And he threatened to kill me . . . I think. Didn't you?"

Noah glances skyward, making a show of trying to remember. "Technically, no, not outright. I'd say it was more of a strong implication."

"Still!"

Reem's face darkens. This time when she speaks, her voice is deeper, more serious. "I'm afraid I may not have effectively communicated your situation, Liv. No one is holding you here. But without the medication we're providing, Adrian will die. Is that understood?"

"The boy is also valuable, in his own way."

As leverage.

"You're threatening Adrian's life, over . . . music?" Reem's plan makes no sense. What could possibly be so important about a few songs?

"Don't make light of the task," she says sharply. "I've guided us through thirty-two long winters here. Lost more folks to despair than to any other danger. Joy isn't just about entertainment. It's how we *survive*. And the boy means nothing to me. He's a tool to help my people. Until he's not."

Hearing her name the very real danger Adrian is in shatters what little defiance I have left. Adrian saved me from a boar, has been working hard to get us to Mount Barton. I can fight for him.

"Understood," I say.

Instantly, Reem's expression lightens again. "Excellent. I'll be watching." She walks away to explain our exhibition to the crowd.

"Well, let's get to it." Noah claps me on the back. "The stage awaits."

■■■

NOAH LASSITER WOULD LIKE TO PAIR. ACCEPT?

My heartbeat drowns out the sounds of the square. What if pairing with Noah brings me as close to him as I feel with Adrian? What if I can't transmit the emotions properly, and he figures out my secret? I give my head a small shake to clear the thoughts. None of that matters right now, not while a deadly infection is creeping through Adrian's veins. With a trembling finger, I press the button, and we're paired. To my surprise, it doesn't feel like much of anything at all.

"There we go!" he says. "That's not so bad, is it? No need to be nervous."

"I'm not nervous."

He gives me a look, and I remember there's no point in lying to him. He can literally feel my jitters.

A handful of villagers have already formed a neat queue. The first in line, a middle-aged woman, holds up a worn leather-bound book.

"This journal belonged to my late husband," she says. Her eyes have already begun misting. "I read it when I miss hearing his voice."

"May I?"

She hands me the book, and I flip through the pages of neat, blocky handwriting until I reach an entry that might comfort her.

APRIL 29TH

Amina and I walked the children to school, then went to the market. Plums were already in stock—feels like they come earlier each year. But I couldn't be too upset about the unseasonable weather, not after the way her face lit up when she saw them. She reached for one, held it delicately in her hand like it was a precious stone. "Should we get some?" she asked, eyes twinkling like we were keeping a juicy secret from the rest of the world. Should we get some? How could we not! Someday when I'm old and gray and down to my last credits, I'll still make sure she has the first plum of spring.

Reading the words makes my throat ache. Noah lifts his violin to his chin, but as soon as he touches his bow to the strings, my mind goes blank. He frowns.

"Is something wrong?" the woman asks.

"No, no, it's—" I meet Noah's confused gaze. "I'll try again." I flip through the pages and find a new entry.

JUNE 17

Jada caught her first fish today, a tiny thing. She was so proud, she almost dropped it as she sprinted to the shady spot where Amina was nursing the baby. Amina beamed at us both. A prize worth more than any five-pound trout.

Again, the man's love for his wife and their children flows through me and swells as I transfer it to Noah. But again, the feeling fades before Noah can play a single note. *What is wrong with me?* I can't remember my life, my home. Now my brain can't even do this?

"You good?" Noah asks out of the corner of his mouth. "Chip on the fritz?" A hushed murmur grows in the crowd, which thins as people leave to do something more productive. Across the square, Reem scowls beside a blacksmith's shop.

"Without the medication, Adrian will die."

"I'm—I don't know, I'm—"

Noah holds up an index finger to the audience, then jumps down from his pylon. He steps closer to me and speaks under his breath.

"Can I talk to you for a second?"

I ignore the crowd's whispers, the feel of Reem's glaring eyes on my skin. "What's going on? Can't you play?"

"It's not me, it's you," he says. "You can't feel it?"

"Feel what?" A cold sweat breaks out on my chest. "Noah, you have to help me. If I can't do this . . . Adrian . . ." I can't bring myself to finish the sentence. Noah's eyes widen as he feels my panic in his own mind. He exhales softly and adjusts his face—back in performance mode. He shouts to the crowd. "Lunch break! We'll be back in twenty."

We unpair. I grab his arm and lead him off behind a row of shops, the chorus of the crowd's disappointment at our backs. As soon as we're alone, I spin on Noah.

"What's wrong with me?" I glance around to make sure no one's followed us.

He rubs his arm, wincing. "You didn't have to dig your claws in so tight."

"Noah!"

"Alright, alright! So, you're rushing. It's almost like . . . you're trying to feel each emotion as quickly as possible, then move on to the next thing. But if I'm going to feel what you feel long enough to get a song out of it, then you have to sit with the feeling."

"Sit with the feeling?" I swallow. I only learned that I could transmit emotions *at all* a day ago. How am I supposed to improve my abilities so quickly?

"Listen . . . take your time. Whatever you're given, explore the sensation a bit. The details may surprise you. Like love, for example. It's not 'just' love. It's tenderness. Nostalgia. Safety."

"Right. Those things." I nod briskly.

Noah lifts a brow. "Well, that was about as convincing as Kenji's vegan pork chops."

"Kenji?"

"Our head cook." He squeezes my shoulder. "I'll find Reem, tell her you need more time."

"You can't! She'll throw us out." I clutch Noah's arm again. He covers my hand with his own, then gently pries my fingers away. "Trust me. She'll understand. We'll start again tomorrow."

He disappears around the corner, and I sink back against the wall. Even if Noah's right and Reem does give us more time, I still have no idea how I'm supposed to hold on to any emotion long enough for him to play it.

Sit with the feeling. Sit with the feeling.

I spend the next two hours walking through the busy streets of the Haven, seeking out as many emotions as I can, and clinging to the thrill, amusement, or curiosity for as long as possible, but nothing lasts for long. Tamping down my frustration, I notice a vendor and her customer haggling over some fabric nearby.

Sit with the feeling.

Their expressions grow more pinched, their words sharper. I pull it all close in my mind. But then the only thing I can think about is Adrian. The way his face twisted as Reem prodded the pus-filled wound on his side. The unflinching steel of Reem's gaze as she explained his situation and what she needed from me. The women's annoyance slips from my grasp like a wisp of smoke.

"Dammit!" I yell. A couple of people shrink from me, confused and suspicious. I fight back tears. I can't do this. I'm going to fail him.

"Having some trouble, it seems," says Reem's steady alto behind me. I turn. The crowd parts for her like rapids around a rock. "I suppose genuine emotions are more challenging than your usual fare. 'Scraps,' pshh. Glorified parlor tricks."

I give Reem a weak smile. "No trouble. Everything's going great. I'm, uh . . . refining my skills."

"Surely we can be honest with one another, can't we? For example: I came to tell you that I've asked Dr. Poulos to pause Adrian's treatment until you get a handle on your abilities."

"What? Noah said you'd understand."

"And I do. But that doesn't change our agreement. I'm not in the business of sharing my resources with outsiders for free." She nods warmly to a passerby, then regards me, stone-faced. "We haven't survived for this long on charity."

The ground drops out from under me. I lurch toward Reem, as if touching her will help her sense my desperation. A fire ignites in her eyes, daring me to take another step.

"Please." I clasp my hands together. "There must be something else you want. Credits? I'll get as many as you want. I'll find a way—"

She tuts, shaking her head. "You can take the girl out of the Metro, but you can't take the Metro out of the girl. I don't want your credits. My top priority is the happiness of my people. Not 'success.'" She sneers. "True fulfillment. If you can't help with that, well . . . maybe the problem is with you. After all, 'It's the beauty within us that makes it possible for us to recognize the beauty around us.'"

I know that line. "'The question is not what you look at, but what you see.' You've read *Walden*?"

"A lifetime ago." She smooths her blouse. "You have until tomorrow. After that, you're better off heading back to the Metro, before sepsis sets in."

Conversation over, Reem hails a nearby vendor and starts chatting with him about preparations for the revelry. I squeeze my fists tight as panic sets in. Adrian's going to die, because of me. Because of this stupid hunk of metal in my head that refuses to do what I tell it to. Adrian's been kind to me so far, but now it's only a matter of time until he realizes I've failed. I'm of no use to him.

I'm of no use to anyone.

22

ADRIAN

"HOW'S THIS?" I STOP STIRRING THE GIANT POT OF SAUSAGE AND KALE STEW so that my teacher for the afternoon, Kenji, can come inspect. My alibi worked a little too well. After Dr. Poulos gave me a round of antibiotics and my fever passed, Reem decided that my VitaBar "experience" made me an ideal candidate for working in the village's community kitchen. Luckily for me, I know my way around a spice rack. Kenji grabs a clean spoon and tastes the soup.

"Not bad! But it's missing something." He pulls his hairnet down tighter around his hair, which is wavy brown with blue streaks. "Needs some heat." Producing a ring of keys from his pocket, he crosses the room to the pantry. There are three separate locks on the door, each requiring its own key. The raiders seem to share everything—the kitchen is open twenty-four hours a day for all to use, and most of their meals are communal. This extra layer of security feels like a contradiction. But I'm a guest here; I won't question their policies.

I try the stew again. Kenji's right, it's a little bland. "Hm. Cayenne pepper?"

He nods, laughing, then goes rummaging through the

cabinet for a small glass bottle. "Bro, what planet are you from? I lived in the Metro for seventeen years, and I don't think I ever even heard the *word cayenne,* let alone heard anyone use it. Wasn't till I got here and had access to the Haven's cookbooks that I really got into making food. You gotta give me some recipes before you two move on." He scoops liberal spoonfuls of the red powder into the pot and stirs. "All right, that's got to simmer for a bit before dinner." My stomach is already rumbling at the thought of soaking up Kenji's stew with some of the cornbread baking in the oven.

"I used to watch old cooking vids," I respond to his earlier question.

"Sure, I understand *how* you know this stuff. What boggles my mind is *why.*"

I've often wondered myself. Why *am* I so drawn to real food, when LifeCorp tries so hard to make us forget about it, in the name of efficiency? Is it because of where—and who—I come from?

Kenji tells me he used to work at an Arcade in Sector Four, tending bar for buzzing patrons whose euphoria needed a little extra push. Given how generous the tips can be, he might have been approaching Upper status. . . . *So why leave?*

"Do you ever miss it?" I ask as Kenji starts work on a salad. "The Metro?"

He chops the vegetables as his mouth quirks to one side. "I miss how certain I felt. How easy it was to belong there. Once I chose to come to the Haven, I knew I'd jumped off that path. And on harder days, I do wonder . . ."

I say nothing but wipe my brow with my forearm. The

kitchen has everything I could dream of: a cabinet full of well-loved cast-iron pans and stainless-steel pots, a spice rack to die for, and a pantry full of basic ingredients. Everything, that is, except air-conditioning.

Kenji continues, "But the truth is, I was a done deal the second my partner asked me to run with him."

The story begins to click into place. Of course someone with Kenji's comfortable setup wouldn't choose to leave on their own. "What made him want to go?"

For the first time, his capable hands freeze.

"I'm sorry. You don't ha—"

"No, it's fine. He, uh—" Kenji clears his throat. "He was arrested. Spent two months in Verch."

"Two *months*?" My jaw hangs open in horror. In LifeCorp's virtual reality prison, time crawls at a snail's pace. You're dumped in a room in the Citadel with dozens of other inmates, each of you hooked up to your own headset, with a personalized simulation of your life uploaded. But it runs at hyperspeed and feels eternal. Two months in Verch is equivalent to eighty years of our time. Long enough to see most of your loved ones in the simulation die, to see the world forget you. To watch your life crumble to dust. It's torture, and that's exactly the point. "Fritzing hell, I'm so sorry."

"To this day, he won't tell me what he did to get arrested. I didn't even know where he was." Kenji's voice is soft. "When he got out, he ran, screaming for the northern border and never turned back. Nobody cared enough to stop him either—so much for LifeCorp's 'humane reintegration process,' huh? By the grace of God, he ended up meeting Reem."

My sorrow gives way to confusion. "Wait. He got out of prison, then he *left* you? And you followed him here anyway?"

He laughs. "Yeah, I surprised myself, too. I was furious. But when he showed up in the Metro again, after all he'd been through, after all he risked to come back for me . . . it wasn't easy, but I love him. Could've held a grudge, I guess, but then we *both* would have gone through hell, and for what? No one wins there."

"Except LifeCorp," I say. "They would've kept their top bartender."

"Exactly." He chops a flame-red bell pepper. "Their loss, for real. I still make a mean old-fashioned. Best in the Haven."

We both smile. The rest of the shift, I'm contemplating Kenji's story, turning it over in my mind like a puzzle box. I don't think I could ever do what he did—forgive someone like that, after they made me feel so alone, or kept such a big secret from me. Could anyone?

Could Liv?

■ ■ ■

IT'S LATE WHEN KENJI AND I CALL IT A DAY, AND MY WOUND STINGS, EVEN WITH Doc Poulos's pain medication. Kenji gives me a small asymmetrical loaf of bread to take home, which he claims he would've thrown out anyway. I'm skeptical, but I don't say no.

As I walk through the town square, I finish munching on my half of the loaf Kenji gave me, taking in the cool night air and the peace of this place as others head home too. Clusters of friends walk arm in arm after a good meal. In the faint light of the windows I pass, parents sing their little ones to sleep. It's nothing like the Metro's chaotic scramble for satisfaction and pleasure. No striving for a higher productivity score, no desperate struggling for the next rung on the ladder. In the Haven, people are . . . content.

Reem has her staff house me and Liv in an unused storage space off the square. Our room is musty, and the ceiling tile is missing, revealing a network of overlapping pipes and ducts. But it has a door, and it's dry, which is a big step up from our last situation. I lift the door slightly off its hinges so it doesn't squeak when I sneak in. The dim light from the square spills into the room, creating lines of pale yellow relief on the curved terrain of Liv's body. She's asleep. Gently, I close the door, wrap up Liv's half of the bread for tomorrow, and unroll a cushioned mat beside her. I'm lying down, ready for rest, when she speaks.

"Are you okay?" she whispers. Her voice fills me with the same comforting warmth I felt on my walk here.

"I think so. My side feels less swollen now. Doc says he wants to pause my treatment, though. Guess he wants to see how I respond to this first dose."

She exhales. The sound of her shaky breath puts me on high alert. I sit up and wait in the silence, listening. Another shaky breath, and then she sniffles.

She's crying.

"Is something wrong?" *Great question, genius.* I put a hand on her shoulder.

Liv doesn't answer, but her body shakes with silent sobs.

"Uh-huh," she finally manages. Her voice cracks, and it feels like someone's taken a hammer to my chest.

"Do you . . . want to talk about it?"

She shakes her head. "Unh-uh."

"Okay." But I can't just let that be *it*. I slide my hand around her waist, pulling her close until my chest rests against her back. She grabs my hand, and our fingers interlock. If I can't comfort her with words, at least I can let her know I'm here for her. "Okay."

"Okay," Liv whispers.

Soon after that, I feel her breathing steady under my arm. Before sleep takes me too, I think of Kenji and his partner one last time, and how miraculous it is that they found their way back to each other despite all the tragic events that stood between them. I could never forgive like that. Because I've never loved like that.

Yet.

23

LIV

I WAKE TO THE HEAT OF ADRIAN'S BREATH ON THE BACK OF MY NECK. THE IN and out of his chest against my back matches my own breathing in a slow, hypnotizing rhythm—like the pull of waves on a shoreline. The pleasure only lasts a moment before I remember Reem's threat. But then Adrian exhales again, and a delicious tingle travels the length of my spine.

Sit with the feeling, Noah's voice says in my head.

I focus on the warmth that spreads across my shoulders and around my waist, to the nook above my hips where Adrian's arm drapes over my body. Electricity crackles at every point where he touches me. I imagine what it would feel like if he pulled me closer, to hear him smile into my hair. The longing deepens until it becomes as real as a jewel in my hand, one that I can rotate to examine every facet: relief, comfort, joy, belonging, desire.

Adrian stirs a few minutes later. An ache of disappointment blooms in my chest when he gently releases my waist and rolls away. I stay perfectly still so he'll think I'm asleep. "Shit, Rao. Get it together," he whispers to himself. I smile into my mat. It's maddening that he doesn't want to give in because of some bodyguard code of ethics. But it's also cute and reassuring to know that he feels at least some of what I do.

Later, we walk to the square together. The sun hasn't fully risen over the pines yet, and the gray-blue light of early morning covers everyone as they hurry to their duties, us included. One girl about my age walks by. She's got doe eyes and a gorgeous pale green headscarf, and she offers Adrian a shy smile as she passes. But he doesn't notice her—not her smile, and not the way her expression darkens as she registers the wires behind my ear.

How long until I fail Adrian, and he views me with the same contempt?

"What is it?" Adrian asks, shaking me from my thoughts. His head swivels to the girl.

"What?"

"You were looking at her."

"I was . . . admiring how pretty she was," I lie.

"Was she?" he asks vaguely. "I didn't notice."

"Oh. Not your type?" I pause. "What *is* your type?" Guessing it's not "brain-damaged girls who wander the woods alone and apparently love asking awkward questions." But I swear my heart stops beating, as if the continuation hangs on his answer.

His neck flushes. "Oh, you know . . ." He breathes the words out in a vague sigh. What am I supposed to do with *that*? Adrian continues. "What about you? Noah's . . . not . . . unattractive." He gestures a few hundred paces away, where

Noah's chatting with a young woman. He turned out to be a surprisingly good guy after I failed yesterday, but I don't feel drawn to him in *that* way. Whereas with Adrian . . .

"Oh, you know . . ." I echo Adrian's earlier carefree tone, but his face doesn't mirror my playfulness. He's watching me carefully. "No," I say, suddenly serious. "I'm not . . . interested in anyone here." *Except you.*

Noah's shouts break the spell between us. "Well, would you look at the time?" he says loudly to no one in particular, checking his wrist screen. "Tell you what: if I were a Proxy with an important job to do, I *definitely* wouldn't want to be late right now!" The woman he's talking to swats his arm and laughs.

"Wow. Subtle." Adrian finally smiles, and a thousand butterflies in my stomach take flight.

"I should go," I say.

"Wait." He grabs my hand before I walk away. "Last night, in the room . . . are you okay?"

"I am. I will be." I glance at his side. Before bed, I tried to see the stars, but they weren't much brighter than back at the lake. My mission depends on us getting to the top of Mount Barton, which depends on Adrian being healthy enough to travel, which means it depends on me saving his life.

With one last squeeze, Adrian lets my hand go and leaves for the kitchen.

Despite his passive-aggressive teasing, Noah's still not set up when I arrive. Instead, he's whispering sweet nothings to that same woman. She tucks her long locs behind one ear. The other half of her hair is shaved into a close buzz cut, revealing a silver scar that matches Reem's—she's had her chip removed. But unlike Reem's scar, this woman's has been transformed into art; tiny silver vines sprout from the main incision, each decorated with delicate leaves and flowers. The tendrils of the tattoo curl around the back of her neck, wild and untamed.

The woman lifts her heart-shaped ebony face to Noah's, and they share a kiss that I probably shouldn't be seeing but can't turn away from. I know what kissing is; I can piece together the fragments of my mind enough that while I've never kissed anyone romantically, I'm familiar with the concept. But this . . . this is something completely different. Their kiss is bold. Voracious. They are devouring each other and enjoying it. Almost a full minute later, they pull away, and Noah brushes her forehead with his nose.

"Metro girl! What did I tell you when you first got here, about staring?" he says, eyes still locked intensely on the woman's face. I snap out of it and walk toward him, my face burning.

"Off to the shop," the woman says before walking away. She's short, and her curves fill out her customized jumpsuit in a way I could never dream of.

"Save me a dance tonight," Noah calls to her.

The woman coyly wraps a loc around her finger. "Only if you wear that shirt I like!"

Noah's gaze is sinful as he watches her walk away. I clear my throat obnoxiously, but it's like he's on another planet. "You have a way with all the ladies, I suppose?" I ask once she disappears around the corner and he finally returns to earth. His eyes are still half dazed. "No. Just with that one," he says. "And she's more than enough, trust me. Candace is our chief mechanic. There's something about a woman in the sciences . . . You think she's gorgeous now, wait till you see her use a multimeter." He crouches to open his violin case, and it's then that I notice a thin band of metal on the third finger of his left hand.

"Hang on. She's your *wife*?" I ask.

"That she is." He waggles his eyebrows with the grin of a dog that stole a soup bone, then inspects his bow.

"You're married?"

"That's what it is to have a wife, yes. You seem surprised."

"You're so young. I guess I thought . . . I mean, you look so . . ."

Noah laughs. "The women of the Haven wept bitter tears the day Candace took me off the market." He makes a show of wiping one eye. "But truthfully, sometimes you just know. With her . . . believe me, I knew. No point in searching anymore."

The square is full of people eager for Noah and me to begin, despite our poor performance yesterday. As we pair and he takes his place on the lamppost foundation, onlookers jostle one another for the first spot in line. But I squint over their heads, until I find who I'm searching for, a few rows back.

"It's still your turn," I say to Amina, the older woman with the journal from yesterday. "Please." The crowd parts, and she steps forward, holding the journal like it's coated in gold. Gently, I take it from her and find the original entry, about her morning at the market with her late husband. The love floats off the pages, and I feel the urge to let the warm glow pass. Instead, I savor it, and gasp as it unfolds itself in a hundred directions. Joy, loneliness, confusion, fondness. All those emotions rise in me as the notes on Noah's violin begin to soar above the crowd, sweet and sustained. Music envelops us. Amina nods, eyes closed, as tears spill onto her cheeks.

"That's it. That's exactly it," she whispers. My own eyes brim with tears.

Busy passersby around the square stop and notice the queue for the first time, and it's not long before we've got four times the interest. The variety of personal items they bring makes my head spin, but I'm grounded by their desires to have their hearts translated to song.

"Lemon is my favorite kind of cupcake."

"She gave this to me after our first kiss."

"His name is Bunny, 'cuz he's a bunny."

I listen carefully to what each item's owner wants to share with me, then do my best to feel what their words communicate, holding everything within me: pain and gratitude, excitement and wonder, and so much more. Noah is an excellent conduit, and each song blossoms on the wind beautifully, raising all our spirits.

Around midday, Reem passes by. She gives a single nod from across the square. Relief floods me, sending the notes of Noah's latest song even higher—a slow, indulgent tune for a girl describing lazy days at her favorite summer watering hole. The crowd applauds. I want to ride this high forever. I can't believe they're cheering for us—for me, and what I can do. For the first time in days, I feel like my chip isn't something to hide, but something to celebrate. A gift that I can share with others.

After lunchtime, most of the adults return to their duties around the village, or home to prepare themselves for the revelry. The children who stay behind are funnier than they have any right to be, making up silly stories about mundane objects like acorns and blades of grass they bring me. Their tales are ridiculous, but the joy radiates from me to Noah's strings all the same. One small girl is telling me about one of her favorite fairy tales as Noah plays a bright, buoyant tune that he introduces as a waltz. She's just getting to the climax when the sky crashes down on me.

Memories blast into my head, sharp as daggers. A place packed with people, so many people, much more crowded than here. There are faces, too—a young man, a brother who's not a brother. Then an older one, who protects me and gives me wisdom. A woman with soulful brown eyes and a warm embrace, granting me tenderness that I don't deserve. And a young girl, with dark skin and even darker eyes, her hair in two gravity-defying puffs atop her head. I clutch my skull, screaming in agony. The village children back away as Noah crouches beside me. He doesn't speak until the episode is over.

"All right now?" he asks quietly, unpairing us. I expect him to ask what happened, but there's no surprise on his face.

"I think so," I say shakily. A name floats to the surface. "Celeste," I whisper. "Kez. Thea. Silas."

Noah stands, then extends a hand to pull me up. "Careful. Take it slow." He pauses to make sure I'm steady on my feet. "You said it's been almost a week since you guys left the Metro? I would've expected the withdrawal to kick in sooner than now."

Now it clicks why he's not surprised. Noah thinks my body is reacting to Mean withdrawal. I decide to play along with that, instead of some jumbled version of *I can't remember anything from more than a few days ago, oh but you can totally still trust us, we're not evil, I'm just mentally defective.*

"Yeah. The pain comes in waves."

Noah nods, and I feel a pang of guilt at lying. "Afraid you won't find any of that poison around here, but we might be able to give you something for the pain."

I smile weakly. "Thanks. I'm okay. We can keep going."

Noah resumes his post on the pylon. I reassure the children that I'm all right, and before long we're back to our games and laughing. But through everything, there's one girl in particular who grabs my attention, with Afro puffs and radiant brown skin like the girl I saw in my mind. Celeste felt like home; I know it the same way I know the ground will catch me if I fall. If she's in that crowded, sweaty place—the *Metro*—then that's where I have to go after we see the stars. That's where I belong.

The rest of the day passes quickly. The square begins to clear as a crew comes to set up for the revelry. Noah and I announce that we only have time for one more customer. A young boy—no older than seven, I guess—runs forward with a shy, playful gleam in his eye.

"Another surprise, Carson?" I ask, used to this one's tricks by now. He nods and smiles, showing off several gaps where his adult teeth will be soon. I hold out my hand, the smallest finger sticking out.

"Pinky-promise me it's not another toad."

His inexplicably sticky pinky links with mine. Satisfied, I close my eyes and hold out my hand for whatever he'd like me to interpret. His footsteps slap across the cobblestones as he runs to retrieve the item, then returns a few seconds later. My interest piques when I hear not only children's laughter rippling through the square, but a couple of adult chuckles as well.

"Noah?" Panic rises in my voice. "It's not a toad, is it?"

"Not a toad," he calls from his perch. "Well, not technically, but—"

"But what?" I ask.

Let's get it over with, I think, and shove my cupped hands out farther. But instead of something being placed in them, they fold up against a warm, muscular wall. I open my eyes to find Adrian, inches away from me, a swarm of giggling children surrounding us. He puts his hands on my hips to steady me, and it's like they've always fit there.

"Liv? What's going on?" he asks, his brows crinkled adorably in confusion. I'm too flustered to speak. He smiles at me tentatively, and my heart does a somersault. The memory of Noah and his wife inhaling one another against the pylon intrudes. Seconds later, Noah lifts his violin to his shoulder, stifling a laugh as he presses his bow to the strings.

"Don't. You. Dare," I snarl at him. That only sends him into more hysterics. Noah doubles over and has to grab the lamppost so he doesn't fall. He can tumble off the platform headfirst for all I care, as long as he doesn't play a single damn note. I'm barely ready to admit my feelings about Adrian to *myself*, let alone expose them to half of the Haven. What would the sound of my heart even be?

Adrian's confusion deepens, and I shift my attention to damage control. "It's a game the kids were playing . . . ," I say. He's waiting for further explanation, so I claw at the first thing I can think of. "They bring me a person from the village and see if I can guess their name."

"But you already know my name."

"Yeah, it's not a very good game. Okay, bye!" I speed walk out of the square, but not before unpairing with Noah, who's still gasping for breath.

■ ■ ■

"TWO KOFTA KEBABS, PLEASE." NOAH PAUSES. "YOU EAT BEEF, RIGHT?"

"I . . . think so?"

He laughs. "I forget you're used to Metro 'food'—" He lifts his hands in air quotes. "This is going to blow your mind. My treat, after that trick with lover boy in the square earlier."

Noah's impatient for dinner after our long day, but I could stay here for hours, watching everyone go by. The street is lined with stalls, and hawkers wander through the crowd, shouting about their wares and services: everything from hair braiding to home repair, games to gardening supplies.

We stand by while the man behind the counter prepares our food. He wears a flowy full-length robe, the top of which is a gray jumpsuit with the sleeves removed to highlight his dark brown biceps. The lower half of the robe boasts a geometric pattern of indigo, yellow, and burnt orange, which matches the beads on the ends of his short braids. A delicious aroma rises from his grill, swirling with the mouthwatering scents from the other food stalls. I'm sure Adrian could name each spice if he were here. Thinking of Adrian makes me worry—did Reem tell the doctor to resume his treatment once she saw me performing in the square? He didn't appear to be in any discomfort, but I should've asked him earlier, instead of running away like a frightened child.

"Ah! Here we are." Noah beams as he hands me a spear of spiced meat and vegetables that makes my mouth drop open. Not only is it the best thing I've ever smelled in my life, it's beautiful. The meat is seared a deep brown, and the heat from the pan has made the peppers vibrant. I'd marvel at the sight some more if my stomach wasn't threatening to eat itself.

I take a bite. If I was in awe before, I've now transcended. Flavors dance on my tongue: the crisp, subtle heat of the vegetables and the tang of the tender beef. Rich golden juice drips down my hand.

"Well?" Noah asks.

"It's . . . even better than bacon," I say out one side of my mouth.

He scoffs. "Now you're just being ridiculous." He tears into his own piece of meat. "So, how long have you and the Great Scrawny Wonder been a thing?"

I nearly cough out my kebab. "We're not."

"Liv, let me help you out: The way Adrian looks at you,

especially when you're not paying attention? That look is reserved exclusively for *things.*"

"It is?"

"Incidentally, that's also the way you look at him. So." He
wipes his mouth and swings on the stool to face me. "Don't
tell me this is your first time with all this?"

"This?"

"Yeah, 'this.'" He curves his hands into a heart shape and
makes annoying kissy faces that I assume are meant to represent me and Adrian. I should smack him, but his question
catches me off guard. *Is* it my first time? I don't have any hard
facts to consider; no names or even the memory of a face. I
can sense that I've had crushes, even a few that were mutual.
When I probe deeper, though, the sensations are shallow, surface level. Nothing as significant as what I feel when I think
about Adrian. This depth, this mutual resonance, is new. "I
think it might be," I say.

Noah nods. "Sometimes it's hard to tell, when it's new.
Your secret's safe with me."

"Thanks." As nice as it is to have Noah to talk to about
Adrian, I need more time to process these feelings on my own.
I change the subject to something else that's been on my mind.

"Speaking of people we give googly eyes to, what does
Candace do all day? Earlier, you said she was the Haven's chief
mechanic, but there are hardly any machines around here."

For an instant, Noah's gaze cools, but then he's back to
his typical charming self. "Fritz if I know, to be honest!" He
glances at my food. "Eat up, Feeler. You'll need your energy
for dancing tonight."

Feeler.

I bristle instinctively, remembering Adrian's strong reaction the first time Noah called me that word.

"Well, so long as we're sharing truths . . . I don't appreciate being called a Feeler. It's insulting."

"That's fair. I don't appreciate being called a raider."

That one's a surprise. I realize that I haven't heard Noah or any of the people we've played for refer to themselves by that word. "I . . . hadn't even thought about that. What should I call you all?"

He cradles his chin in his hand, pondering the question. "Haveners is good, I guess. Or, you know . . . people?"

"Got it." I smile. "People works for me too."

He nods, eyes twinkling. "People it is."

24

ADRIAN

"THAT SHOULD DO IT," KENJI SAYS. WE'VE JUST FINISHED SETTING UP THE LAST of the dessert trays in the square. And not a second too soon, because people are already starting to arrive for the revelry. This early crowd is mostly families with young children, a swarm of whom make a beeline for our table as soon as they spot the sweets. But I also meet a few older couples, and some guys my age whose clothing seems a bit crisper than the Haveners' typical loose, flowing wardrobe. I'm suddenly aware of how drab my own clothes are in comparison. Preston's sweater may have been in good shape when I swiped it from the cabin, but now the pale gray is smeared with stains from sleeping on the forest floor and cooking with Kenji all day. Self-consciously, I run a hand over the coarse curls that my LifeCorp genetic profile tells me I get from my mother's side. They're dry after a week in the forest, not like the well-maintained, product-laden hairstyles of the other guys in the Haven. But Liv won't care—she's not like that.

You're not supposed to care if she cares. Remember?

Right. I concentrate on my main assignment for the night—serving food to hungry festivalgoers while somehow managing not to consume too much of it myself. I eye the carrot cake on the table. When Kenji told me that centuries ago, people often made desserts with vegetables, I'll admit I was skeptical. But then I tasted it: the sweet carrots soaring over the dark notes of clove and cinnamon, with a tangy cream cheese frosting on top. I monitor the inventory of that particular dessert very closely. I can't wait to see Liv's face when she tries some.

The first hour is so busy that I barely have a chance to look up and realize how hectic the rest of the party has gotten. Noah leads a band at the center of the square, featuring strings, horns, and a deafening percussion section. The drums' rhythm thrums in my chest, driving the crowd to a fever pitch of twirling, clapping, and swaying. This way of life is so different from in the Metro—no one's on their wrist screens or hurrying their merriment to get back to work. Life is slow here. Too slow; if the raiders had their way, the advancements back home would never exist. But when I think of some of those advancements—Mean, Proxies, Verch . . . even VitaBars—all I can do is wonder what, exactly, are we supposed to be advancing *toward*? What is the point of the order we're protecting? And what is it costing us?

Someone cheers to my left. "Okay, girl! Bet they don't move like that in the Metro!"

And suddenly there, dancing on a table behind the band, is Liv. My heart stops at the sight of her, her body limned in orange by the glowing torches that light the square. Someone's lent her new clothes: instead of Preston's sweater, she wears a matching skirt and crop top, yellow with deep purple flowers that match the jeweled ones woven into her thick jet-black curls. The matching gray fingerless gloves of her jumpsuit end halfway up her toned arms. Her brown skin shimmers like she's some sort of sun goddess—especially her exposed stomach. Liv moves as if her hips can predict the djembe's pulsing before even the musicians can. She's laughing and shouting happily to another girl who's also on the table, while a group sits on the benches beneath them, watching the band.

Kenji says something, I think.

"Hmm?" I ask, fixated on Liv.

"I've got it from here. Go enjoy the party."

The suggestion sends me spiraling. If I'm released from my duties, there's nothing stopping me from mingling with everybody. Or one body in particular.

"Oh no, I couldn't—" I begin.

"I insist. You guys head out tomorrow, right? Trust me, you won't find another party like this for hundreds of miles." He grins.

"I . . . All right. Thanks, man." I nod at him, then head into the crowd . . . but not before grabbing two slices of carrot cake.

The sea of people around the band parts as I step deeper into the square. Everyone's having a great time, judging by the wide smiles on their sweat-glistening faces. Even Reem seems to be enjoying herself, tapping her thigh as she holds court with a few people to my right. I'm happy they're all making this memory to sustain them through the tough winter ahead. But I don't understand how anyone can concentrate on the music while the fritzing Goddess of All That Is Good and Beautiful in the World is up there, whirling around on a picnic table. I'm vaguely aware that the heat and the tight squeeze of bodies on all sides should bother me like it did in the Towers. But only vaguely. Liv's pull is my singular focus, erasing fear from my mind. Like a moth to a flame, I'm drawn to her. And like a moth to a flame, I'm in danger of getting too close.

I'm nearly through the crowd, carrot cake miraculously intact, when something hard presses against my chest.

"Take this," an older man says. Rivulets of sweat stream down his golden-brown skin, into his scruffy beard. "Gotta piss." He disappears into the dancing crowd, and I hold up the item with my free hand. It's a drum.

"What?" I yell after the man, but he's long gone. Meanwhile, the dancers are glaring at me as the music plays on.

"We need a beat!" one girl shouts. From the bandstand in the center of the plaza, Noah shouts for me to come over.

I don't know how, I mouth over the music—which, I'll admit, has lost a bit of its magic without a percussionist. A pair of dancers push me toward the band. Still clueless, I find Liv in the crowd. She's laughing at the whole scene from a distance. Must be nice. My heart flutters when she smiles at me, but without a beat, she's stopped dancing.

I'll do anything to keep her dancing.

I demolish the cake in two bites. The crowd cheers as I step onstage. Noah stomps out a rhythm as he plays his violin, and I do my best to match it. Even I can tell it's not perfect, but the crowd doesn't seem to care. In seconds, they're whirling and grinding and swaying again to our song. Liv jumps down from the table and dances in circles around the stage. I'm transfixed. She's a celestial being, come down to consort with mere mortals. Noah nudges me to stay on beat, then shouts something to Liv as she passes. They smile at each other. A twinge of jealousy pricks at me. Of course. Liv claimed she wasn't interested in Noah, but they did spend another whole day together. Plus, Liv's incredible, and you could dice an onion with Noah's cheekbones.

No matter. I've got a job to do.

After a few more songs, the drummer returns. Kenji's handing out desserts with his partner, a stout dark-skinned guy with pale blond curls. I find a quiet spot behind the beverage stand before Liv sees me. The bartender takes pity on me, sensing my nerves, but the smell of the pungent drink she hands me turns my stomach even more. I shouldn't want to dance with Liv. But I do, even if she'd rather have Noah.

It's fine. Let her have some fun tonight before we see the stars tomorrow, and then . . .

You're not supposed to care.

Best not to dwell on what comes after tomorrow, when I can't pretend I'm acting on behalf of LifeCorp anymore. I down the drink and feel it numb the edge of my worries. There's a twig by my feet. I take it and absentmindedly draw some designs in the dirt. Soon the lines take shape, transforming into Liv and her wild curls. In less than a week, she's changed my life, challenged everything I thought I believed about the world. But if her memories come back on Mount Barton, then after today, she'll hate me forever. I wouldn't blame her.

"Found you!" says the one voice I don't want to hear, the one voice I'm starting to think of as the centerpiece of my day. I grimace, even as something in me flares like a campfire ember. Liv squeezes herself between the booths to crouch at my side. I don't have the strength to meet her eye. I keep drawing.

"You were great out there!" she says.

I catch an intoxicating whiff of heat mixed with cocoa butter. "Thanks."

"What's wrong?"

"Nothing."

"Adrian. Tell me the truth."

Why start now? I clench my jaw at the guilty thought. Liv takes my silence as resolve and checks out my doodles.

"Those are pretty good!" she says, admiring my caricatures of Icarus, Reem, and Noah's violin. "Did you draw a lot in school?"

"Definitely not." The idea of my Academy instructors even speaking the word *art* is so laughable that I almost forget to cover the sketch to my right, of a girl with big hair and an even bigger smile. Meanwhile, the real Liv's staring at me like whatever I say or do next might shatter her. Of course—I'm the person she knows best in the entire world. Or thinks she does, anyway. I can't shut her out.

"My instructors believed their job was to beat all individuality out of us," I explain. "There was no room for anything that wasn't for the greater good. I remember one time, I was first to the showers. I was alone in there, and the glass was fogging up. I was so tempted to draw the tiniest thing, maybe a smiley face or a stick person." The corners of Liv's mouth turn up, her smile encouraging me to continue. "But I knew that any part of me that was *uniquely* me had to stay buried.

It's dumb, but I still wonder what would have happened if I'd drawn something and it had shown up on the glass when the next guy showered."

"Maybe he would have added a drawing. A doodle revolution." Her smile is in full effect now, and all it takes is one glance for my mind to wave the white flag of defeat. I'm a goner, completely lost to her. But you can't say I didn't try to resist.

Liv leans over and takes the twig from my hand, then sketches something of her own. There's very little space between us. I want so badly to close the distance, but I'm keeping too much from her. It wouldn't be fair.

I swallow. "I actually . . . was born in a place like this."

"What?" Liv pauses, giving me her full attention. How does she always manage to make me feel like I'm the only person in the world?

"Yeah. Another raider settlement, somewhere northwest of here. In Buffalo or Toronto, maybe? I was dumped in the Metro when I was three, with a bunch of other kids. Too many mouths for my birth parents to feed, I guess."

She covers my hand with hers. It's so warm, a respite from the fall air that's already starting to bite. "I'm so sorry, Adrian."

"Yeah. I've been wondering, though. . . . Maybe the raiders—"

"Haveners. Or people."

I pause at the distinction. "Right. Maybe the Haveners aren't everything I've been told. Maybe they're the good guys. And if the good guys didn't want me, what does that make me?"

Liv's delicate shoulders rise and fall. "Well . . . maybe . . . this is a bit like coming home."

Our eyes lock. The band's music is muffled, like I'm underwater. My vision narrows until my entire universe is Liv. "A bit," I manage.

She blinks and starts working on her drawing again. Two stick figures, one with huge wild hair, the other with short springy coils. They're smiling as music notes swirl around them like falling leaves.

I stiffen. Is she asking me to dance? Because if she is, I'm done saying no. Liv lets me be a version of myself that I can't show to anyone else. And I want to hang on to that, and to her, for as long as the world will let me.

I stand. "Come on."

"Where are we going?" Liv asks as she takes my hand.

I nod to the doodle. "Life imitates art."

She beams at me. We head to the dance floor, and I have zero regrets. If Liv's memories do come back on the mountain tomorrow, she'll hate me. This could be the last night we have together. I think of the Haveners, and the way they stockpile joy like a crop. If I'm going to get through the rest of my life without this girl, then I'm going to need a reserve of my own.

25

LIV

CAN TOO MUCH SMILING BREAK YOUR FACE? BECAUSE IF IT CAN, I'M IN SERIous danger.

Adrian is happier than I've ever seen him. There's a light in his eyes as he twirls me, and it's more than the reflection of the torches. Almost like it comes from inside him, and it's contagious. We holler and sway to the music, tripping over one another, laughing when our feet tangle. We're not the most coordinated couple, and the perplexed stares from the people around us only confirm my suspicions. But all it takes is one goofy hip wiggle from Adrian and I'm pulled back into this world where we're the only ones who matter.

When the band takes a break, we do the same. Adrian peeled his sweater off after the first dance, and the bit of brown skin above his undershirt glistens with the heat. We're both panting as we make our way to the table where Noah sits with his wife, Candace, along with Harcourt and a few others.

"Be right back," Adrian says as he heads for the dessert table, leaving me to respond to their raised eyebrows on my own.

"Adrian seems to be feeling better," Candace says slyly.

"I didn't know Doc Poulos could heal a wound like that so quickly." She's fashioned a dress out of an oversized shirt—one of Noah's, I'm guessing—with a gray and maroon print. A small cord of leather ties it at the waist, and it slips off one ebony shoulder to reveal her delicate collarbone. Her moisturized locs peek out from under her maroon head wrap, as do the silver vines on the nape of her neck.

"I don't think it's the doc that's doing the healing, baby." Noah gives his wife a knowing smirk before taking a gulp of beer.

Before I can respond with a quip of my own, Adrian's hand snakes around my waist. The edges of the world go fuzzy as I lean against his warmth and clasp his left hand with my right, securing his hold.

"You have to taste this," he says. His breath is electric in my ear. I bite the piece of cake in his hand. His finger grazes my lower lip, sending a thrill through me that I wonder if he shares. When I look up, his eyes are ablaze.

"Amazing, right?" he breathes. "Kenji calls it carrot cake."

"What? I thought carrots were—"

"A vegetable. I know!"

We giggle, leaning into one another even closer. By the time our laughter fades, the group has dispersed. Noah and the band have started up again. Candace dances through the crowd with a girlfriend. Harcourt and a group of men are playing some sort of card game at one end of the table. Adrian and I grab seats at the other end, to split the second piece of cake he brought.

"I gotta get this recipe from Kenji. It's incredible," Adrian

says, licking frosting from his thumb. I bite my lip and try not
to notice what he's doing, or what it does to me. Between the
sugar high and the rush of being so close to him, I'm delirious
with happiness. I decide to share the best news of all.

"Guess what! I remembered something today." I beam
proudly at him. He freezes, his thumb still in his mouth.

"You what?"

"Yeah. A little girl. I think I care for her . . . like a sister, but
we're not related. If that makes sense?"

"Uh-huh," he says carefully. He straightens in his seat slowly,
like he's moving through mud. The color in his face is gone.

"Adrian? What's wrong? Is it your side?"

"No, I just need to go lie down." He rises and cuts through
the crowd before I can protest. I push through the dancers, re-
playing our conversation in my head. Where did I go wrong?

By the time I get to the band's platform in the center of
the square, I've lost him. Candace has joined Noah onstage,
all flirtatious giggles and roaming hands as Noah tries his best
to concentrate on the music. "Adrian went that way!" she
shouts. "Guess you'll be turning in early too!"

"What do you mean?"

She scowls at her husband. "I thought you said they were
together?"

"It's complicated, or so she claims." Noah smirks. Candace
sighs and leans into me conspiratorially. "He wants you to *follow* him to your room," she overenunciates, like she's spelling
it out for a child.

My eyes go wide. "Oh."

Oh.

26

ADRIAN

PLEASE, PLEASE DON'T FOLLOW ME.

Our tiny room is dark when I enter, except for the faint glow of torchlight that lines the door from outside. Fine by me; I don't need light. I *need* to get ahold of myself. Everything was going fine—better than fine—until Liv brought up Celeste, and the whole glittering façade of the night came crashing down. Have her memories been coming back to her this entire time? I'm such an idiot.

You said once her memories came back, you'd take her in. So take her in.

I can't. I *can't.*

Can I?

A light rap at the door, barely audible over the muffled sounds of the party. Liv's silhouette appears, and my stomach tightens with guilt.

"I brought another slice of carrot cake," she says as she steps inside. I can't believe she's still worrying about me, even though I ran from her. I'm the last person on earth who deserves her kindness.

"Thanks. I'm not hungry right now. Maybe later."

She closes the door and steps inside. "What happened back there?"

I freeze, grateful that she can't see my face in the darkness. What am I supposed to say? That I've been lying to her for a week and only recently decided that it might be a bad thing? That if her memories are coming back randomly, I don't know if I can trust her anymore, which is complete bullshit because there's no way in hell she should be trusting me? That I'm terrified of the moment we become enemies again and she's not "my" Liv anymore, but that I want her to be her full self, because I care about her?

I care about her.

"Too much partying. I'm going to turn in, but you should go. Enjoy." My words sound lifeless. I head for the mats, waiting for the sound of the door creaking open and shut. But it doesn't come.

"Adrian . . ." Liv's voice is thick with emotion, and the idea that I've done something to upset her makes me turn to face her.

"I'm fine. Really." This time, I sound much more convincing. But it doesn't stop the quiet sniffles that I've come to recognize all too well. I wrap my arms around her and feel the wetness of her tears against my neck. "Hey . . ."

"Promise you're okay? I don't know what I would do if anything happened to you. I . . ." She pulls her face from my shoulder. I can't see her, but somehow, I know our eyes have found one another. "I really like you, Adrian," Liv whispers.

I've said it before, but it bears repeating: I am the biggest piece of shit on the face of the earth. A steaming pile of boar scat for not being one hundred percent honest with her. But hearing Liv admit her feelings sparks something visceral in me. Whatever's inside her that's reaching out to me, I need to meet it. I need her to know she's not alone.

The words battle with my rational mind as they push themselves out. "I . . . God . . . I really like you too." And there it is. No going back now.

Liv leans forward. Her nose is feather light against mine, a whisper of a touch. Heat radiates from her hips under my palms. I hold her tighter, move closer, and she makes a noise that sends me out of my skin. But a millimeter before our lips meet, the truth barrels into me, reminding me of the charade I've forced her into:

She doesn't know who I am.

She doesn't know who *she* is.

She doesn't remember who we were—are—to each other.

She has no idea, not really, what she's even asking for.

Against every impulse, I pull back. "We shouldn't do this. You don't remember anything about yourself. What if you've got someone waiting for you in the Metro?"

"I don't. I'd remember anyone who made me feel the way you do."

Oh no. "Well . . . what if it turns out you have an aversion to guys with curly hair?" She giggles in my arms. I relax a little, until Liv tugs at a coil of hair, gently holding it taut.

"I definitely don't." Her voice is husky as she releases my curl and places her palm on my cheek. "I love your stubble," she says as she runs her thumb over my facial hair. "I've been dying to touch it for days." She's so close I can hear the pant of her heavy breaths, which is not helping to deescalate the situation. Mercifully, she pulls her hand away.

"You're treating me like a child who can't make their own decisions. Maybe I don't have all the details filled in, but that doesn't make me any less of who I am. Or any less capable of knowing what I want. I want you, Adrian."

I've dreamt of her saying those words for longer than I care to admit. So why doesn't hearing them now make me feel any better?

"We can't. *I* can't." I drop my hands from her waist. Liv sighs. I hate that I had to disappoint her like this, but—

LIV NEWMAN WOULD LIKE TO PAIR. ACCEPT?

I blink hard, as if that will erase the question floating in my vision.

"Liv—"

"You don't believe what I tell you. Will you let me show you?"

The narrow space between us is charged. Electric. I raise my hand, press my finger to my temple. One tap, then another . . .

Two glowing amber rings in the darkness, and then a wave of desire stronger than anything I've ever felt. My affection for Liv swirls together with her feelings for me, until I can't tease the two streams apart. Liv was right: there's no naivety here, but a confident insistence on making sure I know how she feels. All the tenderness and fondness and . . .

Whoa. She feels *that* for *me*?

A smooth, warm hand runs up the length of my arm. "Well?"

The physical contact sends our desire skyrocketing. She

wants me. But *knowing* about that desire and experiencing it firsthand are two very, *very* different things.

"This feels . . . I mean, it's . . ." My voice sounds far away, and the words come out slurred. If this is Orange Haze, it's a drug unlike anything I've ever known, and one I never want to be rid of. I know I could resist this ecstasy if I really wanted to, but I'm hungry to explore the contours of Liv's mind. Slowly, I intertwine my fingers with hers, gently brushing the inside of her palm with my thumb. The sensation does something indescribable to both of us.

"Say you believe me," Liv breathes. "Say you know this is my choice."

"This is your choice."

She swallows. "And . . . say you want this too."

Understatement of the millennium. "I want this t—" The words are barely out of my mouth before her lips are on mine. *This is wrong,* I think for a fraction of a second. But it doesn't feel wrong. It feels so unquestionably right. The way gravity is right, the way laughter is right, this is *right.* As our mouths deepen against each other, our bodies impossibly close and our shared desire blazing white-hot, I don't care that we've reached a point of no return. After Mount Barton, I will follow Liv to the ends of the earth. LifeCorp be damned. Liv is my law now, and whatever draws the light to her eyes is my justice. We'll burn the bridge and deal with the consequences later.

I'll strike the match myself.

27

LIV

WHAT A DIFFERENCE A DAY MAKES.

For the second morning in a row, I wake to Adrian's breath tickling the hairs on the back of my neck. But this time, he doesn't pull away when he wakes. Instead, he tightens his hold on my waist and brushes his lips against my bare shoulder. A pleasurable tingle blooms over every inch of me. Even better than the delicious sensation itself is knowing I don't have to hide how I feel anymore. For the first time since we met, Adrian and I are on the exact same page.

"Morning," he says low in my ear. I half turn to him, revealing an even more delicate stretch of my neck. I feel a smug satisfaction when he takes the bait, leaving a trail of kisses from my jawline to my collarbone. His arm lies across my stomach, and when he clutches the fleshy part of my hips, something in me catches on fire. I envelop Adrian's lips with my own. Our chests touch; his moans rumble inside me. He deepens the kiss, and I meet his push and pull with the same burning need. A handful of pesky thoughts flutter in my mind like gnats: what time is it, am I expected in the square to sync with Noah, when will Adrian and I gather supplies and provisions before we leave for Mount Barton this evening. But all it takes is Adrian's hand creeping into my hair, and the sound of his breathy sighs, for the annoying thoughts to scatter.

"You seem to have your strength back," I say when we manage to disentangle ourselves many minutes later. Adrian lifts his shirt to inspect the bandage, which appears to be clean.

"It barely even hurts anymore. Doc said it was closing up nicely yesterday."

I smile, but I'd be lying if I said my curiosity was purely selfless. While we kissed, I was careful not to grab Adrian's side, where I know he's still healing. I can't wait until he's fully recovered and I can kiss him harder, grab him tighter. Fully give in to the desire beating at my bones.

He calls my name, tearing me from my thoughts.

"Mmm?" I ask, still biting my lip.

"What are you thinking about? You made . . . this face . . ."

My neck flushes. "Um. Nothing."

"Nothing?" He doesn't wait for a reply, just swoops me up in a kiss that steals the air from my lungs. I'm floating, and twirling, and drowning in him. And I wouldn't want it any other way.

Eventually, the voices and sounds outside alert us that the day has begun. Reluctantly, we separate.

"All right. You're grabbing the jackets from Noah. I'll get water, bread, apples, cheese . . . anything else from Kenji?" Adrian asks, suddenly serious, as he slips his boots on.

"Couple of treats couldn't hurt, right?" I say. "For morale?" Adrian breaks his focus to flash me a boyish grin. I'm smiling like an idiot and he hasn't even kissed me goodbye yet. I remedy that quickly, though, leaning in for one last kiss that puts Noah and Candace to shame. When I open my eyes, I laugh. This time *he's* the one who's flushed.

"I can't believe it's happening. We're really about to see the stars," I say.

"And maybe after Mount Barton, we can come here again. I'll run the bakery and make you all the carrot cake your heart desires." He brushes the tip of his nose against my neck, and my knees buckle. I'm almost lost to him again, when I remember something I wanted to talk to him about.

"Adrian. The girl I remembered yesterday." The name *Celeste* flashes like a beacon in my mind.

Adrian pauses but doesn't pull back. I continue. "I think she's in the Metro. I want to go see her."

He straightens fully now, worry lines etched in his face like cracks in river soil. "I thought, after last night . . ."

He's trying to seem strong, but I can see the panic in his eyes. My heart wrenches. Of course. We only just found each other, and now he's worried that I'm leaving him to go to the Metro on my own. I grab his hands.

"I am happy in the Haven," I say. "I'm happy anywhere with you. That's why I want you to come with me. And from the way you describe the Metro, I'll get eaten alive there without you."

He winces at that. I clasp his hands behind me, inching closer to him. "I want you, and that's not going to change. Stay with me?"

He's far away for a moment, but then he nods. Whatever's troubling him, I'll fix it. I hug him extra tight and whisper my thanks into his chest. I think about what Adrian told me last night, about being abandoned by his people and then growing up in a place where no one cared who he was. He's used to being discarded by people he cares about. In my head, I make a promise: every second that we're together, I'll make sure he knows I'm not going anywhere.

28

ADRIAN

THIS MIGHT BE THE LAST DAY, SO MAKE IT COUNT. THE THOUGHT RATTLES URgently in my brain, edging out the lingering glow of Liv's passion entangling with mine. I'm so worried about how the day will end, I can't concentrate on Kenji running through the supplies he's giving us: "I thought about sorting them alphabetically, but then I decided it would be better to pack them in the most likely order of use, so . . ."

While Kenji runs through his rationale, I go back to the only thing I've been obsessing over since I left Liv this morning. I thought that, even after Liv got her memory back, we could live in the Haven permanently and be happy, despite our differences. The longer we stay, the more comfortable I am. It's where I might have belonged all along.

Yes, I'd have a lot to apologize for. And yes, she'd have every right to be pissed at me. But bit by bit, I could show that the part of her I've fallen in love with—and I fully admit I've fallen in love—is still in there. In the Haven, we'd have time to figure out new roles for ourselves that wouldn't automatically set us at each other's throats. I'm ready—excited, even—to do that work.

But the closer Liv gets to her old self, the less we have in common. Of course, it makes sense that she'd want to find Celeste; she actually has people who love her, no matter what. Whereas I've only got my plants and Nas, who's probably moved on to another partner by now. There's no world where we go back to the Metro and stay in each other's lives as anything other than mortal enemies—a law enforcer versus a law breaker. But I'm not going to leave her. And if that means secretly sabotaging the Force every time an officer tries to arrest her, I'll do that too, for as long as I can.

". . . cover it all with a tarp, and you're good to go!" Kenji finishes his oration, with a pause so heavy I wonder if he expects applause.

"This is great, Kenj, really. Thank you for your help." I clasp his forearm, and we slap one another on the back. I glance at the smooth light-brown skin below the elastic of his hairnet. "Hey . . . one thing I've been wondering. After everything LifeCorp put you and your partner through, why do you still have your chip?"

"You mean besides the fact that it would hurt like a bitch to remove it?"

I laugh. "Fair. I just feel like, if it were me, I'd want to forget I ever had any connection to that place." The words ring dangerously close to true. *Careful, Adrian.*

Kenji gently touches the back of his neck. "I don't know . . . I guess part of me still wonders if we'll ever live in the Metro again, someday. If it could be different. Boston was my home, you know?"

"I do." We stand in silence for a moment before Kenji shakes his head and moves to the counter to prep some vegetables.

"I don't know, maybe I'm a softie. Big on second chances, clearly." He chuckles.

A knock on the door. Harcourt's broad silhouette fills the doorframe. He shifts his eyes between us, at a loss for words.

"Something we can help you with?" Kenji asks.

"Not you." Harcourt points a knobby finger at me. "You. You worked in a factory, right? You good with machines?"

Shit. Of course it would be my luck that our cover's blown right before we leave. But I've got a couple of years of basic mechanics under my belt from the Academy—I know my way around a soldering iron. Will it be enough to take care of whatever Harcourt needs? I guess we'll see.

"Sure," I say.

He leads me out of the bakery and away from the main artery of the village. When we cross an overgrown expanse that I identify as the mall's former parking lot, I start to worry that maybe *Harcourt* is the one who's lying. Maybe they've already found me out, and this mess about machines is a ruse to take me out into the woods and eliminate me. I glance back at the vanishing village as we go farther into the brush.

"Hey, man, I really should be helping Liv get ready to g—"

"Not much longer. This way." He leads us to a copse of oak trees. Something big is nestled against the largest oak's roots, covered by a cloth tarp. Even before Harcourt lifts the cover, alarm bells are blaring in my head. There's something unsettling about the cloth's rumpled shape, the way it stretches along the length of the trunk with long limbs that are almost human.

Almost.

Harcourt removes the tarp, and Nas's frozen face stares at me with lifeless eyes. His arm's been almost completely severed; a few fraying wires are all that keep it connected to his shoulder.

"Found him scouting a ways out. In a forest this big—what are the odds, right?"

"Right." My mouth goes dry. I'm going to be sick. Nas followed the beacon I sent, risking his life to come find me despite Redding's orders. The Haveners beat him senseless. This is all my fault. I've been so busy dreaming up a happily-ever-after in the Haven with Liv, I've forgotten reality. Life in the Metro marches on. My obligations to LifeCorp—to Nas—don't go away just because I fell in love.

"And he's a way bigger score than the farming droids we usually swipe." Harcourt's eyes are crazed, gleaming. Like a vulture with a stolen kill. I shift my gaze to the left slightly so I can avoid seeing the mangled body of my best friend. What I really want to do—what every fiber in my body is screaming at me to do—is sock Harcourt in the face, lift Nas up onto my shoulders, and get the *fritz out of here*. But Harcourt is a big man, with the rest of the village on his side. I'm outmatched. I need a better plan.

"What did you want me to do with him?" It takes all my training to hold my voice level, to stop my shoulders from heaving with rage.

"Usually, I just follow Candace's instructions. But she's busy working on—ah—another project. Chief mechanic business. I thought maybe we could scrap this . . . *thing* for parts? For a generator or something? Dunno, I'm no good with tech. Not really sure what's what in there." He chews his thumbnail, before poking his finger into the gap in Nas's shoulder. The sight sends a queasy chill through me, like I'm watching someone prod the flesh around a bullet wound. Nas doesn't react; he's still powered down, so he doesn't feel a thing. But I do. And I want to beat Harcourt bloody. Before he can notice the loathing on my face, I focus on Nas and cock my head like I'm considering him as a specimen to dissect.

"Not sure there's much to it, honestly—these older models. You might be able to strip a few scraps down for the copper. Barely worth the trouble, in my opinion."

"Thought you might say that." His features twist in a sickening grin. "'Cuz there's more." He points through the brush, where I make out the outline of our cycle and sidecar, partly covered by some shrubs.

A genuine smile spreads across my face as a plan takes shape in my head.

"Now, *that* . . . that, we can use."

29

LIV

"THAT'S LUNCH!" NOAH BELLOWS BEFORE HOPPING OFF THE PYLON. "WE'LL BE back in twenty, for our grand finale. Now would be a good time to consider your final requests! Our maestro is headed out soon." The autumn sun burns hot today, so we find a spot in the shade to split the foot-long sandwich Noah has brought from home. I still can't get over how good food can taste—juicy tomatoes, smoked turkey, and sharp cheese swirl together until all I can do is sigh.

"I'll take that as a compliment," Noah laughs. His eyes catch something across the square, and his brow furrows. I follow his gaze. Adrian's hurrying toward us. He's not running, but the stiff restraint in his muscles tells me he wants to.

"I'll be back," I tell Noah. When I stand, Adrian gestures to the side of the square, behind a food cart that still hasn't been moved from last night's festivities.

"What is it?"

"Do you trust me?" Adrian asks at the same time. He's panting.

I frown. "Of course I do. But now I'm worried. What's going on?" I caress his cheek, and his ragged breathing slows.

He kisses my palm like it's the only thing anchoring him. But when he looks up, his eyes are frantic. Pleading.

"We're not leaving tonight. We need to leave now. Right now."

"What?" Doubt actually does enter my mind now. Not because I think Adrian's hiding something, but because urgency like this—desperation of the sort I hear in his voice—can only lead to mistakes. "Adrian, slow down. Tell me what happened."

"They've got my friend. They've—" His eyes dart wildly as he brings his hands down on top of his head. There's a hoarse whistle in his shallow breaths, and he has to crouch to steady himself. "They'll destroy him if we don't get him out of here."

"Wait, what? I thought you said these were good guys."

"I said I *didn't know* if they were good guys." He grimaces. "I still don't know. I don't . . ." His face pales. Beads of sweat appear on his brow, and I fear he really will pass out if I don't do something. I grab his shoulders.

"Hey, it's all right," I say softly. "Focus on me. Breathe. Slow. That's it." A pause. A flash of Adrian, slowly regaining calm under my instruction.

But not here. Not now.

We've done this before.

"Did we . . . know each other? In the Metro?"

"Huh?" He opens his eyes. Tears spill out, and the question vanishes from my lips. No more questions about the past, or good guys and bad. Only the extinguished blaze of Adrian's smile, and how to get it back.

I take a steadying breath. "What do you need me to do?"

■ ■ ■

A COUPLE STEPS UP TO ME, THEIR YOUNG BOYS CHASING EACH OTHER AS THEY weave between their parents, like planets orbiting twin suns. They couldn't be more opposite—the woman fair-skinned and slim, her husband dark and broad. But their matching grins tell me they belong to one another.

"What have you got for me?" I reflect their calm expressions. But inside, I'm twitchy. Over the crowd's heads, Adrian disappears into the woods to retrieve his friend.

The man reaches into his satchel and pulls out a folder.

"Pictures," he says with a quiet reverence.

I take the folder from him gently and peer inside. There's the couple before children—younger, with eyes shining brightly as they till the village's crops. Someone snapped a picture of them in a sweet embrace, framed by the branches of a dogwood tree in spring. Another photo, the second before the woman dumps a jar of water on her sleeping partner's head. Then their wedding ceremony. Later comes the babies: one soft and roly-poly, his brother long and lean. And the new parents are visibly exhausted. But even though their eyes have bags under them now, they still shine bright. And there are giggles and tantrums and quiet moments alone and louder moments together under that same dogwood. A masterpiece of a life.

"These are so, so beautiful. Thank you for sharing them with me." My eyes brim with genuine tears. "Could I . . . do something a little special for you?"

They lock eyes before nodding. I glance again at the spot

where Adrian ducked into the trees. *Here goes nothing.* I address the crowd. "This family has faced danger, uncertainty, and sadness. But they've managed to make it through to the other side with unbridled joy. And while it's plain on their faces"—I pause to let the couple break out into gorgeous, albeit predictable, grins—"it's a joy that's hard to find, and even harder to seize. Until now." The clock tower looms over the square. Only five minutes until Adrian said I had to meet him, before Harcourt gets back with a tool kit. But the way the crowd is hanging on my every word, I'm starting to think we might actually pull this off. "Will you do me a favor, my friends? When you listen to this song—our grand finale—make it real for yourselves. Remember the moments of your own lives where you felt even a fraction of the happiness you hear. Close your eyes. Embrace it."

"Eyes closed?" A teen boy arches an eyebrow.

I smile sweetly. "I know it sounds strange. But sometimes what we see distracts us from what we feel. Noah, how often do you close your eyes to play?"

"Almost always," he concedes.

This convinces the group. I nod to Noah, and he tucks his violin under his chin. He shuts his eyes.

I begin my opus. I use the pictures, yes. But I also summon every drop of visceral emotion I can muster from the depths of my being. The warmth I feel for Noah, Candace, and the other villagers. Wonder at the woods and the brilliance of Icarus's mind. And so much care for Adrian—his tenderness, his stubbornness. His virtue. The feelings are powerful, both heavy and light, and I swirl them all into a tidal wave that

I hope Noah can translate. He rises gloriously to the challenge, swaying his body as he feels his way through the legato
melody. The crowd is captivated; some have tears streaming
from their closed eyes. I take in the scene one last time, of
these magnificent people who put so much faith in joy—and
me—to get them through the hard winter to come, memories
everlasting.

I make sure no one's watching. And then I run.

The wind in my ears distorts Noah's melody as I sprint silently through the square. I'm over the clearing and almost to
the tree line when my screen beeps—connection lost. Noah's
music stops; soon they'll be searching for us. I push myself to
fly faster as the smooth ground becomes a floor of pine straw
and thick roots. One misstep could be the difference between
getting caught and making it out alive.

"Liv!" Adrian shouts, and I veer toward his voice. The trees
part to reveal him astride a two-wheeled vehicle with an odd
side compartment. Something is slumped over in the compartment. Something . . . alien. My steps falter.

"This is your friend?" I ask, still several meters away from
him. A hazy warning sounds from the locked attic of my mind.
"He's . . . different."

"Yes, he's my friend," Adrian says. His voice is strained. Is
it the stress of the escape, or is he hiding something? Or both?
"I know he's not like us, but we can trust him. I promise I'll
explain soon."

My eyes shift between the thing-person and Adrian, un-
certain. A twig snaps. More sounds of branches underfoot,
under many feet. They're moving quickly.

"Liv. Please." The words are barely more than a breath. I lock onto Adrian's eyes, full of fear but also full of a desperate hope that I'll go with him. He's clinging to me in the face of, what? Danger? Or something worse? A suspicion is strengthening inside me that this is all going to end very badly. But one look at Adrian and I've made my choice. He needs me. He loves me. And I love him. I swing my leg over the cycle, and we zoom toward Mount Barton. Whatever Adrian's afraid of, we'll face it head-on. Together.

30

ADRIAN

WE FLY UP THE MOUNTAIN, RACING OVER THE LIGHT FROST THAT'S BEGUN TO form on the road. I check behind us at every switchback, but no one's chasing us. Good. I've got enough to think about. Primarily, that I'm about to arrive at the top of a mountain in the Outerlands with an enemy of the state who, in all likelihood, is about to be mega pissed at me. Last week, I would've reviewed my training at this point, made sure I remember enough hand-to-hand combat to neutralize her if she attacked. But that was last week.

When I'm not worrying about how many of my ribs Liv's going to break once she remembers everything, or whether the Haveners are planning an ambush at the peak, I focus on Nas. I guess Harcourt wasn't lying when he said he wasn't super techy. If he'd known how much Nas's data core could fetch him on the black market, he'd have sliced him open and yanked it out of the base of his skull casing in a heartbeat. I'm not familiar enough with droid technology to know if my partner will be alright after being off the network for this long, but if the core—the part that makes Nas, Nas—is still intact, we have a shot at bringing him back.

The road ends in a parking lot, about twenty meters below the peak. I cut the engine and the silence overtakes us. Another quick glance down the mountain—we're still not being followed. Maybe Reem and her people will just let us go? I relax a little. Here above the tree line, there's no birdsong, no rustling leaves or babbling streams. Just the whistle of the wind, and the prayers in my head. *Please let her stay. Or if she can't stay, let her remember this part, too.*

Liv catches me watching her. The sinking sun reflects in her hair and eyes, setting them on fire. She misreads my expression for something else, and then the fire in her eyes is lit from within too. She lifts her face. I wish I could let myself enjoy this kiss.

"Did we know each other? In the Metro?" Even hours later, the question stops me cold. I go still as her lips touch mine.

She pulls away with a quick smile, then turns to Nas, slumped in the sidecar. "Should we bring him up with us?"

I shake my head. "Too heavy. He'll be all right here."

"Are you sure? What if you switched him on so he can walk on his own?" I almost chuckle. Even worse than Old Liv trying to kill me would be Old Liv trying to kill me *and* Nas trying to kill her. As much as I want to know if my friend is okay, it's better to wait until we're back in the Metro, so Liv can get to safety first. The murkiness of my plan terrifies me. Can I really protect her from the Force forever?

Liv waves a hand in front of my face. "Anybody home? Don't make me kiss you again."

"Wait, that's all it takes?" I slacken my face and stare off into the distance. When she doesn't take the bait, I lean toward her slightly. "Any day now," I mumble through puckered lips.

She gives me a peck, then laughs. I wish I could bottle the sound.

"Come on, sun's setting. This could be it!"

With a twinkle in her eye, she begins the short, steep hike to the peak.

"This could be it," I repeat, and follow.

We're panting when we reach the top. The view is absolutely breathtaking. Mount Barton is the southernmost peak of a range of mountains that extend in a northwest arc. Now, each of them glows fiery orange in the sunset, like a string of embers. Behind us, the Metro's chrome opulence ripples in the sunlight—more mirage than city.

"Wow," I say.

Liv nods reverently. "Wow."

I glance down the slope to make sure Nas remains safe, then sit on a flat rock that's wide enough for both of us. Liv takes in the view. She teeters for a moment, like she's standing at the edge of an abyss. This must be overwhelming for her, to see such vastness when she knows so little of the world we come from. I take her hand and squeeze. I'll be her anchor, for as long as she lets me.

The last hints of sunlight disappear over the horizon, and we wait for true night. Liv hugs her knees to her chest, shivering. I grab our sweaters, then point to a trio of stars, the first to appear.

"Looks like a slice of carrot cake," I say.

She laughs, then gnaws the inside of her cheek. I rub her shoulder. "More stars will come."

She nods, looks toward Nas. "Do you think they'll forgive you?" I wait for her to be more specific. I've done a lot of things that need forgiveness, from a lot of people.

"The Haveners," she clarifies. "For stealing your . . . friend."

The Haveners' forgiveness is solidly in the middle of my Reasons Adrian's a Piece of Shit list, if not somewhere toward the bottom. But I humor her.

"Dunno. Does it matter? We're headed to the Metro, right? Not back there."

Liv checks the sky. A couple of faint twinkles, but it's barely dusk.

"We *might* go back someday," she says. "And even if we don't, you like them, right? You wouldn't want them to hate you forever, even if you never see them again. That matters."

She's right. I'm slowly learning to accept the fact that as soon as Liv regains her memory—whether it's tonight or a month from now—the best place for her will be as far from me as possible. Which means I'll have no chance to explain myself or apologize for lying to her every second of the past week. We'll live out the rest of our lives in two separate orbits. And she will, most likely, hate me forever.

"It does matter," I say, more to myself than to her. "The truth is, I kind of always assumed they'd hate me eventually. As soon as they figured out who—*what* I really was. A relationship between Haveners and those in my profession . . . doesn't work."

"Bodyguards have strong opinions about outsiders, huh?"

"Something like that."

She leans her head on my shoulder. "What if the Haveners knew you were born in the Outerlands?"

I shrug. "I've spent fifteen years in the Metro. I'm more a product of that place than anywhere else."

"Well . . . maybe the way they met you makes a difference. They got to know you for *you*."

I can't have this conversation right now. My stomach is in knots. Liv is right, but she's also so wrong. Things aren't that simple—not between Haveners and Forcemen. Not between me and her.

The warmth of her head on my shoulder scalds me, like a brand marking me for my crimes. I'm about to wrench myself out from under her, when she lifts her head on her own and gasps. I look up.

Stars.

A blanket of them, as vast as an ocean. It feels like I'm standing at the edge of the glittering bay, instead of staring up at the sky. I sway at the expanse of all that light, in all its contradictions. The beauty is grand, but also so simple. I feel like the tiniest speck of nothing. I feel like the luckiest guy on the planet.

"I want to keep this," Liv whispers, her eyes pinned on the heavens. Her face is glowing so brightly I wonder if one of the stars fell and landed beside me.

Me too, I think. How is it possible for someone to change your life so completely in only one week?

She glances down at her screen and fumbles with the controls.

"Nero, record Scrap," she says. Her screen chirps in the affirmative. I freeze.

"What?" Liv asks.

"How did you know to say that? To call it that?"

She pauses, frowns. "I'm . . . I'm not sure."

An earsplitting screech from above. The source is almost impossible to see against the night sky, but then a winged streak of black cuts across the white of the stars. Icarus circles the top of the mountain, his spirals getting closer as his cries echo. I skitter toward the peak's edge. I can't make out any Haveners, but that doesn't mean they're not there. And if their group's big enough to surround us, we're fritzed.

"We have to get out of here," Liv says, reading my mind. She takes my hand and we run for the cycle, gravel and dust flying as we go. One hand grips the chilled rubber of the handlebars, and I think we're home free, until I see them. Shadows emerging from shadows. Dozens of faces shrouded in darkness. Icarus screeches as he makes his final descent, so close that the wind from his wings ruffles my hair. He disappears into the black and lands on one specter's shoulder.

"Always trust a Forceman to steal and deceive," Reem's voice sneers.

"You stole him first," I shout at her. Strong words, but my shaking voice betrays me. Liv clings to me, fear rattling her breath. I slowly reach across my body with one hand.

Somewhere to my left, Noah makes a *tsk* sound. "Another

blaster hidden somewhere? I urge you to reconsider, Adrian. I assure you that you are outmatched." The cold click of a blaster's safety latch sends my heart into my throat.

He's wrong, though: it's not a blaster I'm reaching for. Why would I need such a tiny weapon, when there's an enormous one right behind me?

If only he'd wake up.

I feign like I've heeded Noah's warning and clutch my wrist instead of my holster. I find the button on the side of my screen, the one for Nas's beacon, and mash it until my thumb aches. Out of the corner of my eye, I can see the three green LED lights behind his ear flash once, then start to blink. It's working. But will it be fast enough?

"We don't want to hurt you," Liv says. That earns her a chorus of sucked teeth and skeptical scoffs.

"Oh no? That why you send your robodogs to ruin our food supply right before the first snow every year? Why so many of our children go missing each summer?" Kenji's voice calls out with surprising sharpness.

Liv and I frown at each other. *"What?"* I shout.

What the fritz is he talking about?

Suddenly Reem's hesitance toward outsiders and the locks on Kenji's pantry make sense. He's not protecting their food from other people in the Haven. He's protecting it from the raiders—the *real* raiders. LifeCorp, and my team. Another tumbler in the lock slides slowly into place: me as a toddler crammed in a truck with other young children, the Forcemen who helped us when we arrived at the Metro.

I wasn't abandoned. I was *taken.*

My head swims. The questions will have to wait. Nas's foot twitches; he's rebooting. I just need to buy us a little more time.

"We're going back to the Metro." I swivel, desperate for anyone in the crowd to listen.

"That's right," Liv adds. "And we swear, we'll stay out of your way—"

"Until you tell your Forcemen buddies exactly where we are, and how to get into our stores," Kenji says. The pain I feel at his accusations surprises me. I bury it.

"Kenji. Please. Once we're home, I can help. I can send more supplies—"

"We don't want anything from you," Harcourt spits out. The shadows edge closer, weapons glinting in the starlight. Liv and I step toward the cycle. She's trembling now. I'm terrified too, but I hold her close. "It'll be okay," I lie. Two of Nas's three lights glow bright green as the third continues to blink. *Almost there.*

Noah steps forward until we can see his face, at last. Sympathy flashes as he regards Liv, but at the sight of me, his gaze hardens to cold steel.

"Give him up," he says.

"I only want to get him home. He's hurt."

"He's a droid."

I lift my chin. "He's my friend."

"Droids don't have friends," shouts Harcourt.

A mechanical whirring behind us, so quiet anyone unfamiliar would mistake it for the wind.

"Dumb *and* ugly," Nas says. "What a pity."

I tackle Liv to the ground and out of the way as Nas jumps out of the sidecar, raining smoke and rubber bullets on the Haveners. As I cover Liv's body with my own, I pray the Haveners don't do something stupid, like retaliate. Nas's programming prohibits him from firing anything lethal, as long as his targets haven't used force against him. If Noah and Kenji can get their tempers in check, they might actually survive. And against my training, I want them to.

Seconds later, Harcourt yells, and blaster fire lights the mountain up. *Dammit.* Liv screams and I drag her behind a nearby boulder as Nas lifts his arm. I can't see Nas's attack, but I hear the Haveners' screams as they flee, hear the blaster beams shred the trees. My eyes sting as my nose fills with the cloying smell of tear gas. *Please, let them all make it out.* I don't know who I want to win. But if anyone gets seriously hurt, we'll never have any chance at peace.

When the smoke clears, I make sure Liv's okay, then peek over the boulders. The Haveners are gone. There are no bodies in the woods, no sign of blood. A minor miracle. I run to where Nas kneels, still operational but in bad shape.

"'In and out in less than a day,' my ass. What'd you do, go rogue?" He smirks at me, but his smile flickers when my own is unconvincing. I change the subject.

"Is that . . . your arm?" Behind him, a chunk of metal twitches on the ground. Nas examines the sparking socket where his shoulder should be and chuckles. "Who knew the raiders had blasters that could do *that*? Grab it for me?"

"Yeah, sure." I jog to the detached limb, pick it up, and

freeze. Nas has gone perfectly still. The fans in his processor speed up as he senses a new visual input.

"Hands up! You're under arrest," he booms.

Liv jumps up, confused. "What? No, I'm—agh!" She slumps to the ground. Her face is crumpled in pain as she clutches her chip.

With his available hand, Nas pulls out his blaster and trains it on her. "Target is uncooperative."

I don't have time to explain, or plan, or even think. All I see is Liv, helpless on the ground, and Nas's blaster pointing at her face, and there's no other choice but what comes next. I drop Nas's arm and sprint toward him, digging my hand like a blade into the exposed wires at the back of his neck. I find his data core and yank hard. The shell of his body slumps to the ground.

"I'm sorry, man. I had to. I had to." I pocket the core. Someday we'll laugh about this. I hope. Movement above catches my eye. A shooting star?

A satellite. Liv cries out. Suddenly her episodes and offhand comments over the last week make sense. With every rotation around the Earth, this machine has been redepositing bits of memory in her mind, slowly sealing our fate.

Liv groans as she writhes in pain. I sprint toward her. Her eyes are shut tight, but she reaches one hand toward me.

"What's happening?" I ask, as if I don't already know. As if avoiding the truth might leave space for some other reality to enter.

"Everything." The word grinds out slowly from behind

her clenched teeth. "I can't . . . tell . . . what's real . . ." Her
hand clasps my arm like she's grabbing a lifeline. I pull her up
so she's half sitting, cradling her in my arms. She buries her
head in my chest as she cries. I check the sky, searching for
the satellite like it can offer any help, but it's gone. In place
of the slow-moving white light is a frantic flashing of red and
blue, careening through the sky. A Forceman copter. Nas must
have signaled it when he spotted Liv. The idea of returning to
that world, of seeing Liv locked up by people I used to trust,
makes my stomach turn. We should run. But if I can see them,
they've spotted us too. It's too late.

"You're real. And I'm real. I promise this has all been real."
I say the words over and over, hoping they sink in. It's not just
Liv's pain my voice has to overcome, not just her cries, but
every memory that's come flooding back, every neuron and
synapse that tells her what someone like me is supposed to
be: cold and heartless. Whatever she thinks of me from this
point on, I need her to remember that I was real with her, in
every way that mattered. My love was real.

The copter's so close I can hear the propeller now. The
full reality of what I've done to Liv hits me. The decisions I've
made for her. The future I've trapped her in.

"I'm sorry. I'm sorry, I'm so sorry." I rock her gently.

"Adrian?" she whispers, still terrified. Her eyes fly open,
and there's a battle waging inside them. They flicker between
the brightness of the girl I've come to know, and something
darker, shrewder, that sizes me up instantly.

This is it. I'm losing her.

So I kiss her, slow and deep. A kiss, I pray, that's strong enough to hold this version of her here, no matter how her old memories demand control. The trembling in her chin quiets. We pull apart.

And then her fist connects with my jaw.

31

LIV

IF I LIVED A THOUSAND LIFETIMES, I'D SPEND ALL OF THEM DESTROYING ADRIAN Rao. Each lifetime could be reserved for a different form of punishment. One for drowning. One for dropping him off tall buildings. And one for punching, because the hit I landed on the top of Mount Barton, before the copter landed, and they swarmed me, felt *so good.*

So maybe two lifetimes for punching.

A robo-dog enters the custody office, a VitaBar packet clipped to its back. They stopped sending actual officers with my meals a few days ago, once the third one came back with a black eye and a bruise on her face in the shape of a vitamin-fortified brick of kelp. The bot enters the cell through the mechanized doggy door and waits patiently for me to take the food. I groan and lean my head on the wall, starting the five-minute timer in my head. I guess legally they have to offer me the meals, but I'm tired of the game. I haven't been able to talk to anyone since being detained. And my stomach rumbles for Kenji's cooking. This feels like the cruelest joke. Archiving my memory was supposed to be an escape from the Metro's oppression. Instead, my mistake cost me my freedom, literally trapping me within LifeCorp's system.

At the two-minute mark, another compartment slides open on the bot, revealing an injector of Mean. Condensation beads on the vial, brightening its aquamarine glow. *Teal? That's new.* I can't deny the fact that part of me practically starts salivating at the sight. But I'm not the same person I was a week ago. Mean isn't the key to our happiness; it's simply another one of LifeCorp's tools. And it controls us far more effectively than any Forceman ever could.

Four minutes and thirty seconds. "You want me to eat? Bring him to me," I say to the bot's camera lens eyes. It's all I want, all I've asked for since they dumped me here. I glared at Adrian the entire ride back to the Metro, bored a hole in his head with the heat of my hatred. But he couldn't even do me the courtesy of looking at me, not once. The coward. I need to see him so that I can make it clear that I never, ever want to see him again.

Two more days pass. Hunger gnaws a hole in the center of my body. Interrogator droids ask me questions through the bars of my cage—about Silas, about the Riveras, about the Haveners. They wait for me to speak, or for my pulse to race or heat to crawl across my chest and give me away. I say nothing, betray no one. Later, in the middle of the night, I can't sleep. I pass the time by counting the beats of the mysterious dripping noise on the other side of the room. Somewhere around 1,400, the door to the room creaks open. A tall, slender silhouette slinks down the stairs, a hololantern balanced on his palm. I don't move as he approaches my cell, just keep staring at the ceiling, arms folded across my chest.

Adrian stands on the other side of the bars. He looks, to put it delicately, like total shit. Like he hasn't been eating or sleeping much. Good.

"Um . . ." He shifts on his feet. *Um?* As if it's not enough to take my dignity, now he has the nerve to be shy? "Liv?"

Drip. "Fourteen hundred and forty-two."

Silence. Then "Liv, please."

Drip. "Fourteen hundred and forty-three."

Silence. More silence. Is that really all he's got?

Drip. "Fourteen hundred and forty-four."

"I'm— Sorry doesn't even begin to cut it. I . . ."

Drip. I wait for him to go on, but he doesn't. Stunned, I lift myself on to one elbow. *Drip.* "That's it? That wasn't even a full apology. It was the *implication* of an apology. God, you— and you made me lose my count. Get fritzed."

Our eyes lock for the first time since I became myself again. He's shaved since we got back. The new smoothness of his face is yet another thing that makes him feel like a stranger. The bones in my jaw threaten to split, I'm clenching my teeth so hard. Anger crackles inside me like a bonfire. I don't care if it consumes me whole eventually; I only need to survive long enough to get my revenge. I tear my eyes from Adrian and look toward the ceiling. The heat creeping along my skin fades.

"Uniform suits you," I say, referring to his white and gray tactical armor, the LifeCorp logo etched on the left breast. He lets out a breath of laughter, and the hairs on my arm stand up.

"Something funny?"

"Just that I've never felt less like I belonged in these clothes."

I suck my teeth. "Uh-huh."

"I'm serious," he whispers, eyeing the surveillance camera in the corner. "I spent my whole life believing I was preserving peace and prosperity. But after . . . everything in the woods . . . I don't think that's what we're preserving at all. Lowers spend every second of the day toiling for LifeCorp's bottom line. The Uppers may have credits, but nobody's happy, not like the Haven. And everyone just thinks this is the way life has to be."

I roll my eyes. This moment of growth would be a lot more believable if he hadn't spent the past week *lying* to me about literally everything. "Compelling stuff, Officer. Well, while you're on your path to enlightenment, some of us actually suffer the consequences of your choices. Thanks for giving Celeste the money for her mods, by the way. Now she can 'toil' like the rest of us. Sounds plenty prosperous to me." My voice wavers as I mention Celeste. Did she go through with the operation while I was gone? Part of me wants to beg Adrian to track down the answer, but I kill the impulse. I'm done depending on him.

"Celeste . . . I forgot about that." Adrian presses his lips together as his eyes close. "But that's exactly what I'm saying. Her life should be about so much more. We could be fighting for more."

"Not in that uniform, you can't. Let me guess, you want to 'change the system from the inside'? That's just something people say when they want to climb the ladder without feeling bad about it. You don't believe any of your 'epiphany.' Not really."

Adrian opens his eyes. "Fine. You don't have to agree with me."

"True. I don't have to do *anything* with you." My rage takes hold again, and I fly to the cell's bars. "Ever again." We're inches apart now. The flames of my anger lick my skin as I stare down this enemy who's witnessed me in my most naive state. At my most vulnerable. I let him see the hatred behind my eyes, and his face falls.

You hurt me, now I've hurt you. How does it feel?

"I get it, okay?" he says. "It was wrong to lie to you about who I was and why I was in the Outerlands. I'm sorry. You have every right to hate me."

"*Do* you get it, though?" I say, ignoring the pained warble in his voice. "Do you really? Because you talk a big game about changing, but so far, I'm the only one you seem to be extending that shriveled-up olive branch to. What about the thousands of other prisoners in the Metro? Or is your newfound quest only reserved for the ones you daydream of playing house with?"

He reels. "I don't—I didn't—"

"And by the way, saying 'I'm sorry'—which, it bears repeating, you *barely* did—isn't some magic spell that suddenly makes everything okay. Actions speak louder than words, Adrian. And I can hear you"—I gesture to the bars between us—"loud and clear."

I lift my chin, triumphant. But the same anger I'm nursing now burns in Adrian's eyes.

"What about you?" he asks, his voice low.

"What *about* me?"

He steps forward, and I have to let go of the bars to avoid touching him. "You wrecked Jonah Rivera, from the inside out. You screwed with his life—and his wife's—forever. But all you've talked to the interrogators about is vengeance against me. Where's Rivera's justice?"

The memory strains against the current of time, and everything that's happened since that night in the alley. Sobbing in the stairwell before Thea found me, wishing I could claw my chip out of my skull. I dig my nails into the flesh of my hand so I don't cry. It works, a little. "You have no idea how sorry I am about that."

"You can't have it both ways, Liv. You're either the same as me: all words and no action . . ." The briefest hesitation flickers on his face. "Or you're the heartless criminal I thought you were from the start."

And there it is. Whoever I was in the woods, she's gone now, sealed away in a lightless tomb. And Adrian's words placed the final stone.

"Guess you've figured me out, then," I say.

A faint buzzing from his wrist screen. I catch a flash of Redding's face before Adrian can hide it. Of course. Less than a week back in the Metro, and he's on the Force's leash again. The space between us is heavy with regrets. His, or mine? I face away from him, resting my forehead against the wall's cool metal.

When I turn around, he's gone.

32

ADRIAN

MY CONVERSATION WITH LIV PLAYS IN MY HEAD OVER AND OVER AS I CROSS the Citadel's courtyard, toward our LifeCorp-sponsored residential suites. Some cadets spot me from a distance and cheer across the lawn. The whole Force knows our story now, or at least the version of it I told in order to keep everyone as safe as possible: *Yes, Liv had her full faculties the entire time; she came willingly. No, we didn't run into anyone else while we were out there. And I'm not sure who tore Nas up, but they must have beat him up pretty bad for his data core to fall out on its own like that. Good thing I recovered it for him.*

How long will my lies hold up, with my guilt weighing me down?

My screen buzzes again. I groan when Redding's face appears beside the message icon. I can't keep ignoring him.

> *Redding: Any progress?*
> *Rao: Not yet, sir.*

I chew the inside of my cheek. If I don't show progress, Redding won't let me visit Liv again. That means I won't be able to get her out once I think of a plan.

Without me home to water them, my herbs have started to wither. I don't bother to tend them now, either. VitaBars are good enough when I remember to eat. As I pass the dying plants, I rip off my uniform, claw off my signet ring so I can finally breathe. I reach for some joggers and a white sweatshirt. In the sterile light of my apartment, the shirt looks almost blue—the same shade of blue as the sweater Liv wore in the woods, which is probably crumpled in some evidence bag in a metal locker somewhere. Almost every remnant of our week together—except for Liv's copy of *Walden*—is in custody. I couldn't bear to let them have that; it felt like locking up part of her soul.

I take the book with me everywhere, read it late at night when my self-hatred and my worry for Liv won't let me sleep. Hearing the author's descriptions of the woods, how communing with nature helped him see his life with perfect clarity . . . it makes me feel like I'm back there, with Liv and the breeze and her eyes shining brighter than any star. I write notes in the margins to help me remember.

der what
v thinks
kes a book
"true"?

To read well, that is, to read <u>true</u> books in a true spirit, is a noble exercise, and one that will task the reader more than any exercise which the customs of the day esteem.

YES!!

<u>Our village life would stagnate</u> if it were not for the unexplored forests and meadows that surround it. We

Look
this up

need the tonic of wildness,—to wade sometimes in marshes where the <u>bittern</u> and the meadow-hen lurk, and hear the booming of the <u>snipe;</u> to smell the whisper-

Tl

ing sedge where only some wilder and more solitary fowl builds her nest, and the mink crawls with its belly close to the ground.

Look, a bittern!

Adrian, you incurious buffoon, that is clearly a snipe!

The luxury of one class is counterbalanced by the indigence of another.

whoa

Whatever I can do to pretend I'm there, and not here.

Thoughts of Liv are everywhere I turn. I could pick anything in this apartment, or anything in the world, and my mind would find a connection to her. A bizarre game of chess played between me and my brain:

Plants, spices, Haveners, Liv. Checkmate.

Window, sky, stars, Liv. Checkmate.

Toothbrush, mouth, lips—

Enough. This isn't helpful. If I'm going to figure out what the fritz to do about the mess I've made, I need sleep. Or whatever passes for sleep these days.

■ ■ ■

FIVE HOURS LATER, I'M BACK IN UNIFORM, WALKING INTO THE CITADEL, WHEN my screen chirps. Redding wants to see me.

"How are you, son?" he asks as I enter his office. It's the first time someone's asked me how I'm doing since I got back, and the question catches me off guard. "A little, uh—"

"Like someone's put your ass on backward, eh?" He laughs, gesturing for me to sit. "I felt the same way after my first extended stay in the field. Really scrambles you for a bit. It'll pass."

Will it, though? There's been a thick knot in my stomach ever since we arrived at the Haven, a feeling that maybe the truth is different—or at least bigger—than what LifeCorp has led me to believe my whole life. Now I know how the communities in the Outerlands are plundered by the side I *thought* was good. Now I know that *I* myself am part of the bounty they steal.

"You wanted to see me, sir?"

His brown eyes twinkle. "Got a new mission for you, Rao, if you think you're ready?"

Strangely, his words bring relief. If Redding's got a new assignment for me, he still trusts me. The hairline cracks in my façade haven't yet begun to show.

"Absolutely, sir. What's the situation?"

"Orange Haze."

"Sorry, sir . . . Isn't that already my mission?"

"Same objective, new strategy. We've tried eradicating the threat of Orange Haze by targeting its distribution. While it's certainly of note that there have been no new incidents since Newman's disappearance last week, we can't be sure other dealers won't pop up soon."

I nod. "Of course." My toes curl in my boots. During my

debrief, I told Redding I didn't learn anything new about Orange Haze while we were out in the woods. Lying was my only choice. What if Redding found out the drug he's after is nothing but a natural reaction to Liv's Scraps—and the way she sees the world because of all the books she's read—rather than something lab-made? Instead of being one of many potential dealers, Liv would become the drug's sole manufacturer. Then getting rid of Orange Haze would be as easy as getting rid of her. Not an option.

"So we're switching gears," Redding continues. "While we work to weaken our enemies' defenses, we can strengthen our own position."

"Strengthen?"

He pulls a large black case from beneath his desk and unlatches it. Under the fluorescent lighting glisten hundreds of vials of teal Mean, identical to the one that Nas gave Jonah Rivera before Liv's attack.

"I call it Ambrosia." Redding's face glows luminescent turquoise from the vials' reflection. "Employee Care says it enhances compliance by up to eighty percent. A new resource in our arsenal."

Enemies. Defenses. Arsenal. He speaks like we're at war. Maybe we are.

"Excellent, sir." I swallow the bile in my throat. "What would you like me to do with these?"

"Our pilot program in the Towers has been astonishingly successful. We're ready to roll this out to every Arcade in Boston. You'll oversee distribution and ensure the transition goes smoothly."

"Smoothly?"

"There have been reports of a few . . . adverse side effects. Rare, of course." His jaw ticks. "No matter. I've assigned you to sectors one through ten, as well as twelve and thirteen."

I frown. "What about Sector Eleven?"

"Market Research has decided that Eleven needs a more . . . organic approach." Redding waves a dismissive hand. "Something about regional differences in receptiveness to institutions. We've got someone on it. Anyway—" He closes the case with a *snap* and thumps the outside loudly. "If this rollout goes well, there's plenty more where that came from. Employee Care is riding Research and Development hard to make enough of this for the entire Metro. This is only the start."

Something he said earlier prods at me. "Sir, these side effects—"

"Irritability, indigestion, the odd bout of psychosis . . ." He continues to list horrendous symptoms. The puzzle comes together. What Liv did to Rivera wasn't right, but his extreme reaction—the way he smashed the bottle on his head to get the voices out—wasn't because of her. This new Mean, Ambrosia, poisoned his mind, made the ghosts in Liv's memories a vivid reality he couldn't ignore.

"Anyway, if you could see this week's productivity scores from workers in the Towers, Rao, trust me, you'd agree it's worth it."

Worth it for who?

"One last thing." He purses his lips, suddenly serious. "We've tried being gentle with Newman, as you suggested, but I'm getting impatient. I've put in a request for a Verch pod. If she doesn't talk soon, let's increase pressure, hmm?"

"I . . . What?" My heart pounds in my ears.

"I know she's cute, but don't go soft on me, son. You've always been a team player. Loyal, almost to a fault. If we win this one, I see a promotion in your future. Can I count on you . . . Sergeant?"

Redding slides a vial of the teal poison across the desk, and I hold it under my palm. I'm tempted to smash it.

Ambrosia, Orange Haze, Liv. Checkmate.

33

LIV

I'VE FINALLY GIVEN IN TO A FITFUL SLEEP WHEN THE DOOR ABOVE THE STAIRS opens again. The same lanky silhouette with the same bouncing black coils descends the stairs.

I grit my teeth. "Come to twist the knife a little deeper into my back?"

Adrian says nothing in response, but the look in his mournful brown eyes ratchets up to the highest level of "puppy dog."

"Oooh, good, that's very good," I say, shifting my jaw. "Practice that face. Maybe Silas will let you off with debilitating torture instead of killing you outright. Kez too."

The corners of Adrian's mouth twitch down. "And you'll watch, I suppose?"

"No." I lift my chin defiantly, ignoring the flicker of hope in his eyes. "I'll help." I glare at him with an intensity that should wither him on the spot. But he doesn't move, just stands there, staring.

"What?"

He takes a step closer to the bars between us, and I feel the tiniest increase in temperature from his body heat. "How does it work, exactly?" he asks softly. "Do you remember everything from . . . before?"

The question wheedles its way into me like an injector full of Mean, uncovering the thoughts I've been working hard to ignore. The truth is I remember it all, and my feelings for him aren't even the deepest betrayal. When we were in the Outerlands, Adrian let me believe the world could be something beautiful, even though he knew better. He let me love my life, and I hate him for it. When my memories came back and I saw myself for what I truly am, what LifeCorp made me: one replaceable cog in its ever-grinding machine . . .

He doesn't deserve any of me after what he did.

"No. I barely remember anything," I say, my face hardened steel. "Except your lies."

"One lie. One."

"That you told repeatedly. Let's not get into technicalities, Officer." My heart jumps at what his words imply, that everything else about the last week might have been true. But it doesn't matter. He's a Forceman, and I'm . . . me; what are we supposed to do from my prison cell?

"Why *did* you do it, Liv? Erase yourself like that?"

My breath hitches. The answer feels impossibly heavy, too big for this tiny cell. A few days ago, Adrian would've been the only person in the world I could explain myself to. Now he's worse than a stranger. I study the pinched skin between his eyebrows, the way his chest broadens with every slow inhale. All the way down to his waist, and the Taser that's a hair's width unclipped. He's smart enough not to make a mistake like that, which means it's not a mistake. What the fritz is he doing? Does he think letting me escape is going to win me over? That we'll ride off into the sunset together?

Moron.

"Fine," Adrian says. "Maybe I don't deserve to know why. But whatever happens from here . . . it *was* real, Liv." His voice cracks, but I'm too busy plotting my next move to acknowledge his words. Let him blubber on the cold cement floor. Maybe they'll even give him the courtesy of a mat.

I step up to the bars, opposite Adrian. His breathing slows, lips slightly parted. Those *damn* eyelashes flutter as he raises his eyes to mine. . . .

"I love y—"

Liar.

Before he has time to say anything else that only half of me wants to hear, I slip my hand through the cell's electric barrier. The pain is excruciating, but only for a second, as I grab the Taser and use it on the electric lock. Then the cell is open, and the pain is gone.

For me, that is.

Adrian doesn't even move into a defensive stance as I punch him in the gut. Still, it hurts me to hurt him—probably just my temporal lobe enhancements artificially magnifying my empathy. Whatever the reason, I can't bring myself to land another blow. I shove him into my empty cell right as the alarm system's backup generators come online, trapping him inside and blaring an alarm that security's been compromised. Flashing emergency lights bathe everything in red.

"Don't you dare think, for one second, that we're even now," I say.

Adrian opens his mouth to speak, arms wrapped around his stomach, but I don't have time to listen. More importantly, I don't want to spend another second watching him writhe on the ground, when half of me wishes he weren't in pain and the other half wishes it were so much worse.

I hide in the shadows as I make my way to the Citadel's exit, only moving between flashes of the emergency beacon. A couple of turns in the labyrinthine halls, and then I'm outside, by the dumpsters behind the building. The Towers' lights glitter golden on the horizon. I wonder how Noah would transcribe the way my heart swells at the thought of returning home. But home will have to wait. The Towers are the first place the Force expects me to go. And anyway, I have a payment to collect, if I'm not captured first.

It's surprisingly easy to travel the mile between the Citadel and the Estates undetected, with everyone searching for me in the maze of the Towers. I cling to the darkness, scurrying from one pylon to the next under the elevated train tracks. I figure I've got about an hour before the Citadel's surveillance catches up with me. But there are almost no security cameras in the Estates, so if I play this right, I'll be long gone with a bank account full of Mr. Preston's credits before officers even check this direction.

I flip the Scrap of the stars over in my mind, examining it like a precious gemstone, as I near the Preston estate. A memory like this is unquestionably rare, and therefore valuable, but still, I doubt anyone else would pay as much as Preston has promised—*one hundred thousand credits.* My pulse quickens at the thought. As soon as the money is in my account,

I'm transferring it to Celeste so she, Thea, and Kez can get out of here and choose a different path for themselves. Even if Adrian and his oafs catch up to me, I'll know my friends will be living for something more.

The Prestons' complex is eerily dark as I approach—no lights anywhere. Jasmine flowers glow pale white in the night, bobbing gently with the breeze. I frown at the scene. A trap? No. A trap would have kept everything the same, luring me in with a false familiarity. Something else is going on.

The doors are locked, but there's a loose first-floor window on the side of the main house. I wiggle it open and slip inside. The empty rooms are pristine, guest-ready as ever, except for Mr. Preston's quarters. A used tumbler on a side table, a throw blanket out of place. And several stacks of discarded books on one desk, like he was sorting through them. Like he was leaving in a hurry.

Mr. Preston's not here, and neither is his money.

34

ADRIAN

BOTS WHIR THROUGH THE MEDICAL WING AS THEY PATCH ME UP. LIV GOT ME good; that one punch cracked some ribs, but it's nothing a bot's serum can't handle. I'm almost disappointed when the pain fades away like a bad dream. It was Liv's retribution for what I did to her, and it could've been—*should've* been—much worse.

People still smile at me in the hallway, but the adoration is gone now. In an instant, I managed to go from being a promising young upstart to a bumbling rookie again. Fine by me, as long as Liv's anywhere but here.

A droid I haven't seen before approaches from the other end of the hall. I give a polite nod, expecting him to pass. Instead, he crosses the hallway, beaming, with arms outstretched.

"Is that any way to greet the guy who saved your life?" His mouth lifts in a lopsided grin. "Where are your manners, rookie?"

I blink at him a couple of times, until the pieces snap into place. "Nas?"

His eyes—hazel now—warm to me. "Good to see you,

man." We embrace in a bear hug, before I push him back to get a better look at him. His new body is almost as tall as my six-foot frame, and even more muscular than his previous bulky build. Add his wide nose, rich brown skin, and strong chin, and I already know he'll be insufferable from now on. As if his ego wasn't bad enough before.

"I—good to see you too! But, uh . . . as long as we're comparing notes, I saved your ass first."

"My rescue was cooler, though. Points for style." He smiles, and I'm genuinely relieved. He's really okay. I've still got one potential ally in this mess. That is, if I can come clean about everything I've done.

"Redding briefed you on the new mission, I take it?" Nas asks. "It's wild down there, man."

"Down where?"

"R and D, in the basement. That's where they fixed me up. I could hear all the lab guys in the room next door, scrambling to put as much Ambrosia into as many cases as possible."

I take in his words. They're making Ambrosia *here*? Not in some LifeCorp lab? But then, of course they are. Redding would never let them go far. Control is everything to him. Ambrosia for the Lowers, promotions and accolades for me. The same leash in different colors.

"Right. R and D . . . in the basement." I nod. "Was heading down there now, actually."

"Without your partner? Still gunning for star pupil, huh?"

My thoughts race as we walk to the stairwell. We need time, for me to tell him what I've done and learned, for me to figure out what to do about the stockpile of Ambrosia sitting below our feet, threatening to ruin the Lowers' sanity even further. But with Redding's new mission and Liv on the run, more time isn't an option. Maybe I can—

"What's up with you?" Nas asks, a few steps ahead on the stairs.

"What? Nothing. What?" *Smooth as rusted metal.* We stop on the landing.

"Normally you'd be busting your ass trying to beat me to the basement, but you're like ten steps behind. So again, what's up?"

No more time for lies. But I can't find the words to tell him the truth either. Nas studies my face, then lets out a slow breath.

"Ever since we were assigned to each other, you've been obsessed with being better than me. But you can't be. Do you know why?"

I search for signs of aggression in his stranger's face, but there are none. "Why?"

"Two words: *discursive programming,*" he says. "Not only are my mental algorithms better than yours, but I can tell you *exactly* why I make the choices I do. No matter how complicated. I know my mind." His processors whir as he cocks his head. "In the last ten days, how often have you been able to say the same?"

My first reaction is to tell Nas to go fritz himself, but the anger only swells because he's right. I can't articulate who I am anymore, or what's driving my decisions. From the moment I met Liv, my actions have been one impulse after another. Like if I just keep moving, I won't have to face the contradictions, or what they mean.

"And as long as we're on the subject of my features, I've also always been equipped with full-circumference situational analysis," Nas says pointedly. My stomach sinks as his meaning becomes clear: He knows no one else was on the mountain that night. He knows it was me that pulled his data core.

"Nas. I'm . . . I—"

He brushes me off. "You don't have to explain anything to me. We both know your squishy little brain can't handle it." He claps a hand on my shoulder, his tone only slightly mocking. "As for me, I'd be happy to lay out in line-by-line detail why I continue to trust you, despite my sense that whatever you're planning isn't, strictly speaking, protocol. *You* are my prime directive, Adrian. Your mission and safety. Before your ego inflates to the size of this stairwell, technically every Force droid's prime directive is centered on their partner. But I like to think I lucked out. Because as muddled as your mind may be, I've never known your heart to miss its mark."

Again, Nas surpasses my expectations. I always think that all these battles are mine alone to fight. But Nas is my partner— my friend. So I tell him the whole truth. How Liv and I met, then met again, and how my love for her has upended everything I thought I knew. Nas listens, no questions asked.

And together, we plan.

35

LIV

ALL RIGHT, YOU SON OF A BITCH, WHERE THE HELL DID YOU GO?

In the last fifteen minutes I've turned Mr. Preston's office upside down, searching through his drawers, the papers on his desk, even the creaky cot in the adjacent back room. There's nothing—no hints at where he might have gone, not even a sign that he was packing to go anywhere in the first place. He's simply . . . vanished. Meanwhile, a pair of mechanical hands are clicking away at his computer, maximizing and minimizing windows, typing inane phrases like *engage market leaders*. Guess he didn't bother to tell LifeCorp he was leaving either.

Think, Liv. If you didn't want LifeCorp to find a message, where would you hide it? Mr. Preston's eccentric, but he's no cheat. He wouldn't send me on a dangerous mission and then abandon me.

Would he?

In the corner of the room, the air regulator dutifully puffs out a calming scent for the tenth time since I got here. My eyes drift to the methodically arranged books on the back wall's floor-to-ceiling shelves. I step up to the library, noting the cracked spines of the well-loved collection. How did Preston find time to read all these when LifeCorp demanded so much of their VP? I think of the last book I borrowed from here, the copy of *Walden* with the mysterious inscription from R: *"I went to the woods because I wished to live deliberately. . . ."* My fingers find the gap where *Walden* belongs alphabetically, and something catches my eye. The back of the bookshelf here isn't the same pale gray as its front; there's art printed on it. A painting? The rest of the books scatter to the floor as I uncover the design. Not a painting, but an enormous map of the night sky that extends to the shelves below this one. A golden overlay outlines various constellations over the stars. Even illustrated, the sight rouses a familiar yearning in me, pulling other memories from the woods with it like a dragnet.

I trace the designs with my fingers, and an item bulges under my hand. Frowning, I press again, confirming the unmistakable presence of something small and rectangular. Tearing at the poster reveals a tiny brown paper parcel underneath, maybe as long as my finger and twice as wide. I flip the small package over and almost drop it when I see the writing on the other side.

For Liv. Live deliberately.

I gasp. *A credit chip?* I rip the paper open clumsily, and my heart sinks. It's not my payment, but a memory card.

A shuffling sound down the hall. *Shit.* The Forcemen found me early. I kill the lights and think through my options for escape. This room is at the end of Preston's upstairs hall; the only way out is back where I came from. I position myself beside the door, my back flush against the wall, and wait.

Someone stumbles in the dark, and another someone shushes them. My blood runs cold. I'm outnumbered. The steps grow closer. I tense my muscles for attack, wondering for a second if maybe I shouldn't. What if the footsteps belong to Mr. Preston, or one of his servants? A creak in the floorboards jolts me to my senses. Anyone who belonged here wouldn't be skulking around in the dark.

I crouch low, like Kez taught me. The officers come closer, their footsteps just around the corner now. I squint hard, but the darkness yields nothing. I can't tell how many of them are here or where they're positioned. My best bet is to tackle the leader at the knees and run while the rest are distracted by the commotion. If I get the timing right, I may be able to send the first one barreling into his buddies.

Another creak outside the door. I push off with my legs and rush the person's knees. But it's not legs I hit. My forehead collides with something rock hard. Our hands grappling for one another, my attacker swears as he lands on his ass in the hall.

I know that voice.

"Hell was that? That's it, I'm getting out the flashlights." Thea sucks her teeth as a beam of light slices through the air. Her annoyance fades to a poorly masked chuckle as she sees both Kez and me gingerly rubbing our foreheads. Kez is blinking the world back into focus, while I wince at the knot already forming beneath my skin.

Celeste peers around Thea's side. She gasps. "Liv!" The pain in my head fades as she rushes to me. Her arms wrap around my neck—soft and warm.

"Your surgery. You didn't—?"

"I couldn't do it without you, Liv." She whimpers into my clothes. My shoulders slump with relief as I put an arm around her waist. I may not be back in the Towers yet, but I'm home.

"When she heard we were coming to find you, she pestered us till we let her come along," Kez says. "Well done, by the way. You've got the Citadel lit up like a damn Arcade."

"No thanks to you," I say over Celeste's head. Her presence is the only reason I dull the bite in my voice.

He laughs sheepishly. "We were gonna get around to rescuing you. Right, Thea? Weren't we just talking about—" His open mouth collapses into a thin line as he reads Thea's face: two point five liters of pure, unfiltered *Don't bring me into your foolishness.* Kez tries again. "But when Silas got out, he said the Forcemen were already scrambling to track you down. We headed to the Towers to lose them, then came here."

My mind snags on Kez's words. "When Silas 'got out'? From where?"

"They didn't tell you?" Thea helps me stand. "Y'all couldn't have been more than two floors from each other."

It takes me a second to comprehend. "They arrested him?" The air in the room vanishes as I imagine every horrible scenario at once. "No . . ."

"Few days ago. Liv . . . they put him in Verch for a day," Thea says softly.

I shake my head slowly. "All that time, I was right there. I could've helped him if only I'd known." *If only Adrian had told me.* Anger blazes in me at the thought of that liar lying again.

Uneven, shuffling footsteps approach us. I jump to my feet, but the rest of the group is calm.

"That'll be the boss," Thea says, a note of sadness in her voice. "He's a little slower after what they did to him."

Before I can ask her what she means, Silas turns down the hall, a slight limp to his steps. Pain has tightened the muscles around his eyes and mouth, but all that dissolves when he sees me. I run to him, taking in his dusty but impeccably tailored pants, his secondhand jacket that drapes awkwardly off his slanted shoulders. Both the clothes and the man have seen better days, and my heart breaks at the bruises and scars that adorn his skin. But there's no mistaking the man himself, whose laughter matches my own as we crash into a hug.

Silas Bekele, the Dagger of the Towers.

"You can squeeze me tighter than that, can't you, Livvy? May be a little banged up, but I'm not dead yet." Silas's laugh rumbles against my chest. Tears prick the corners of my eyes.

"Are you hurt? What did they do to you?" I whisper.

He shakes his head. "No need to dwell on the past. We've got work to do."

After one last squeeze and a pinky promise that we'll see each other soon, Celeste agrees to go with Thea back to the Towers, for her own safety. Silas fills me in on his latest plan. As he predicted, Sector Eleven is on the brink of collapse as the local crew continues to water down the Mean supply. Silas was prepared for this: he's got an extra stash of Mean hidden at an Arcade, right on the border between Ten and Eleven. He wants to march into Eleven with the Mean, touting himself as Sector Eleven's savior, on the condition that they swear fealty.

The job is straightforward enough, except for the one piece of the puzzle he won't let me have.

"But where did you get the Mean?" I ask, weaving to hold his avoidant gaze.

"A trusted source, with . . . shared interests." Silas says. "Livvy, you know how I appreciate you pressure-testing my schemes, but we've got five minutes until your face is on every Forceman bulletin in the Metro. Are you in?"

I fiddle with the memory card Preston left me, which is lodged safely in my pocket, not the credits he promised but surely some piss-poor excuse and an overly cerebral goodbye message. I'll watch it after I forgive him for letting me down. So maybe never.

I don't have Preston's credits. I don't have any other way to get Celeste and the others out of this lifestyle. So I don't have any other choice.

"I'm in."

"Thank goodness. You know I'm nothing without you." Silas smiles proudly, and I can't help but bask in his approval. He walks on.

Kez squeezes my shoulder. "We'll do great things once we control the Eleventh. Give people the lives they deserve."

The lives they deserve. I take in the sunken circles under Kez's eyes, remembering Noah and the other people our age at the Haven. Life there wasn't glamorous, or flashy. But it wasn't this—constantly striving and hustling for even an ounce of stability. Both options seem impossible; it's not like I can wave a magic wand and move everyone in my life to the Outerlands. But if we stay in the Metro, do our lives revolve around credits, productivity scores, VitaBars, and Mean forever? And will I always be watching over my shoulder for another Forceman attack?

Kez goes on. "For example, the life *I* deserve includes an apartment that doesn't smell like the Sector Thirteen canneries on a hot day. Let's dream big. What do you say?" He picks a sprig of jasmine off a vine and hands it to me. I take it, smiling. When I was alone in the woods, after I first wiped my memory, I could never have imagined having so many people who cared about me. My family. I'm still not sure the Metro has the future I dream of anymore, but wasn't this my dream too? To find my crew, find where I belong?

I let the jasmine's musky scent eclipse my doubts, and we head toward the Arcade to kick off Silas's plan, under a starless night sky.

36

LIV

WE TAKE THE ROUTE SILAS HAS MAPPED OUT, UNDER BRIDGES, THROUGH GUT-
ters, and along the darkened side streets that hardly anyone
uses anymore. Silas swiped us some extra RelaProxy uniforms
from Mrs. Preston's part of the compound. The pale pink
jumpsuits are snug on Kez and Silas and huge on me, but I
can't complain as long as the disguise works. It's not unusual
for RelaProxies to be sent out on errands in the middle of the
night; the handful of people we do run into quickly avert their
eyes, assuming we're engaging in some illicit tryst on behalf
of our clients.

The closer we get to carrying out this plan, the more it
gnaws at me. I'm still parsing everything that happened in the
Outerlands (everything that doesn't have to do with a certain
tall, dark, and lanky someone, anyway), but one thing I know
for sure now is that there's another way to live if we choose.
Maybe if Silas knew that, he'd think differently about using
LifeCorp's drug to subdue these people.

"I'm gonna drop back," I tell Kez. "Check on Silas." I glance
over my shoulder, where Silas limps about eight yards behind us.

Kez nods me back. As I approach Silas, I can hear his labored breathing, the faint grunts anytime he puts weight on his left foot. He's refused our help with walking, snapped at us whenever we slowed our pace. I erase the grimace of sympathy from my face before he can catch it. Damn the man's pride.

"I know you're fine," I say as I take his elbow. The tightened muscles around his eyes relax. "I wanted to review the plan."

"I *am* fine," he says, too quickly. "Your mere presence has me feeling a hundred percent again. But I wouldn't say no to a chat."

"Me neither." I squeeze his arm. The traffic noises ahead get louder; we're almost to the Arcade. "Boss, about this plan . . . maybe we should rethink it."

He frowns. "Don't tell me you're chickening out?"

"Never. But—Mean is *LifeCorp's* tool. Using it for our own gain might change things for a little while, but in the end, isn't it still their game we're playing?"

"Not just playing, Livvy." Silas smiles, and he's instantly ten years younger. "Winning. I want to win. More than that, I want to see *you* win. All four of you, in comfort and security. With everything you've ever wanted."

Memories beckon against my will: Dancing in the firelight. Smiling in a field of flowers. Kissing in the dark. "There's more out there. I've seen it. A different way to live." I picture the Haveners' shining faces. What could we build if we had joyful songs to keep us going instead of Mean? Love and connection instead of pleasure and greed?

"A different way, eh? Well, once we're kicking our feet up on a new leather chaise, you can tell me all about it."

Ahead of us, Kez freezes, then sprints behind a building. We follow him, managing to get out of sight seconds before a Forceman cruiser hums past. My heart hammers in my chest. *Way too close. And I was just getting somewhere with Silas too.* They keep pushing in on us—LifeCorp on one side, the Forcemen on the other—suffocating our dreams. How could Adrian be one of them, when the dreams we shared—dreams of finding a place where we belonged—seemed so real?

Not real, I remind myself. *Just convincing.*

Evading the Forcemen cruisers adds another twenty minutes to our route, but eventually the neon glow of the Arcade comes into view. The electronic music's bass thrums under our feet as we approach the back entrance. The door's cracked open, as Silas said it would be.

"Wait here," he says as we duck into the utility room. "I need to make a call."

"To who?" I step closer. "Silas, who are you working with?"

"I'll just be a minute." Silas leaves the room before I can press further. The door to the alley bangs shut. Kez gives me a shrug and flips a crate over to sit. He pulls out an injector vial of his own, filled with same teal liquid I was offered at the Citadel.

"You tried this yet?" he asks. "Mean two point oh. I got it from another Sprinter, who said it cut his delivery time *in half.* Ladies first?" He wiggles the Mean in my direction.

"No thanks," I say, remembering the violent withdrawal shakes my second night in the woods. "I'm . . . clean, actually."

"No shit?" He sounds almost amused. "What's that like?"

"It's . . ." *Painful. Beautiful. Tedious. Clarifying.* None of the words I can think of fit quite right. "Different."

Silas bursts back into the room, and Kez pockets the vial, still full.

"Okay, let's get to work," Silas says. He's sweating heavily, eyes looking everywhere but at us. "The dispenser by the bar had a fresh delivery this afternoon. Should be plenty to carry over to the Eleventh."

Kez's eyebrows rise sky high.

"We're going to *steal* the Mean from right under the patrons' noses?" I ask. "I thought there'd be an extra stash in a closet or something."

Silas gives a dismissive wave. "The people inside are so dazed, they won't even notice. Besides, once we're over the border into Eleven, folks there will rally to our cause." That's Silas: an incurable optimist. He continues. "Meanwhile, back here, the Citadel will disperse troops to deal with the ruckus. With more Mean, or some other methods."

I gape at him openly. This is not the man I know. The Silas I know, whatever else he may be, would never have talked so lightly about the Forcemen's abuses.

"How can you say that?" I ask. "Those same Forcemen had both of us behind bars this morning. And now you're teaming up with—"

Realization dawns, loud and sharp. It can't be. But it's the only thing that makes sense.

"They cut you a deal, didn't they?" I ask. "Let you out on

the condition that you do their dirty work. This whole plan is for them, isn't it, Silas?"

Kez's expression falls as his eyes swivel between us.

Silas steels his face. "I am not a man who is accustomed to captivity. All your talk of doing bigger and better is wonderful, Livvy. Pure poetry. But how are we supposed to do *any* of that, if our lives are not our own?" He steps toward me, eyes so sincere, and suddenly I'm eight years old again. "I'm not proud of what I did. But Inspector Redding made it very clear: if I don't get Ambrosia into Sector Eleven, I'll be locked up in Verch for years. That is not poetry, that is my reality. Now, will you help me?"

As long as I've known Silas, I've never seen this kind of vulnerability on his face. He's made various asks of me since I was a kid. But this feels different. He's not just asking. He's begging. And I would do anything for him. So I do.

It's half past two a.m. There's no one on staff at this hour; the Mean dispensers are self-serve, and patrons can connect their own neurochips to the wireless hub in the corner. "You are *powerful*. You can do *anything,*" a woman coos sexily over a driving beat. On every screen, the words WORK HARD. CHANGE THE WORLD pulse over a kaleidoscopic background.

We slip carefully into the main space of the Arcade, but honestly, it wouldn't matter if we had air horns tied to our boots. The patrons are walking zombies. Eyes glossy, mouths drooping open, everyone nodding to the beat like the living dead. I stare at them, seeing the madness with fresh eyes.

"Liv, focus!" Kez hisses between grunts as he and Silas

yank the dispenser from the wall. I tear my gaze from the patrons, blinking away the ache in the pit of my stomach. We get the back panel off the dispenser, and dozens of aquamarine vials of this new Mean shimmer in greeting.

Kez's eyes shift to Silas. "Think it'll be enough?"

"It better be." Gently, we stack the trays in Silas's duffel bag.

"I'll carry it, Boss," I say, before Silas has a chance to pretend he can handle the weight. He grabs my wrist, a little too tight. "No, let Kez carry it."

I frown. "Why? It's not *that* heavy—"

"Livvy . . ." He's watching me with a sad expression I can't quite pin.

"To be fair, it *is* literally my job to deliver things. I got it!" Kez hoists the bag onto his shoulder, a little too rough. It doesn't sound like anything breaks, but the vials inside clink loudly enough to get the attention of a handful of patrons nearby. Their heads snap toward the only thing that could shake them from their chemical-induced reverie. I hold my breath as they take in the scene—the dismantled dispenser, the bulging duffel bag on Kez's shoulder. Silas doesn't wait for them to put the puzzle pieces together.

"Go, go!" he shouts as the group runs toward us. Soon every patron in the Arcade is aware of our theft. Their stupor makes them clumsy, though, and a few drop off after being distracted by the screens again. But about a dozen Lowers pursue us doggedly as we overturn stools behind us.

"We can split up when we get outside. I'll take Silas. Kez, you make for—"

The wail of sirens stops my words cold, getting closer with

every second. They skid to a stop at the end of the alley. The patrol-car lights wash our bodies in red, stunning the Arcade patrons trailing behind us.

"Liv Newman, come out with your hands up!" a man's voice calls over a megaphone.

How did they know I was here? Unless . . .

I whirl on Silas. "What did you do?"

That same remorseful look. "Livvy . . ."

"What did you do, Silas?!" I wipe away angry tears.

"It was part of Redding's deal. We were never all going to make it. But *I* have to, Livvy. I have to. You're young. Once you're out, you'll still have plenty of life left to live. But Verch for me . . . if you only knew what I've seen, what they made me live through."

"No fritzing way," Kez whispers.

Hot tears spill onto my cheeks. This is the man I thought of as a father. Who took care of me, fed my stomach and my mind when I had nothing to offer. But now I see, his generosity only extended as far as his own selfish pursuits. Silas Bekele will cut down anyone who stands in his way, myself included.

The Dagger indeed.

Again, Forcemen call my name, but I'm not moving until Silas dares to raise his cowardly eyes to mine. Maybe that's why I don't notice Kez take a deep breath, lift the hood of his RelaProxy disguise over his head, and drop the duffel bag to the floor with a crash. The Arcade's front door swings open as he vanishes into the street, nothing but a blast of cold night air in his wake.

"Kez!" I shout into the wind.

"There!" the Forcemen yell as Liv Newman gives chase, a blur of pale pink zooming down an alley. They take off in pursuit of Kez, their chorus of sirens fading. I mouth a silent prayer. Kez is fast, but is he fast enough?

"Stupid boy!" Silas yells as he sinks to his knees. He unzips the duffel bag Kez dropped to reveal shards of glass and a spreading pool of sickly sweet–smelling Mean. I watch as Silas cuts his hands, rummaging through the bag for even one vial that hasn't been broken. His breathing becomes ragged as he realizes the plan has fallen apart.

"I can't, oh God, they're going to—" He stands again, the whites of his eyes blazing as he yanks at his collar, struggling for breath. And then he too flees from the Arcade, into the dark underbelly of the Metro. I wish I could feel sadness, or even anger, as I watch him go. But all I feel is an empty pity.

With the Forcemen's flashing lights gone, the aggravated patrons notice me again. The sugary smell of Mean drifts through the Arcade, jolting more of them from their daze and toward the duffel bag. They scramble over one another, tearing, biting, for even one drop of the liquid seeping onto the floor. I watch in horror. This is what LifeCorp and its methods have reduced us to—worse, this is what they *want* us to be. Mindless zombies hunting for their next fix. I was almost one of them, before the Haven. Before Adrian.

One of them is still standing and cocks his head at me, dull eyes searching my face.

Jonah Rivera?

I stare as he loses interest and walks into another room, surgical tape still shining on his stitches. Not yet fully healed, and he's already back where he began. My heart breaks for Mae. Does she even know he's here, wasting the little money they have on more Mean?

Enough. We can't live like this anymore. It's not worth it.

I step away from the mob, into the corner. The sensory hub digs into my back. I want to smash it to bits so it can't pump any more junk into our heads, can't numb us further to the world's beauty. But then I remember Reem's words in the market:

"It's the beauty within us that makes it possible for us to recognize the beauty around us."

The beauty within us.

The sensory hub pushes sensations out to the patrons, but where does it get them from? I mash the keys until I find what I'm looking for.

SELECT INPUT SOURCE:

DATACHIP

WIRELESS CONNECTION

Will this even work? Broadcasting joy helped the Haveners, but are we too far gone?

I hold my finger up to my temple and pair with the hub. I have to try.

The effect is instant, on the lights, the screens—everywhere. Gone are the harsh neons and strobing images. Now every wall hosts a piece of my heart, of memories I fashioned into a song of my own. Close-up, sweeping images of Celeste's gap-toothed grin as she shows me a new invention, and Thea singing low when I can't sleep. Raw emotion pulses under my skin like a current as I watch. Kez's loyalty and warm safety. The sorrow and devotion and hope I feel for the Towers. The wonder of the stars. The all-encompassing, soul-fortifying power of Adrian's love, of his belief in me. I even summon a strand of Noah's music, soft and melodic in my head, but it soars through the speakers and rumbles in my bones.

Outside, the puddles on the street transform from black to golden, cornflower blue, deepest crimson, depending on the images projected on the walls. The grunts of struggle near the duffel bag stop as dozens of sunken faces crowd the screens like starving whelps.

"What is this?" asks one man who's gaunt and angular with shaggy hair. His mouth falls open and his eyes go wide, glistening with unshed tears. I hold my breath as he slowly wanders the Arcade, taking in every sight and sound that I've poured myself into. He pauses in front of one screen—the field of daisies from the first time Adrian and I paired.

I say nothing as I join him, just take in the way the flowers bob, like a fragrant whitecapped ocean. A breeze rustles their petals, and the leaves of the surrounding trees. At the edge of the screen, if I squint, I can make out the wing of a very clever hawk circling overhead. The whole scene glimmers in golden light.

"I like this one best," the man says, his voice gentle, but laden with something powerful. "It feels like an invitation. Like a fresh start."

I watch the memory with him as Icarus flies in lazy figure eights before disappearing into the tree line. And I have to agree. It's time for something new.

37

ADRIAN

NAS AND I EMERGE FROM THE STAIRWELL, INTO THE CITADEL'S BASEMENT. THE ceiling here is lower than the tower's other floors, the walls a dingy beige instead of the Force's trademark white and chrome. The lack of the sleek grandeur makes my hair stand on end. The Force has more than enough of a budget to fix up this level. They've chosen not to in order to send a clear message: *Nothing to see here.*

We reach the room where Nas said he heard R&D scrambling earlier. The door is closed, and there are muffled voices on the other side.

"I count two officers," I whisper. "You get them into a corner, and I'll collect as much information as I can. Maybe we can find out where else they're making Ambrosia."

Nas nods, but then sincerity clouds his features. "Wait, Adrian. Before we go in there . . ."

"Yeah, man?"

He exhales. "If you ever tell anyone else about that nice stuff I said in the stairwell earlier, I'll deny it. And I'll put fish guts in your protein powder. Cool?"

"Cool." I shake my head. Clearly Nas's personality profile is still set to maximum levels of smartass.

The voices on the other side of the door grow suddenly louder. We move just as the door swings open, hiding ourselves behind it. I can't see the officers, but the strain in their voices tells me they're pushing something heavy.

"My productivity score better be sky-high after this," says one woman. " 'Last load of the day' my ass." More grunting and the squeak of a cart's wheels under lots of weight.

"Don't look at me," her companion says. "Bekele's the one who blew the mission. If he'd gotten the shipment to the Eleventh without tripping over his laces, you'd be in an Arcade right now with a shoulder full of the good stuff."

I'm so stunned, I almost let go of the door handle. Silas Bekele was Redding's inside man for the Sector Eleven op? As in, the man who all our intel says raised Liv like one of his own? And he failed his orders, which means whatever punishment Redding has planned for him is coming, and soon. If Liv's anywhere near him when that happens . . .

The women's voices fade as they round the corner. Nas and I duck into the room. He locks the door and starts casing the rest of the place.

"Let's make this quick," I say. I need to get to Liv somehow. Keep her safe. My eyes scan the beakers and test tubes covering the laboratory counters and land on the two computers in the corner. There could be important records here, of the formula for Ambrosia, or where else it's being manufactured. I press a few buttons on my wrist screen and begin transferring the computers' data to my local storage. I flip through some of the documents on the screen as the transfer continues, until I reach a file labeled *CONFIDENTIAL—Internal Testing Protocol.* I click it open.

SYNTHETIC DOPAMINE COCKTAIL ("MEAN") VERSION 2.7.3.3—"AMBROSIA"

INTERNAL TESTING PROTOCOL

Abstract

The injectable liquid solution colloquially referred to as Mean has led to immeasurable increases in LifeCorp's annual profits. However, concerns about the chemical's sustainability in response to corporate expansion and more exigent production schedules has inspired LifeCorp to pursue development of a new Mean, with greater efficacy (as measured by financial returns). While testing of any replacement candidates on the average Metro citizen could be harmful for productivity levels as well as potentially erode shareholder value if discovered, LifeCorp Research & Development has found a great deal of success in testing on incarcerated individuals currently engaging in LifeCorp's virtual imprisonment program ("Verch"). By leveraging these existing resources, we have seen gains in compliance and efficiency, without risking any negative impact on our valuable workforce.

I hate them.

The second the data transfer completes, I smash the computer on the ground. Those monsters. Those evil, repulsive—

"Adrian?" Nas emerges from the next room, clocks the shattered machine at my feet. "Everything . . . okay in here?"

"They're using Verch prisoners as lab rats," I pant. "They're testing new versions of Ambrosia on people who aren't even conscious enough to consent." I kick part of the computer's hull across the room. Verch is hell as it is; I can't imagine experiencing it under the influence of this poison.

Nas grimaces in disgust. "Well, as long as we're in the

mood to destroy things . . ." He leads me into the back room, and I freeze at what surrounds us: fifteen carts that I assume are identical to the one the two officers pushed out of here, each of them burdened with dozens of trays of at least a hundred vials of Ambrosia each.

The sight wrings something worn and ragged in my chest and reminds me of Liv lying feverish and weak on the cave floor. I'm done searching for the middle ground, done hoping that someone in this viper's nest will miraculously acknowledge their humanity. It's time for us to turn the tables. For all of them. For Liv.

Without a word, I grab a cart and push, hard. Fritz loyalty. It topples easily under the weight of the trays. Vials shatter by the thousands on the hard tile, in a shrill crash that sounds like the world coming apart. That'd be a good start.

Nas joins me on the next one, and soon we're down to one more cart. He looks at me. "Together?"

"Together."

We push—

"What in the *hell* do you think you're doing?" A baritone voice cuts across the room. Inspector Redding stands in the doorway, a blaster in his hands trained on our faces. A vein twitches in his neck.

I don't bother explaining, because what we're doing is obvious. I don't bother asking him if he knew about the testing, because you don't make it to his level of seniority without covering up a dirty little secret or two. The only thing on my mind is making it out of here so that I can protect Liv.

"Hands up!" Redding shouts. "You too, Davani!" Nas does

as he's told, but I notice a few vials missing from the tray closest to his hand, and a telltale tinkling sound in his pocket. Whatever he's thinking, he's about to get us both killed.

"Hey, Adrian," Nas says loudly. I shift my eyes to his face.

"Yeah?"

"Don't forget what I said about the fish guts." With a grunt, he pulls the last cart down, blocking Redding's blaster rays. Nas pushes me behind him as he sprints for Redding, tackling him at the knees. Redding's blaster flies across the room, bouncing off the wall and landing in the shards of glass that litter the floor. Redding struggles against Nas's superhuman strength to lift his wrist screen and call for backup. I move to help Nas, but he waves me away.

"Go!" he shouts.

"But—"

"Go!"

I run, glass crunching under my boots. There's panic in Redding's voice as he asks Nas what he's got in his hands, but I don't turn to see. The last thing I hear before I slam the door behind me is the hiss of an injector of Ambrosia. Then another. And another. And another.

38

LIV

I LEAVE THE ARCADE PATRONS WITH A RUNNING LOOP OF SCRAPS THAT I EX-ported to a memory card. Everything that happens after I step out onto the street is a blur. I stumble, exhausted, through the alleys, unsure of my destination. Kez. Silas. Adrian. Three different kinds of grief, but each one has taken another piece of who I was before that night on Preston's dock. The losses are stacking too high, and I can't carry them anymore.

I'm leaving before anyone else gets hurt.

My fist hesitates on the door of Silas's hideout, a spare apartment he rents for when things get too hot. Thea and Celeste will be inside by now, but maybe I shouldn't let them know I'm here. Even if it is just to say goodbye.

The door creaks open. "Liv? That you?"

I lift my head at the sound of Thea's warm alto. That's when the tears come, and I don't have the energy to stop them. Thea sweeps me up in a hug, and I bury my face in her shoulder, feel the reassuring heat of her palm rubbing my back.

I'll miss her comfort.

Inside the apartment, I tell Thea and Celeste what happened at the Arcade. Thea tuts and makes small humming noises to herself as I talk, while Celeste grows more and more horrified. By the time I'm done, Celeste's eyes are wet with tears. My heart breaks for her. Silas was as much a parent to her as he was to me. News of his betrayal hits her hard.

Thea, on the other hand, sits calmly. "Wish I could say I'm surprised," she says after a long silence.

"You're not?"

Celeste puts her head in Thea's lap, and Thea smooths her curls. "A man like Silas has one interest, and one interest only: himself. The rest of us were just lucky to factor into his designs for as long as we did."

I marvel at her evenness. Thea's a natural CareProxy, always watching out for the others in her life. Never shaken— forever an anchor. Wherever her miraculous inner strength comes from, I'm grateful for it now. She watches me, no doubt noticing the resolve on my face. "Celeste, go get yourself a tissue, 'kay?" Celeste obeys, and Thea raises her brows at me, expectant.

"I'm glad Celeste has you," I say.

"She also has you." Her words are quiet but pointed.

I glance over Thea's shoulder to make sure Celeste is still wiping her eyes. "You know I can't stay here. I'm the only reason the Forcemen are in the Towers in the first place. I can't make you a target too. We've already lost enough—"

Thea reaches to cover my hand with her own. "Exactly. We've already lost enough." I pull away. She sighs. "Always running."

There's a knock at the door, forceful and insistent. Celeste squeaks and runs to hide in the cabinet like Kez and I taught her. Thea and I lock eyes, silent. I scan the room, then gesture behind her, to a broken chair in a corner. Thea nods and makes quick work of two legs, prying them off so that the splintered ends are dangerously sharp. She tosses me one, and we approach the door.

More banging from the other side. Thea and I nod to one another. *One. Two . . .*

I fling the door open and lift the chair leg over my head, then bring it down hard. Adrian's beautiful eyes meet mine as his hand grabs the weapon, stopping it midswing.

"It's you," we say at the same time.

My arm slackens. I don't know how long we stand there, frozen, staring at each other. Long enough for Thea to tell Celeste it's safe to come out. Long enough for me to bring myself back from the brink of wanting to collapse into his arms if he so much as brushes my shoulder. I—or at least, Outerlands Liv—may have loved Adrian when we were together in the Haven. But that version of me didn't understand what love really is. In the Metro, LifeCorp demands our time, our energy, our bodies. But Adrian's love asked me to surrender a much greater part of myself: My trust. My hope. My heart.

No more sacrifices. Rather than love, than money, than fame, give me truth.'

Thea shifts her stance behind me. "Well . . . I'm Thea. And you are?" Finally, Adrian tears his eyes from mine. He introduces himself, then enters the apartment, and I can't stop sneaking glances. Him, here. I expect him to disappear any moment, like a flickering hologram. But he's real, so real I can see the shadow of stubble on his face. My hand twitches.

I want to feel the scratch of it under my thumb. Against my cheek.

"How did you find us?" I ask.

Adrian frowns. "How—? Celeste messaged me the address." He looks past me, confused, to where Celeste is slowly backing away. "You said she wanted me here!"

"She does!" Celeste turns to me. "Don't you?"

"I—" Irrelevant. "Celeste, *why* did you do that?"

"And wait a second," Thea says. "If you knew it was him, why did you hide when he knocked?"

"He messaged me first!" Celeste whines to me. "Said he had something important to tell you. And I wasn't hiding from him, I was hiding from *you*! I thought you might be mad. Are you mad?"

I take in Celeste's enormous bright eyes as she chews her lip. After tonight, I might never see her again. I don't want to spend our last few minutes together fighting.

"Come here." I open my arms, and Celeste curls into my lap. Once she's comfortable, I cool my gaze and turn to Adrian. "What did you need to tell me?" It better not be some variation of *I love you* again. Because I'm still so, so pissed at him. And because if he says it, I might not have the strength not to say it back.

Adrian exhales. "Something Redding told me at the Citadel. He's been working on developing an extra-strength Mean, called Ambrosia."

"Teal, glittery stuff?" I say, my voice distant. I shudder as I remember Kez rolling the vial between his fingers before Silas's plan fell apart. Did he end up using it, wherever he is?

"Right. Apparently, it makes the mind more supple, increases compliance." He sneers.

I think of the zombielike Arcade patrons. Another wave of hatred for LifeCorp courses through me. They already have the Lowers trapped, and they want more control?

"Here's the thing though, Liv: the night you—the night with Mr. Rivera. Nas and I had given him a vial from that same batch, an hour earlier. I don't think what happened to him was your fault."

I scoff. "Yeah? Must have been some other Liv Newman who put those awful thoughts in his head." There's more truth in the words than I'd like.

"You had no way of knowing he'd react like that. You were just trying to survive, like everyone else."

"So . . . I'm not a monster?" I whisper. Our eyes meet, and I wish we were back in the woods again. I want him to hold me, to hum into my ear as I drift off to the sound of cricket song. If only it were that easy.

"You never were," Adrian says softly. He clears his throat and addresses the rest of the room. "I destroyed as much of the Ambrosia at the Citadel as I could, but who knows how much more is out there, across the Metro."

"You *destroyed* it?" Thea's eyes widen, matching mine. A move like that would cost LifeCorp millions of credits. New possibilities swirl in the space between us. Maybe some part of him is exactly who I believed he was. Maybe it wasn't all a lie.

Adrian continues, eyes blazing with conviction. "And I thought maybe, if we could get outside the Metro, we might be able to find someone who could help us stop production."

"Outside the Metro?" Celeste's eyes light up. To her, Adrian's words sound like adventure. But I know better.

"In a brilliantly ironic twist, you seem to have lost *your* memory," I tell him. "Because last I recall, the Haveners attacked us and accused us of stealing from them."

"Haveners?" Thea asks.

"Raiders," Adrian and I both explain.

Thea's eyebrows disappear behind her bangs. "*Excuse* me?"

Oops. "I was going to tell you, Thea, promise." Eventually. Maybe.

"I *do* remember," Adrian says to me. "And, Thea, it wasn't as bad as it sounds, really. Eh, maybe it was. But anyway, I've got something that might win their favor back. I downloaded everything the Force had on Ambrosia: how to make it, where they're storing it. It's all here." He taps his wrist screen. "We could take it to the Haven. Join them."

"You keep saying 'we,'" I tell him. "What makes you think I'm going with you? That any of us are?"

He turns sheepish. "Well . . . are you happy here?"

Time stands still as he waits for my answer. My mouth feels dry. "Since when has that mattered?"

"It matters to me." Plain and simple. Like him caring about my happiness is the most natural thing in the world. I'm too tired to untangle the knots that form in my chest after that, so I talk around them.

"Celeste and Thea are better off in the Metro."

"We are?" Celeste and Thea ask at the same time.

My jaw wobbles. "A-aren't you?"

"Liv." Thea leans in, takes my hand. "For as long as I've

known you, you've been running away from something. A place, a situation. Yourself. Hell, what are all of those books you read, if not a way to escape? If you're telling me you were *happy* in the Outerlands, then I'm packing my bags."

"I'm going where Liv's going!" Celeste wraps her arms around my neck. A burst of warmth blooms from my core. When Silas asked me to join his plan, I'd been willing to pick up my old life right where I left it, in order to stay with my crew. It never occurred to me that they'd be willing to start a new life just to stay with me.

"What about Kez?" I ask.

"We can leave word," Thea says, already getting up to find a pen and paper.

If he survives, I finish in my head.

"All right, that's done." Thea finishes the note and puts it under the trick panel in the kitchenette's second drawer. "Now, how do we get to the Outerlands?"

"Do you have a vehicle?" I ask Adrian. He shakes his head. "Even if they haven't turned off my access yet, there'll be trackers in any Force vehicle I could get my hands on." Anxious heat burns in my chest. Our plan isn't even underway and it's already falling apart. *Think.* There's nowhere near the Towers where we could get a vehicle; no one around here has that kind of money. . . .

"The Estates," I say. "Mr. Preston's place is vacant. I drove one car into the Outerlands, but maybe they left another?" I look around at the three of them, who all respond with different variations of a shrug that says *What other option do we have?*

"I like it," Adrian says. I ignore the proud flutter in my chest. "Assuming we can get all the way to the Estates without getting caught."

"Already did it once tonight," I say, more than a little boastful.

"Yeah, but that was from the Citadel. And now they're on the hunt for you and a defecting officer. There'll be even more sharks in the water," he says wryly. "We could go north, by the riverports?"

"Hm. Or east and cut a wide circle around?" I offer.

"I thought grown-ups were supposed to be smart," Celeste says, slinging on her backpack. Her eyes are twinkling the way they only do when she's thought of something brilliant. "All this 'west, no, wait, east' stuff. You guys are overlooking the only direction that could actually work."

"Which is?" Adrian raises an amused brow.

Celeste grins. "Below."

■ ■ ■

"I CAN'T BELIEVE NO ONE COMES DOWN HERE," CELESTE SAYS, HER BOOTS sloshing through the brackish brown water. The T train has run aboveground for as long as I can remember, but lucky for us the abandoned subway tunnels are still here . . . mildew smell notwithstanding. Celeste points out a mosaic map on the wall. "See! So cool! Adrian, you've seriously never been underground?"

I glance back at Adrian, who's too busy trying to keep down whatever he had for lunch to answer.

"I, uh, prefer being aboveground. Yeah. Big fan of above-ground, where the air is fresh and open," he says shakily. I have to hand it to Celeste, though; her plan's a good one. And according to her, as long as the tide is out, we won't meet our untimely demise in a watery grave.

"Should be another thirty minutes this way," Celeste says, then swings her flashlight toward the map to double-check. We drop into a comfortable silence, the only sound the steady drip of water around us. In the calm quiet, I almost let myself believe that we'll make it out of this safely. First to Preston's cabin, then to the Haven, if Reem and her people will have us again.

Stop. You're not free yet. Don't let down your guard . . . like you did with Silas. Instantly, I'm myself again. Mask on, armor secure.

Behind me, in the darkness, Adrian mutters to himself. "Two things you can hear. Come on. Come on . . ." I want to reach for his hand, help him breathe through the fear. But that would mean forgiving him, softening myself. That's not the Liv we need right now.

Adrian whimpers. If he doesn't get his claustrophobia under control, we're going to be delayed, or maybe even get caught. Feebly, he tries again, "Two things you can—"

I start to hum a passable version of the shaving cream jingle he hummed for me in the cave when I was sick. I'm not great at carrying a tune, but it's good enough to slow his breathing. After a few rounds, he joins in. When his voice is the smooth tenor I remember, we let the music fade. Adrian catches up to walk beside me.

"Great song," he says appreciatively.

"I've always thought so."

Silence in the dark. Then, "So you *do* remember it all."

Shit. "Doesn't change anything," I say softly.

He sucks in a breath. "It changes *everything.* You can choose, Liv. You can be who you were before the woods, or you can be your true self."

I stifle a laugh. "And who's that? A starry-eyed sociopath? No one wants her back."

"I do," he says without missing a beat. My stomach flutters in a way I'd rather forget. "And you weren't a sociopath."

"You don't know what you're saying."

"Don't I? I've seen you at your worst—" I cringe as the memories of what I did to Joe Rivera seep into my mind's eye. Adrian takes my hand in his, rubbing it with his thumb. "—and at your best. When I look at you, I see someone who dreams of better days for the people she loves, who's not afraid to fight for them. Someone who cares so deeply about the world and everything in it that she had LifeCorp believing her feelings about her home were *a literal drug.* Someone who's generous with her talents . . . and her heart—"

"Enough." I pull my hand from his. "Enough. This is . . ." My breath shudders as I steady myself. "Back at the Citadel, you asked why I archived my memory. I did it because I was tired of being trapped by my 'talents,' as you called them. LifeCorp demanded almost all of me, and Silas took whatever was left. I won't be trapped again, by you or anyone else. Whatever happened in the woods, forget about it. I'm not that Liv any-more." I speed up toward Celeste and Thea, ignoring the way my traitorous body still longs for his. Halfway to them, spots appear in my vision. I lose my bearings in the darkness. My skin goes clammy as I lean against the tunnel's slimy wall.

"Liv!" Celeste shouts in the distance. The echoes of her voice make me even dizzier.

"I'm all right," I say, woozy. "Guess I haven't eaten much in . . . the past five days or so."

Small boots slosh through the water, but it's Adrian who reaches me first.

"Here," he says, lifting one of my arms over his shoulder. A crinkling sound. "Take a bite?" I open my mouth and he feeds me a VitaBar. It tastes, quite frankly, like blueberry-flavored ass. But it's got the nutrients my body so desperately needs.

"Better?" he asks after I take a few more bites. His brow is crinkled in concern.

"Well, it's not Adrian Rao's world-famous bacon and eggs," I say weakly.

He smiles. "There she is. If you're feeling good enough to roast me, I'll count that as a win any day." He sits with me a few minutes more, making sure I finish the whole VitaBar. Slowly, he helps me stand as Celeste and Thea lead the way.

"One more thing," Adrian says, before I join my friends. My hand tingles where he held it. "You can hate me all you want, but don't deny yourself the truth."

"What truth is that?"

When he speaks, his voice is so soft it hurts. "You were 'that Liv' long before you were anyone else."

39

ADRIAN

AIR. SWEET, GLORIOUS, FRESH AIR.

We emerge from the tunnels as dawn breaks. The streets of the Estates are practically empty; unlike the Lowers' bustling commute in the Towers, the Uppers start their day with early-morning meetings from their home offices. Ten yards ahead, Liv's walking with Celeste and Thea, not even bothering to glance back to see if I made it out of the tunnels in one piece, which is fine. She may never forgive me for lying to her, but that's not why I'm trying to save her. I'm saving her because my life won't be worth living if I don't.

Just as Liv said, the Prestons' Estate is a ghost town, but we stick to the inside walls of the courtyard anyway. Dawn bathes the gray cobblestones in pink light, and the scent of jasmine carries on the wind. Liv brushes her fingertips over the flowers as we walk, an almost mournful expression on her face.

"Kez should be here," she tells her friends.

Celeste takes her hand. "He'll come back to us. Like you did."

The Prestons' garage is bigger than my whole apartment.

Against one wall are gardening bots caked in mud and grass clippings. Almost all of the garage is dedicated to what I can only describe as toys—bicycles, golf clubs, ice skates, a pottery wheel. All of them unused, most still in half-opened LifeCorp boxes. I'm sure the Prestons bought these with good intentions, hoping to sneak in a brief respite from their workdays. But all I can think of are the Lowers in a warehouse somewhere who scrambled to get these packed up before their productivity scores fell, or the SprinterProxy who delivered the products within an hour of purchase, only for them to collect dust for weeks or maybe years. The whole thing seems so . . . thoughtless.

"Look!" Thea says, pointing across the cavernous room. Behind a squat rack still encased in foam, I catch a glimpse of a chrome car door. We rush toward the car, but slow when we hear two voices arguing.

"I can't *see* anything!" a guy says through gritted teeth.

"Then maybe you should get those pretty silver eyes checked out," responds a girl. Two figures stand.

"Kez!" Liv whisper-screams, dashing through the lacrosse sticks and snorkel equipment at her feet. They collide in a peal of laughter, with Celeste close behind. Even though I know there's nothing romantic between Liv and Kez, I can't help but feel jealous as I take in her wide, uninhibited smile. The only strong reaction this Liv's ever given me is a punch to the gut. Not saying I didn't deserve it, but still.

"And Sophie!" Liv hugs the woman next to Kez. She's slim, with light brown skin and thick brown hair that falls in loose ringlets. Like Liv and Kez, she wears a pale pink RelaProxy jumpsuit, though unlike theirs, hers looks like it was actually tailored to her.

"How did you lose the Forcemen?" Thea asks Kez after she hugs him. Kez sucks his teeth. "Please. Who do you think you're talking to?"

Sophie opens her mouth, a clever retort on her tongue.

"*Rhetorical* question, Duchess," Kez says, smirking.

"I was here the first time you came through, but I hid," Sophie explains. "Thought you were robbers. It wasn't until this brainiac came back and almost set off the car alarm that I realized what had happened." She gestures to Kez, rolling her eyes.

"Oh, please. You were relieved to see me," Kez says.

"Never said I wasn't."

"Sophie, where is everyone?" Liv asks. "Where's Mr. Preston?"

"Last week, I heard him screaming on a conference call, late at night. I woke up the next morning and he was gone. No explanation, no note—at least, not for Mrs. Preston. She packed up the whole staff and headed back home to Raleigh. But Mr. Preston did leave me a message: all it said was *stay.* The next day, a package arrived by drone. A memory card, with instructions—"

"It was you," Liv says. "You put the envelope behind the stars in his library."

Sophie nods. "No idea what's on it, but it seemed important. Have you watched it yet?"

"I was waiting until we got somewhere safe," Liv says. There's a reluctance in her voice.

"'Get somewhere safe.' Great idea!" Kez barges in, wrapping an arm around each of their shoulders. He jabs a thumb at the car. "Duchess and I were trying to hack the car's scanner to accept my chip so we could pick y'all up and get the hell out of here. But my hacking skills are a little rusty. And *someone* wasn't holding the flashlight properly."

"There is only one way to hold a flashlight," Sophie says, voice dripping with honey. "Whereas there are a million ways, Kez darling, for you to be a giant asshat."

Kez feigns a swoon. "I could listen to those sweet nothings forever." He hands Celeste the screwdriver in his hand. "Celeste, could you . . . ?"

"On it!" Celeste examines Kez's screwdriver with a disdainful frown, then takes a smaller one out of her bag and unscrews the panel under the steering wheel.

Kez notices me standing to the side, still in uniform. The mood shifts. Liv hugs herself shyly. "Oh, um. Kez, this is Adrian. Adrian, this is Kez."

I give a small wave to Kez and Sophie. Kez's face is careful as he studies me. "And Adrian is . . . ?"

"Liv's friend!" Celeste offers as she works, a screw pinched between her lips. "Or they used to be friends, and Adrian wishes they were still friends. But Liv doesn't want to be friends, or at least she *says* she—"

"*Celeste,*" Liv snaps.

The kid huffs out a breath.

Kez shifts her eyes between Liv and me, noting her standoffishness, my nerves. Suddenly, his face relaxes, and his confusion gives way to boisterous laughter.

"Oh my God, this is too good. It's too good!" He cackles. "Liv! You? And a—a—" He's still doubled over laughing when Liv shoves him to the ground and goes to check out the car. I help him up.

"Thanks," Kez says. "Man, I don't know your story, but the fact that you're in that uniform and Liv hasn't decked you yet? That says a *lot*."

Liv huffs from the other side of the car. "I *did* deck him. Twice, actually. Fritzer won't stay down." But even as she says the words, the corner of her mouth twitches with a smile. I'll take it.

"All set!" Celeste chirps, securing the final screw back on the panel. Liv tugs on one of the girl's long coils and releases it. "Hey, smarty. You've known how to hack car scanners this whole time? Why haven't you ever done it before?"

Celeste shrugs. "Never had a reason to try."

Kez leans against the vehicle. "So, where we headed? DC? Atlanta? I know a guy in Philly who could put us up for a few days."

"The Outerlands. I'll explain everything," Liv says, before Kez's words catch up with his face.

"I . . . okay, Boss." Kez swivels the car's front left chair around into manual drive mode. Pain flickers on Liv's face. Kez called her *Boss*. Is she thinking of Silas? I'm not sure exactly how he let her down in the Eleventh, but I'd give anything to make it so she never feels that way again.

Kez mock bows to Sophie, inviting her to enter the car. She gives him a deadpan look, before shrugging and getting in. As a RelaProxy, she built her whole career around Preston's life, his relationships. Without him, there's nothing left for her here either.

"A road trip, just like in the movies! Eeeee!" Celeste squeals. She's so excited that she hugs the closest person to her, which happens to be me. I laugh as her tiny arms wrap around my waist, one of the Prestons' tennis balls in one hand. But regret follows soon after. I'm the reason she almost lost these arms. It's time to leave that version of myself behind, forever.

We start to get in the car. Liv sits shotgun, while Thea slides into the back, beside Sophie. I'm about to sit beside Thea when Celeste climbs in, waiting expectantly in the last seat. Thea and I stare at her.

"What?" Celeste asks.

"Celeste, there's six of us," Thea says. "You can sit in my lap for a couple hours, can't you?"

"No way! You guys are always making me cram in places just because I'm little—"

Thea pinches the bridge of her nose. When she gazes up, the rings around her pupils glow navy blue. "Please don't do this right now."

"Don't do that mod thing! I'm not a baby!" Celeste whines.

"We don't have time to argue," Liv says over their squabbling. "Adrian, come here." She steps out of the car as I walk around to her side. "Sit." Confused, I do as she says. Then, like it's as natural as breathing, Liv Newman sits on my lap.

"Go, Kez," she says.

As Kez pulls out onto the road, Liv holds her muscles taut, hovering above my chest instead of lying flat back against it. That can't be comfortable.

"I don't bite, you know," I say.

"I know. I'm fine like this." Her abs tremble visibly.

"The Force will be watching the main border checkpoints closely," Kez says from the driver's seat, his pupils glowing silver. "Can't go through the city. I'm going to take us over to the riverfront." Smooth as an oil slick, he navigates the Prestons' car north, then east. I haven't been to the ports in years, and I'm surprised how much they've changed. There's not a human in sight as we drive along the road that hugs the river, only an army of rustproof bots and droids transporting LifeCorp goods from massive autonomous cargo ships. The shipping droids aren't humanoid; they look more like the robots in illustrations of what people *thought* the future would be like, a long time ago. They don't even have eyes—the only things they can "see" are the radio waves from the other machines around them. Either Kez is a genius, or he's unwittingly brought us to the perfect route for our escape.

"Whoops!" Kez says as he swerves to avoid a bot crossing the street. I'm buckled in, but Liv's not. Instinctively, I grab her waist so she doesn't hit the dashboard.

"Sorry about that, everyone!" Kez says. "Wish I could tell you it won't happen again."

"It better not, *David*," says Thea.

Kez grips the steering wheel a little tighter. "Do *not* call me that."

Sophie's eyes widen with revelation. "Oh, I will *absolutely* be pocketing that information for later," she whispers to Thea.

"What was that?" Kez strains to see them in the rearview mirror.

"Oh nothing, David!" Sophie calls. As they bicker and Celeste giggles, Liv turns toward the window, voice so low that only I can hear.

"Thanks," she says. "For the, um, assist."

"Anytime." *Always.*

"I was wondering: where's your . . . friend? The one we saved."

"Ah." My heart clenches at the sudden mention of Nas. Did they hurt him? "He's . . . back in the Citadel. He helped me destroy the Ambrosia, and then he attacked Redding so I could get out. . . ."

"Whoa. I'm sorry."

"Me too."

A long silence passes between us, and then she leans back, her body warm against my chest. My heart soars higher than Icarus ever could. I miss being close to her like this. I drink in the smell of her hair like it's oxygen. Citrus and honey, even after all this time.

"This doesn't mean I forgive you," she says, voice heavy with sleep. She wraps my arms tighter around her middle.

"I know."

"I'm just tired."

I hold her close and sigh. Maybe some part of me is finding respite too.

"Then rest."

LIV

WHEN I WAKE UP, THERE'S SNOW ON THE GROUND OUTSIDE. LIGHT DRIFTS FLY across the windshield. Adrian's smiling at me like the fact that I fell asleep on him automatically makes him king of the universe.

"Hey," I say, still groggy as I slide over to the seat beside him.

"Hey."

"Where are we?" I rub the sleep from my eyes and peer out the window. Preston's car—the one I drove to the Outerlands over a week ago—is right beside us, buried under a foot of snow. "Oh."

Adrian and I are the only ones in the car. Outside, Thea and Sophie talk quietly. Celeste is throwing snowballs at Kez that immediately disintegrate once airborne. Fat white flakes nestle themselves into her Afro puffs. I've never seen her so happy.

"Guess we should get going to the cabin before the snow picks up." I reach for the door handle.

"Hang on. Please."

I've known this conversation was coming from the moment

Adrian appeared at Silas's hideout. I thought maybe after I blew him off in the tunnels that he would've gotten the message. But here he is, his doleful eyes sucking the air from my lungs, the heat from his nearness making my pulse pound in my throat.

"Yes?"

"I. You . . ." He closes his eyes. Breathes. Opens them again. "You are worth saving."

"What?"

Adrian continues like he didn't hear me. "You are worth saving, not because of what you can do for anyone, or your chip, or your bullshit productivity score. You are worth saving because of the way you never lose hope, even though you like to pretend you're a cynic—"

Rude.

"And the way you lose yourself completely in a book. And your courage. And the way you trust people, even after they fail you. *I* failed—" His mouth contorts with unspoken pain. "You're worth saving, Liv. You. Not the Liv from the Haven. You, right now. And I know this is cheesy as hell, but I'm saying it because sometimes, I don't think you understand. I *need* you to believe you are worthy."

The walls I've built around my heart sway and shudder. What is it about Adrian that makes me want to tear them down?

I'm wondering how to respond, when he suddenly sits up straight, like a commanding officer has called him to attention. He turns his ear to the window.

"What is it?"

Adrian's eyes widen in fear. "Get down. Whatever you do, don't leave this car." He bolts outside and yells at Kez to lock the car, then run.

Above, a terrible buzzing sound, like someone's sawing the sky open. Kez picks up Celeste, who's screaming for me. Then he, Thea, and Sophie sprint for the forest as three Forceman copters emerge through the blanket of white clouds like enormous birds of prey. Forcemen leap out of them from a height that would shatter any human's femur on landing. *Droids, then.*

Adrian's fiddling with his wrist screen beside the car. He's jittery on his feet as booted footsteps trample through the woods around us, but he doesn't run. Why doesn't he run?

My wrist screen buzzes.

INCOMING FILE TRANSFER FROM ADRIAN RAO. ACCEPT?

I press yes, and a file called *Ambrosia Manufacturing and Distribution Plan—Phase 1* starts to upload, crossing through space from Adrian's wrist to mine. Seven Forcemen droids burst out of the tree line, their bodies entirely covered in tactical armor. They've each got to be at least six feet tall, giants come to swat an annoying pest into submission. They'll make quick work of Adrian if they catch him. But his eyes are locked on his screen.

"What are you doing? Run!" I yell, hunched low on the floor of the car. *Go. Survive, or I don't think I can.*

"I love you, Liv." Without warning, Adrian darts left, zooming into the forest with the droids hot on his tail. My wrist screen chimes over the silence of the falling snow.

TRANSFER COMPLETE.

Outside, all is calm. Movement in the sky draws my eye. Not copters—not mechanical, but animal. A hawk.

Icarus?

Please let it be.

I clamber out of the Prestons' car. The cold air hits me like an electric shock, but I can't let it slow me down as I track the bird against the white sky. I don't know if Reem will hear me, don't even know for sure if it's Icarus I'm following. But if LifeCorp's sending droids into the woods now, we've got no chance of surviving.

Not on our own.

42

ADRIAN

A LITTLE FARTHER, THEN I'LL LET THEM CATCH ME.

"Target acquired," the droids say in unison behind me, pounding the forest floor like a herd of wild boars. Chipmunks scurry across my path. Birds squawk and take flight as every creature in the woods is made aware of these lethal intruders. *I'm sorry,* I tell them all in my mind. *They'll be gone soon.*

Liv's friends ran toward Preston's cabin. I'm leading the Forcemen in the other direction, out of the woods and away from Liv and her future. Whatever's next for her, it won't include the Force.

Or me.

My breath burns in my chest as I trudge through the snow. My feet tangle in something—underbrush? I look down at my legs as I sink into the wet snow, at the tight black cable tying my ankles together, pinning my hands to my sides. In the distance, one of the Force droids lowers his hand. They've snared me. I wriggle backward a few feet, my back numbing from the cold. *Dammit.* I wanted to get farther than this, give Liv and her crew a bigger head start. Just one more way I failed her.

The Forcemen slow as they reach me, lifting their masks to

reveal smug grins. They can take their time now. All of them raise a hand to their foreheads, turning off their auto-record settings with three quick taps. They've apprehended the traitor who destroyed LifeCorp property and helped attack their superior officer. They'll bring me in, but not before torturing me to their hearts' content. Even through my fear, I'm disgusted.

With my hand pinned, my fingers graze the handle of my holstered blaster. The cords around my arm dig into my skin as I strain against them, reaching for my weapon without drawing attention to my hand. It doesn't work: one of the Forcemen notices and draws his own blaster. I get the message, lower my hand.

"That's more like it," he snarls. "The audacity of you humans never ceases to amaze me. As if that puny thing could—"

He doesn't get to finish before a beam of blaster fire punches him right in the chest. Not from me, but from somewhere behind me. His circuits fried, the droid slumps to the ground with a sickening *thunk*. The Forcemen droids get into formation and draw their weapons. I swear I note the tiniest bit of fear on their faces.

"What the fritz was that?" one asks.

Another droid wipes the snow from his eyes. "Not sure."

"Never seen a blaster take a droid down like that."

The answer to their question makes itself known. A swarm of Haveners descends from the trees, hooting and hollering as their blaster beams soar through the woods. The droids fight back, but they're no match for the Haveners' souped-up weapons, or the way they dart through the trees like they're riding the whipping wind. The droids are on unfamiliar terrain, tripping over roots and running into low branches as they retreat. These woods are the Haveners' home, and they've come to defend it.

I scramble behind a large pine to avoid the cross fire. A massive blaster beam whizzes by, singeing my shoulder before it takes another droid down. Where did the Haveners get weapons like these?

Before I even turn my head, another cluster of Haveners appears. Noah's wife, Candace, is in the rear, an enormous chrome cannon over her shoulder. She pulls the trigger, and a stream of blaster fire takes down two droids at once.

Damn.

Candace isn't just the Haven's chief mechanic. She's their weapons specialist.

I shut my eyes tight, praying I'll make it through the turmoil, when something tugs at my boots. I open my eyes to see Kenji sawing through my restraints with a steak knife.

"Waste of a good knife," he mutters. "Blade will never be the same."

"Kenji. Thank you," I say, angling my arm toward him so he can cut the restraints there, too. "I'll make it up to you, man, I swear."

"Hell are you talking about?" Kenji looks at me like I'm a stranger. I guess I might as well be, now. He leaves my arms bound as a squad of Havener soldiers flanks me. Eyes cool as steel, Kenji flicks his knife tip north, away from the fighting. Toward the Haven.

"Walk."

43

LIV

"ISN'T THIS AN ESPECIALLY LOVELY CASE OF DÉJÀ VU?" HARCOURT CHUCKLES
as he nudges his blaster into my back. Thea, Celeste, Sophie,
and Kez each have their own Havener guard. Celeste's face
is streaked with tears, and her wet eyes glimmer in the low
lamplight as we reach the village.

"Move it!" Celeste's guard bellows. Kez and I both step forward, but he's faster, of course.

"Do *not* talk to her like that," Kez growls to the guard. The
silver rings around his pupils cool to brown.

Harcourt steps between the two men. "Let's see . . . you've
got the cuffs, we've got the blasters. So we'll be talking however we want." Kez shoots daggers into Celeste's guard's head
with his eyes as we walk on. The only sound is the crunching of our boots on the snow. Through the flurries I can make
out the familiar brown stone buildings and tattered flags I remember so well. For a brief moment in time, I thought of the
Haven as my home. But now it's just as likely to be our prison.
I feel sick with guilt. When I pictured us all together in the
Outerlands in the car, this isn't what I had in mind. My friends

never should have left the Towers. At least then they would've had a chance at staying alive.

The snow is blinding as the guards lead us through the empty streets. Wind bites through the thin fabric of my jump-suit. Where is Adrian? I hope with everything in me that he somehow escaped, that he's on his way somewhere safe. In a weird way, I'm glad I didn't have a chance to respond to his kind words in Preston's car. Adrian can invent a story in his head that helps him move on. He can imagine an ending where I break his heart. Something that makes it easier to say goodbye.

The faint vibrato of a violin cuts through the gray winter morning. The music grows louder as we approach a large building with warm yellow light spilling from the windows and onto the snow. When Harcourt opens the door, my senses feast. Noah's music, the smell of hearty stews and sticky baked treats, the sight of the Haveners in all their vibrant glory.

"Whoa," Celeste says, eyes wide. Even as I smile, my heart twists. They can do whatever they want to me, as long as they let her stay.

The building is a large storage space they've apparently converted into a communal gathering place, away from the cold. Long tables line one wall, half a dozen stew pots on top. In the center, about fifty Haveners of all ages lounge on floor pillows, some with thick blankets up to their necks. Reem sits in the center of the group, along with Noah. She lifts her hand, and he stops playing.

"Harcourt, I believe I was clear: they are to be deposited

at the nearest Metro checkpoint, where they belong." Reem is as regal as ever, but there's a quiet rage bubbling under the surface.

"It's this one." Harcourt jostles my arm roughly. "Says she has something you might want."

"I doubt that very much." But she stares at me, inviting me to speak.

I step forward. "The first time we met, you told me you'd been waiting for the day when Proxies would wake up to Life-Corp's abuse." I turn to my friends. "Here are three Proxies who refuse to be mistreated anymore, and one I've saved from that fate."

"Touching. Does treachery run in your little group?"

"They've done nothing wrong. They will work hard and love this community the way I—" I stop myself. "The way it deserves to be loved."

"And what way is that?"

Her meaning is clear; she doesn't think I understand anything about the Haven, or what it represents. So I tell her what I know. I tell her about what happened at the Arcade, and how I used my memories of my time here to give the patrons something real that could withstand not only Ambrosia but LifeCorp itself.

"I owe it to you," I say as the excited whispers in the room die down. "You're the one who first taught me to broadcast joy to the masses. These four will work hard to maintain that joy and wholeness in the Haven. If you let them."

Reem considers Thea, Sophie, and Kez, but her eyes linger longest on Celeste, who's been biting her lip as she struggles to focus on the conversation at hand and not the tray of sweets on the table. My heart pounds in the unending silence. *Please, Reem. Please let them stay.*

"For heaven's sake, someone get the girl a sweet bun," Reem says at last. She points to Thea. "And you. I know those boots are pinching your toes, you're not fooling anyone." She beckons to a handful of Haveners, who sweep Thea, Sophie, Kez, and Celeste into their midst. My knees wobble with relief. They're going to be all right. I did it.

"Thank you," I say.

"And you?" Reem asks. "What choice will you make?"

I frown. In a way, my choice has been clear since that night on Preston's dock. "I want to fight back," I say. "I have a file that shows where LifeCorp is making more Ambrosia," I say. "Adrian gave it to me before he . . ." A flicker of pain in my chest. "We know you have the weaponry to take them down. The blasters you used on Mount Barton."

"Oh yes, those. Candace's handiwork. You didn't think we survived out here all these years on buckwheat and kumbaya, did you?" A smirk crinkles her eyes. "You've done well, sugar. But that's not the choice I meant." With a flick of her fingers, the guards behind me open the door to the blustery gusts of snow outside. Three men enter, the two guards on either side flanking—

"Adrian!" I run toward him, but one of the guards lifts his blaster in a silent threat.

"The Forceman can't stay, of course. So you must choose. Stay here with your friends, or try your luck out in the cold, with him."

"Don't be s-stupid, Liv," Adrian says. His lips are pale, his nose and ears raw from the cold.

"But—" I scramble to think of every reason Reem should keep him here. "Adrian was born in the Outerlands! If Life-Corp hadn't stolen him from his family and forced him into the Academy, he'd be one of you."

Reem's eyes narrow. "A lie."

"N-not a lie," Adrian says, teeth still chattering. "But inconveniently d-difficult to prove."

"Say that's true, their lies have seeped into your bones by now."

"No," I say. "He's renounced the Force. He helped us get here—"

"And one act is enough to absolve him of a lifetime of enforcing their crimes?"

"Eh, 'lifetime'? Really?" Beside Reem, Noah wrinkles his nose. "He *is* just a kid." One raised brow from her, and he shuts up.

I glower at Reem. How can she be so hard-hearted, with everything she proclaims about the Haven's joyful lifestyle? "Listen to yourself," I say. "You hate LifeCorp so much, you're willing to turn away one of your own. You talk a big game about community, but you're doing exactly what your enemies do: pit us against one another. You'll never win that way. You're falling into their trap."

Reem narrows her eyes at me, before looking over my head to the guards. "Search him before you have him removed, please. He may have something of use."

"You can't!" I scream as I rush to clutch her arm. But it's

too late. One guard grunts his approval as he unclips Adrian's blaster, empties the VitaBars from his pockets along with his— that is, my—that is, Mr. Preston's copy of *Walden*.

"Where did you get that?" Reem asks the question at the same time I think it. She stands and closes the distance between her and Adrian in long, graceful strides. I follow, peering over her shoulder as she takes the book and opens to the inscription on the inside cover:

> *To Arthur, until we meet again. "I went to the woods because I wished to live deliberately . . ."*
> *Love always, R.*

Reem gasps when she sees the worn elegant handwriting. I remember what she told me when I asked if she'd read *Walden* before. *Yes,* she said, *a lifetime ago.*

She thumbs the faded ink, then clears her throat and begins to recite from memory. "'I went to the woods because I wished to live deliberately. To front only the essential facts of life, and see if I could not learn what it had to teach, and not, when I came to die—'"

At this phrase, my memory pricks. "'. . . discover that I had not lived,'" I finish, then explain as her curiosity is piqued. "My client, Mr. Preston, said that line to me before he gave me my last assignment. He was sick. He wanted to see the stars one last time."

Reem's eyes glisten with unshed tears. "Arthur . . ." She flips through the pages. Standing beside her, I'm surprised to see not only the printed words, but handwritten notes in the margins. Adrian's own thoughts as he read the book after our time in the woods. And doodles, so many doodles. Of flowers and hawks, bacon and carrot cake, a girl and a boy under the stars.

Reem's tear falls on the open page. "This reminds me of us. Long before LifeCorp took over, and the world turned upside down. We were so young. Anything seemed possible. Maybe it still is. . . ." Her voice fades as she scans Adrian's notes. To the guards, she says, "Let him go."

Adrian darts out of their grasp, and we embrace. The rest of the room goes back to their affairs, but my entire world is right here in my arms.

"I'm sorry," I say, my forehead pressed to his. His skin's still cold.

"Nothing to be s-sorry for."

"Yes, there is. I love you, and I should have said it sooner. If only—"

"Hey, L-Liv?" Adrian brushes our noses together. "I'm pretty c-cold. Can you think of any way to, I dunno, warm me up?" He gives me the most adorable puppy eyes.

I make a face like I'm thinking hard. "I may have *one* idea. Not sure you'd be into it, though."

"No? Why's that?"

"For one, there's no bacon involved." I frown. "Though technically, I guess there *could* be bacon involved. There's no rule against i—"

He kisses me like he's on fire and I'm a bucket of ice water. Stars explode behind my eyelids, interrupted by familiar words hovering in my vision:

NOAH LASSITER WOULD LIKE TO PAIR. ACCEPT?

Smartass. I decline, of course. This moment is pure, raw—no technology, Orange Haze, or Ambrosia in the way. Still, Noah still plays for us. With my eyes closed, my chest pressed to Adrian's rapidly warming body, I sigh as violin music swells to fill every corner of the hall. The melody sings of contradictions—at times playful, then tender; joyous, then somber. Complex. Peaceful. I was afraid that Adrian's love might ask me to sacrifice myself. I didn't realize he was willing to give as much of himself to me, and more. Like trees that intertwine in the woods, we make each other stronger, and I want Adrian to be an enduring part of my growth. I want to break and rebuild with him. I want to laugh and cry and feel it all. Good and bad. Easy and hard.

And real.

LIV

"... NASTY STUFF, THAT AMBROSIA. OH, LIV, I HOPE YOU AND YOUR FRIENDS haven't taken any. But the attached file should have all the information you'll need on LifeCorp's distribution routes. Every drop-off point and delivery schedule. If you found Reem, show her the file. She'll know what to do, how to prevent Ambrosia from ruining any other lives," Mr. Preston's thin voice says. On my wrist screen, he holds up a credit chip. "The chip I'm hiding in the cryo-fridge should have enough credits to help the cause considerably. Good luck, Liv. Thanks for the memories, eh?"

His sable face disappears from the frame as a cough racks his body. Behind him is the kitchenette where Adrian cooked for me for the first time. Octavia Butler's *Parable of the Sower* sits on the table behind him . . . the same book the Haveners found him holding in his bed a few days ago, his chest still, with a restful smile on his face. I wish Mr. Preston had had more time to enjoy his life instead of working nonstop. What's the point of success and long hours if you never get to enjoy the fruits of your labor?

I vow to live my own life fully, for his sake.

I take the memory card out of my screen and pocket it for safekeeping. I've already given Reem the files Mr. Preston mentioned, and she's started putting a plan together. My head spins at the thought of what one hundred thousand credits could do, not for me, but for everyone else who's still in the Metro. Now, instead of just paying for my own bookshop with a cat-bot, that money will pay for the supplies and support we need to eliminate Ambrosia for good. Yes, Liv and Crew got the hell out, and we're going to help others do the same. Maybe even Silas someday . . . if he wants to change.

There's a soft knock at the door of the new, larger room Reem assigned me and Adrian. We're in the same corner of the Haven as Celeste and her workshop, and just a few doors down from Thea, who spends most of her time helping with the new children's theater. Sophie's and Kez's homes are on opposite sides of the Haven, though if the rumors of them sneaking across the square in the middle of the night are true, Reem could probably find a more efficient use for one of their rooms. Those two may squabble nonstop, but they're not fooling anyone. I can't judge, though. I've been known to do crazy things in the name of love myself.

Adrian enters, silhouetted against a backdrop of stars, and quickly shuts the door to block the chill of a quiet winter night.

"Bedtime snack?" he says, balancing two sandwiches and a thermos of tea.

"Yes, please!" I scoot over on our mattress to make room for him.

"One hundred and fifty more refugees just arrived from the Metro. They've set up so many more tents in East Haven," he says. "Over three thousand new people, in the week that we've been here. All were either at the Arcade that night you broadcasted your Scraps, or they know someone who was. I heard some of the factories have even had to shut down. Not enough output."

"That's incredible."

"*You're* incredible. Everything's happening because of you. The world's really changing, Liv. Reem says there are even reports of refugees in other camps." His expression darkens slightly.

After she took us in, Reem sent a message to the other nearby rebel settlements—apparently, there are dozens—to see if anyone knew anything about Adrian's parents. No word-Adrian'syet.

"We'll find your family," I say, squeezing his arm. "Nas too." I know Adrian's happy here with me, but as long as he's giving me his heart, I want it to be whole.

He smiles, then pours some tea and hands it to me. I can't tell which is more comforting: the drink, or the idea of more refugees finding a new life in the Haven. I wish them an ounce of the happiness I've found.

Adrian joins me under the blanket. "So cozy," I say. "I wish we'd had a blanket and tea up on Mount Barton."

"I'm glad you brought that up, actually. Been thinking we should visit again in the spring. We need a do-over." His mischievous grin makes my toes curl.

"Oh?"

"I mean, yeah. Last time I kissed you up there, I got my jaw rocked—"

"Rightfully so!"

He brushes my forehead with his lips. "Definitely. I'm just saying, I imagined it going a little differently."

"And exactly how did you imagine it going?" I ask, the picture of innocence.

Adrian takes my tea and sets it aside. "Hmm, I dunno. Maybe kind of like . . ." He leans forward and kisses the tender spot where my shoulder meets my neck. Pleasure radiates down my back. Outside our window, the stars twinkle as I bite back a smile. There's still a lot to figure out, a long way to go before we're truly free. But in a world determined to isolate us, Adrian and I have found each other.

And that is worth everything.

ACKNOWLEDGMENTS

Glory to God for all things!

Just as no words could ever truly describe the wonder of a sky full of stars, it would be impossible to fully articulate how grateful I am to everyone who helped make *The Dividing Sky* a reality. Still, I'd like to take a moment to thank the constellations that have burned brightest on this journey.

To my agent, Jen Azantian, as well as Ben Baxter and the rest of the ALA team: thank you for championing my heart-filled adventures from the start. I'm so fortunate to be a part of this crew.

To my editor, Bria Ragin: you saw through to the swoony heart of this story and guided me there with Dagger-like precision. Thank you for boosting my productivity score.

To David and Nicola Yoon. Thank you for making a place for stories like *The Dividing Sky*. I'm grateful to be Joy Revolution's first science fiction title, among a growing family of books that shows young people of color falling love across the world, across history, into the future. I'd journey to the Outerlands with you any day.

To everyone at Penguin Random House who helped champion and shape this story: Wendy Loggia, Beverly Horowitz, Barbara Marcus, Colleen Fellingham, Tamar Schwartz, [More RHCB names TK]. Special appreciation to Liz Dresner, Shorsh, and Kenneth Crossland for making the world of *The Dividing Sky* come to life visually. You're all so fritzing talented!

To the friends and family who have supported my writing journey, even thirteen years ago when I was an associate consultant reading *The Artist's Way* in my Manhattan apartment instead of working on my slide decks. An extra special shout-out to the friends who read early unpolished drafts of *The Dividing Sky,* some before it even sold: Baylee, Belinda, Blair, Christy, Clare, Colin, Emily, Etta, Maelan, Monique, Niki, and Ruth. Your feedback was a rush of Orange Haze when I needed it most.

To my mother. I never could've gotten here without your expert orienteering.

To the original Afronauts, especially Chelsea and Beatrice, for being a safe Haven for dreaming. The world is not ready. And to KL, whose absence is felt every day. I kept my promise.

To Diana, who first showed me what good editing looks like, and made me believe my books could go the distance. You are one clever hawk.

To the Black women authors who have offered encouragement and advice over the years: Nicola, Ayana, Karen, Bethany, Tracy, Nia, Liselle, Jess, and so many more. Thank you for your incredible, starlit stories.

To the podcasts that kept me going when none of my friends wanted to talk about publishing anymore: *Deadline*

City, *Basic Pitches, Writing Excuses, Print Run, Write or Die, First Draft, Shipping & Handling, Publishing Crawl, Of the Publishing Persuasion,* and *Publishing Rodeo.* There's not enough bacon and eggs in the world to express my gratitude.

To Michael, for letting me quit and un-quit as many times as it took. I'm so lucky I heard your song over the chaos of the Metro.

To the babies: my life came into sharper focus the first time I held each of you in my arms. You are the glow I'll gladly follow to the end of my days. I love you.

And lastly, to the readers: I hope you've enjoyed! Thank you for picking up this book, and for giving me memories that will last a lifetime.

Nero, end Scrap.

ABOUT THE AUTHOR

Jill Tew was destined for speculative fiction nerddom from childhood. She grew up watching *Farscape, Hercules,* and *The 10th Kingdom,* and always had the latest copy of Animorphs tucked in her backpack. Now she writes the kinds of stories she loved as a kid, with characters she wanted to see more of—Black heroes asking big questions, saving the world, and occasionally falling in love along the way. A recovering business school graduate, Jill enjoys belting show tunes and baking in her spare time. She lives in Atlanta with her family.

jilltew.com